ΛAQA

A DEMONIC THRILLER

OMAR M .AHMED

Published in the USA: ISBN 979-8-218-70782-8

https://wraithsandwizards.com
info@wraithandwizards.com

ACKNOWLEDGMENTS

To **Maryssa Gordon** (Pocket Editing)—your pen is a wand, your
edits a spell. Thank you for sharpening
the blade of this story with your wisdom and care.

To **Muhammad Waqas**, whose cover art conjured the first
enchantment—your vision opened the gate
before the first word was ever read.

To my daughter, the keeper of my tales and the spark behind my
fire—your belief turned whispers into worlds.
Thank you for walking beside me through every imagined land.

And to you, brave reader—thank you for venturing into these
pages, for lending your eyes to this dream, and your
heart to this journey.

If this story left a mark upon your soul, consider leaving behind a
trace—a review—for those yet to
follow.

The tale continues. More worlds await.

ABOUT THE AUTHOR

My name is Omar M. Ahmed, and I live in New Jersey with my wife and three kids. Professionally, I am an Information Technology (IT) Systems Engineer, a career I've pursued with passion and fulfillment. Yet, alongside my professional life, I've always been a dreamer.

From an early age, I was enchanted by the fantastical worlds of orcs and elves, drawn to the magic of storytelling. However, it wasn't until I watched *The Exorcist* that I truly understood the incredible power of this medium. That film left me sleepless for nights on end, and I vowed to stay far away from anything, even remotely connected to horror.

And yet, here I am—writing a horror book.

While I don't claim my work rivals the sheer terror of *The Exorcist*, I can assure you that every ounce of effort went into crafting a story meant to thrill, spook, and unsettle. I hope you experience the same chills I felt while writing it.

Happy reading—and happy haunting.

CONTENTS

CHAPTER 1

HOMECOMING

The lamp was an enigma—elongated and forged from pristine glass, its surface etched with ancient, cryptic markings. It gleamed faintly under the dim light as if harboring secrets beyond comprehension. Josh, a young man with unruly black hair and a wiry frame, clutched it tightly. He stared intently as though the lamp had cast a spell on him.

Behind him, the bed groaned under the weight of an over-stuffed backpack. Clothes and trinkets threatened to burst from its seams, chaos in stark contrast to the neatly arranged room. The green flannel shirt hanging from Josh's lean shoulders appeared as weathered as he was, draped over a graphic tee so faded it was hard to make out its original design.

"What's that?" Kevin's words broke the silence, his tone a mix of curiosity and amusement. He stood at the doorway, freshly scrubbed and radiating the calm confidence of someone who knew how to command a room. His golden hair caught the light, framing his chiseled features.

Josh turned but maintained his grip on the lamp. "Just some decoration piece," he remarked nonchalantly, placing it on the nightstand. "Picked it up at Dad's."

Kevin smirked, leaning casually against the doorframe. "You mean you stole it."

Josh shrugged, flashing a half-smile. "Borrowed, technically. He is my dad, after all."

Kevin chuckled as he started down the stairs. "Well, I gotta jet. Later, man."

Josh turned to face the staircase and yelled, "Hey, thanks again for picking me up." But Kevin was already gone. Josh fell silent as he returned to his backpack, though his gaze lingered on the lamp for a moment longer.

Kevin had been Josh's best friend since kindergarten—one of those rare bonds that managed to survive growing up. Josh had just returned from a long trip to Washington, DC, where he'd been staying with his dad. Kevin, being Kevin, took time off work just to pick him up from the train station. They only had a few minutes to catch up, laughing and talking like no time had passed at all before Kevin needed to rush back to work.

The room was a strange blend of order and nostalgia. Feminine curtains fluttered gently in the summer breeze, their delicate pattern at odds with the rugged posters of movie stars and wrestlers that dominated one wall. A bulky sitar hung in the corner, its intricately carved wood exuding an ancient dignity. But despite the neatness, the lamp now on his nightstand seemed to draw all attention, its presence quietly unsettling.

From downstairs, his mother's voice rang out, warm yet insistent, "Josh, sweetie, lunch is ready! Don't let it get cold!"

"Coming, Mom!" Josh called back, tearing his sight from the lamp and racing down the stairs. They sat next to each other at the table and started eating. Josh was hungry; he hadn't eaten all day.

"I missed your food," he said without stopping eating or looking at his mother.

His mother, Carol, ate slowly, admiring her son with a gentle smile. She would usually poke him and remind him of his manners, but she had not seen him for a month and was happy to have him back.

"Emily doesn't cook?" she asked as if it didn't matter.

"She does," replied Josh, grabbing some salt. "But not like you!"

Carol tried to hide her smile, but it didn't matter because Josh wasn't looking. Emily was Josh's stepmother, who married his father, Matthew, a few years ago. They had a daughter named Samantha, who was two years old. During this trip, Josh saw Samantha for the first time and became fond of her. Emily did not care about Josh. She had gotten increasingly defensive since Samantha was born and saw Josh as competition to Samantha and wanted her husband's full affection and fortune for her daughter. Josh got the hint but didn't care. He was just happy to spend time with his father and half-sister.

After lunch, Josh returned to his room, exhaustion tugging at his limbs. He collapsed onto the bed, but his mind refused to rest. The lamp loomed in his thoughts, pulling him toward it with an almost magnetic force.

He stretched out and picked it up again. There was an element about it—its craftsmanship, the way the etchings seemed to float between the layers of glass. He could just make out a subtle, wispy swirl of smoke within. He blinked and it disappeared.

His heart quickened as he inverted the device, examining it from every angle. The smoke was then gone like a figment of his imagination, teasing the edges of his vision. "What are you hiding?" he murmured, running his fingers over the gilded symbols. They were mesmerizing, their texture almost pulsing under his touch.

Without thinking, he rubbed the lamp, his manipulations slow and deliberate. "Open sesame," he whispered, his voice trembling with nervous excitement. Nothing happened. Undeterred, he tried again, each stroke fervent to a greater degree—desperate. His breathing grew uneven as a strange warmth coursed through his veins, intoxicating and otherworldly.

That cautious part of his mind tried to stop him, but he ignored it. His demeanor had turned serious; it was as if something else was controlling him, showing him the way. His smile was gone, his face turned stiff, and words he never knew, and a language he did not understand, came out of him.

His body jerked, and he uttered three unknown words.

"Daksinabandha anuprabhusati madarthe."

There was a shift in the air—a charge that raised every hair on his body. Smoke erupted from the lamp, thick and swirling, consuming the room instantly. The unearthly presence plunged the once-bright space into darkness, filling the air with a heavy weight. Patterns danced within the smoke, hypnotic and chaotic, as if alive.

Josh's chest tightened. His gut feeling told him to flee, but his legs refused to cooperate. Before him, the smoke coalesced, forming a shape—vaguely human, yet entirely otherworldly. Two pupils blazed through the haze, feline and fierce, their glow a searing orange that burned into his soul.

Behind those eyes was a very ancient being. It seemed intelligent and calculating. But the glare betrayed something else— deep-rooted hatred, anger, and a longing for revenge. The irises were glowing deep orange, and sometimes red. The creature took a deep breath and the smoke expanded. As if it weren't observing but sensing its surroundings, it looked around. The smoke barely condensed as it exhaled. The smokeless being closed its luminous eyes, experiencing its sense of freedom, the free air, the earth, and the space for the first time in a long time. And then it froze, but only momentarily, opening its eyes with burning rage, glaring at Josh.

An utterance, guttural and ancient, shattered the silence.

"Ulskfre nabfrels lomphrd."

Josh's lips moved but no sound escaped. The words came again, louder and with increased urgency.

"Ulskfre nabfrels lomphrd."

Josh's mind raced; he hated his curiosity for putting him in this deadly position. A wave of nausea washed over him, making his legs buckle and his hands shoot out, desperately searching for support as the impending vomiting intensified.

"I-I don't understand!" he stammered, his voice barely above a whisper.

The creature's gaze flared crimson, its rage palpable. The smoke tightened around him like a vice, suffocating and inescapable.

Josh's vision blurred as fear clawed at his mind, leaving him trembling and weak.

He collapsed onto the bed, his breaths shallow and labored. With the last of his strength, he whispered, "I freed you..." before darkness claimed him.

The being loomed over him, its form crackling with malevolence. For the first time in centuries, it was free—and it hungered.

IT WAS LATE AT NIGHT, AND JOSH URGENTLY NEEDED TO GO TO THE bathroom. Blinking groggily, his vision adjusted to the darkness, but a sudden sensation froze him in place. Two glaring red orbs pierced the shadows, staring at him from the TV in his bedroom.

A chill coursed through his body as he clamped his lids shut, his breath catching in his throat. When he dared to look again, the TV screen was black and empty, the faint hum of electronics the only sound. His chest tightened. I must be imagining things, he told himself, though the unease lingered like a shadow in the corner of his mind.

Josh struggled to get out of bed. His limbs were sluggish, like unseen chains weighed them down, and his grogginess made every step heavy. Still half-asleep, he stumbled into the bathroom. But as he stood by the toilet, a detail was amiss.

His hands brushed the fabric of his clothing—not my pajamas. The thought hit him like a cold slap. His gaze darted around the unfamiliar room, panic blooming in his chest. I don't have a TV in my bedroom. And there's no attached bathroom in my house.

A low noise from outside cut through his thoughts like a knife. Scratching, shuffling, the sound of a sizable object moving through the backyard.

Josh stiffened, his pulse quickening. Those damn groundhogs again, he thought, irritation momentarily overriding his confusion. But then a whisper brushed his mind, faint and questioning. What garden? You don't have a garden.

The noise grew louder, a deep, guttural sound that didn't belong to groundhogs—or any small animal. Josh's irritation melted into dread, but instead of retreating, he let a surge of defiance take over. He made his way to the garage and grabbed his shotgun. His hands shook some-what as he loaded it, his mind repeating the same thought like a mantra: Whoever it is, they will regret this.

The chilly night air hit him as he stepped into the backyard. The noise had stopped, replaced by an oppressive silence that made the hairs on the back of his neck stand on end. Then he saw it—a hulking shadow behind the shed, too big to be anything normal.

"Who's there?" Josh yelled, his vocal cords cracking but forceful. He raised the shotgun, his grip unsteady. "Come out! I've got a shotgun and I'm not afraid to use it!"

The shadow shifted, and a massive wolf-like animal entered the dim moonlight. It was like nothing Josh had ever seen—its pupils glowed crimson, its fur matted with filth, and long threads of saliva hung from its snarling jaws.

Josh froze, his body betraying him as primal terror rooted him to the spot. The beast's gaze locked onto his, and the world seemed to stop for a moment.

Then it lunged.

Josh let out a strangled yell as he fired the shotgun. The blast tore through the creature's side, and he saw blood spray across the grass. But it didn't stop. It didn't even slow. The wolf barreled into him with terrifying force, knocking him to the ground.

The next moments were a blur of pain and horror. Razor-sharp teeth tore into his flesh, rending skin and muscle like paper. Josh screamed, the sound raw and primal, as the beast's jaws clamped onto his arm. He felt his bones splintering under its crushing bite.

His vision blurred, the edges of his consciousness dimming. Somewhere in the distance, lights flicked on. Neighbors' voices shouted, and he thought he heard sirens wailing, but it all appeared distant—like another world.

The wolf released him suddenly, its ears pricking at the commotion. With one last, blood-chilling snarl, it turned and disappeared into the shadows.

Josh lay there, his breath shallow, his blood pooling beneath him in a dark, warm stream. The pain was unbearable, but even worse was the cold creeping over his body, spreading like ice through his veins.

As the sirens grew louder, his vision went black, and the world slipped away.

JOSH WOKE WITH A START, HIS CHEST HEAVING AS IF HE'D BEEN running for miles. His throat felt dry, and cold sweat drenched his clammy skin. The memory of the wolf—its blood-red orbs, the searing pain of its fangs—lingered in his mind like a dark cloud, heavy and oppressive. His heart thudded painfully against his ribs as he struggled to ground himself in reality. The dream seemed so real, like he was being torn to pieces by that monstrosity.

He glanced at the clock. Dawn had just broken, its pale light weakly illuminating his room. Then his sight landed on the lamp. The glass shimmered innocuously, but Josh recoiled as though it might spring to life. He scrambled out of bed, his movements frantic, uncoordinated.

"Get it together," he muttered, his tone a hoarse whisper. Yet his hands trembled as he pushed himself upright, retreating from the table where the lamp sat.

The wolf's glare flashed in his mind again—those terrible, burning embers of hatred. And then there were the other images, half-formed yet no less vivid: the sound of the shotgun, the eerie silence of the garden, the sensation of teeth grinding into his bones. Josh clutched his arms, his fingers digging into his skin as if trying to reassure himself he was still whole…still alive.

His gaze darted back to the lamp. Was it watching him? Waiting for him to make another mistake?

He reeled out of his room, his bare feet thudding against the stairs as he made his way down. His grip on the banister was unsteady, and halfway down, his foot slipped. He tumbled, landing hard on the floor below with a cry that reverberated through the house.

"Josh!" Carol called out, filled with alarm. She emerged from the kitchen, her face a mixture of worry and confusion. "What happened? Are you okay?"

Josh groaned, pushing himself up onto his elbows. His limbs were weak, his head spinning. He barely registered Carol kneeling beside him, her hands fluttering as if unsure whether to touch him.

"You're sweating," she murmured, her voice rising in panic. "Oh, honey, you don't look good at all. Are you sick? Did you hit your head?"

"I'm fine," Josh mumbled, though the words sounded hollow even to him.

"No, you're not," Carol insisted, helping him into a chair. She pressed her palm against his forehead, her touch cool against his fevered skin. "You're burning up. Let me get you some water. And aspirin. You need to rest—maybe I should call the doctor."

"Ma, stop," Josh uttered, his voice cracking. "I'm fine. I just… didn't sleep well, that's all."

"Didn't sleep well?" Carol frowned. She hurried to the kitchen, returning with a glass of water and two aspirins. "Take these," she said, setting them on the table.

"I came by last night around dinner, wondering where you were. But you were out cold. I figured you were tired from the trip."

Josh obediently swallowed the pills, his hands shaking as he lifted the glass to his lips. The cold water was a slight comfort, though it did nothing to still the storm raging inside him.

"Eat something," Carol urged. "You'll feel better."

"I'll be fine, Ma," Josh commented, avoiding her gaze. "You should get to work. Don't worry about me."

"Don't be ridiculous," Carol said, her tone sharp with maternal authority. But subsequently, she sighed, her shoulders slumping. "Fine. But call me if you're unwell, okay?"

Josh nodded, grateful when she finally relented and left the house. The moment the door clicked shut, his composure crumbled. He buried his face in his hands, his breathing ragged.

JOSH WOKE UP THREE HOURS LATER, SLOUCHED IN THE CHAIR, HIS neck stiff and aching from the awkward position he'd slept in. He groaned as he sat up, rubbing his sore neck. A faint hunger gnawed at his stomach, but a different concern loomed larger— the memory of last night.

Was it real? A dream? It seemed so vivid and raw that his mind couldn't let it go. Shaking his head, Josh stood and walked to the fridge, absently grabbing a drink to wash down the remains of the sandwich his mother had left him.

Yet the questions gnawed at him more than hunger ever could. Placing the empty glass on the counter, he ascended the stairs almost unconsciously. He needed to know.

Josh's bedroom door creaked as he pushed it open, his heart hammering in his chest. There it was—the lamp—sitting on the side table as if mocking him. His breath quickened as his gaze locked onto it, scanning every inch.

The wolf, the garden, and the lamp all appeared too real. His mind swirled with unanswered questions and gnawing fear. His body ached, not just from the fall but from the weight of the unknown pressing down on him.

And yet, despite the fear clawing at his chest, his vision

returned to the lamp. It sat there, still and unassuming, but Josh had a suspicion it expected him.

Waiting for something more.

But then he froze. The etchings—those intricate carvings he was sure he'd seen—were gone.

He stepped closer, his eyes narrowing. His fingers brushed the smooth surface of the lamp, searching for any trace of the markings, but there was nothing. Yet the white smoke inside still swirled faintly, teasing him with its mystery.

Panic and curiosity collided in his mind. He slammed the door shut, leaning against it as thoughts raced through his head.

Should I? Shouldn't I? If this thing were dangerous, wouldn't it have killed me last night?

What about the fever? Was it a coincidence?

And the etchings—where did they go? Am I losing my mind?

He stared at the lamp, its unassuming exterior hiding something far more sinister—or wondrous. His hand trembled as he picked it up. *If I don't do this, I'll never know.*

Josh's heart pounded as he gripped the lamp and, just like before, rubbed its side with hesitant fingers. The smoky swirl inside stirred violently.

This time, the smoke didn't fill the room. Instead, it gathered before him, a blurred figure slowly materializing. Two eyes, glowing like molten coals, pierced through the haze.

Josh's breath hitched. His left hand shook violently, clutching the lamp, while his right hung limp at his side. Then, from the formless smoke, an arm extended—long and grotesque—ending in claws sharp enough to tear flesh.

A cold sweat drenched Josh as he stumbled backward, muttering, "Why do I listen to myself?"

The clawed hand reached toward him, the arm waved toward the right, and the lamp flew effortlessly back to the side table. The arm vanished, leaving only the smoke to stare at him.

Josh gasped, his back pressed against the wall. The creature bowed, its fiery gaze fixed on him with a chilling intensity.

Then it spoke. Its tone was deep and resonant, carrying an otherworldly power. "My deepest apologies for last night, Aaqa."

The word hung in the air, heavy with meaning. Josh's body trembled, his mind fighting to process what was happening. He swallowed hard, his utterance barely a whisper. "You… you speak English?"

The creature's eyes flared, its presence exuding malice and disdain. "Speak is for your filthy kind. I think, and you hear," it growled, its tone devoid of warmth.

Josh's instincts screamed at him to run, but his legs refused to move. He compelled himself to meet the creature's gaze, though it was like staring into the abyss.

"Who are you?"

The being responded as if it was prepared for this question.

"I am the one you freed."

Josh's fear didn't disappear—it twisted into something colder, something sharper.

For a moment, he felt foolish, like a child being toyed with by something far more dangerous than he could grasp. The answer had been too obvious, too simple, and that realization only made the knot in his chest tighten.

Panic clawed at the edges of his mind, but he fought it down, his hands trembling at his sides. He had to be better. Stronger.

"What does 'Aaqa' mean?"

The being tilted its head, its lips curling into something that might have been a smile—or a sneer. "Aaqa," it rumbled, "means my lord."

Josh's back pressed harder against the wall as if he could sink into it and escape. The creature seemed to revel in his fear, its glowing pupils expanding and contracting with every heartbeat.

"My lord?" Josh repeated, his words barely audible. "What do you mean, 'my lord'?"

"You freed me from my prison." The creature's voice was a low, ominous growl reverberating in Josh's bones. "I am bound to you by ancient magic. You are my master."

Josh blinked, his mind struggling to keep up. The words appeared unreal, like a figment from a twisted fairy tale. "Bound to me? Like… like Aladdin and the magic lamp?"

The creature offered no words but stared at Josh intently. This was no fairy tale with friendly genies serving the commands of their master.

Josh swallowed hard, his thoughts racing. *What have I done?*

The entity remained motionless except for the patterns of smoke, which moved gently in all directions and disappeared near the edges. New patterns would follow the old ones and disappear near the edges, and this repeated. There seemed to be a face, but it was impossible to say if there was a mouth. Josh could hear the creature but didn't see any movements except for the patterns in the smoke. Even the pupils remained still unless the creature redirected its attention. When the creature communicated with Josh, its locked and focused eyes made his hair stand on end.

"You owe me…" Josh tried to swallow, "three wishes…right?" The creature stared back at Josh, which instilled in him a sense of disdain. Maybe he didn't want any of those wishes. His face cringed as he averted his gaze.

"Three wishes?" the creature's deep voice inquired. Then, to answer his question, it said, "If I had locked you up for four thousand years in that lamp, would you have come out to grant me three wishes?" The being's eyes turned dark red; it didn't take long to recognize it was angry.

Josh offered no words but looked away, occasionally glancing at the creature. "I didn't lock you up," he mumbled.

It seemed the creature wanted to say something; there was a moment of anger, but it subsided.

"But you freed me, and therefore, I am bound to you, at least until you die," the creature said, looking intensely at Josh.

"Until I die?" A worried look etched across his features.

"Correct," boomed the creature.

"What happens to you when I die?" asked Josh as he tried hard to swallow.

"I am free," replied the creature, completely emotionless.

An icy knot formed in Josh's stomach. The implications hung heavy in the air. "So…if you want freedom," he began cautiously, "wouldn't it make sense to…kill me?"

The creature leaned closer, the smoke pulsating with menace. "An ancient and powerful magic binds me to this lamp," it explained. "If it weren't for this magic, you, Aaqa, would already be dead."

Josh nearly buckled at the knees. He recoiled, his back hitting the wall, the impact anchoring him to the present. "I am confused. What kind of ancient sorcery is this?"

The thing tilted its head, considering him. "Do you understand the laws of your physical world?"

"Yes, somewhat. I think you mean like laws of physics?" asked Josh.

"Like your physical laws are bound to your physical being, ancient magic is bound to the magical or unseen world," replied the creature uninterestedly.

"You said bound to me until I die? What does that mean to me?" Josh inquired.

"It means," the creature answered spitefully, "that you are my Aaqa, and you may command me."

"So, if I request something of you, you have to obey?" asked Josh.

He swallowed again and continuously rubbed his hands. This is what he was trying to get to—the answer to this question mattered. But he was also worried he would anger this thing and ask the wrong question or ask the right question the wrong way. And yes, it was worth the risk. Josh wasn't stupidly brave, but he was brave enough to avail himself of an opportunity.

"Within reason," the creature slyly remarked.

"Reason? Aren't you immensely powerful?" Josh inquired, his facial expressions tightening with tension.

"Very!" the being bellowed. "But within reason! If you ask me to get you the moon, I will destroy this house of yours and everything within it!" The stare was so intense that Josh slid to the floor.

"But you can't hurt me. You admitted it yourself," Josh remarked while swallowing yet again.

"I can't physically touch you," the being seethed. "That is not the same as hurting you."

Josh studied the creature for a moment. One thing Josh understood right away was that this thing was intelligent—as a matter of fact, probably surpassing the intelligence of anyone Josh had ever met. But its intention felt malign. Part of him was telling him to get rid of this being, but his curiosity was getting the better of him. Josh stood up and tried a more friendly approach.

"Hmm…my name is Josh. What may I call you?"

The being spoke with disdain. "Only your kind would be arrogant enough to think they could speak my name!" It stared at Josh, not blinking or letting him out of sight. But its eyes showed the slightest amount of patience.

Josh changed his approach, his objective being to get as much information as possible.

"Okay then, what are you?" Josh asked.

"I," the creature announced, moving closer to him, its gaze shifting from dark orange to dark red, "am an ifrit...the mightiest being in your universe, and perhaps beyond!" it roared.

"Oh!" blurted Josh. "Then how did you end up trapped in a lamp?"

This touched a nerve, and Josh immediately realized he probably should not have asked that. Despair washed over him as he heard whispers around him, repeating words like 'treacherous, vile, abominations.' He dropped to one knee, whispering, "I command you to return to the lamp," as he gasped for air.

The smoke condensed into a long, blurry string and filled the lamp. The room emptied of the smoke and returned to normal. Josh got up on his feet and took deep breaths.

He stared at the lamp, its surface cool against his trembling fingers. He was still conscious of the creature's presence, even as it retreated into the swirling smoke. Sweat drenched his body, and his hands were clammy. Yet, his curiosity pulled at him stronger than fear.

I'm in control. I have to be.

With a determined breath, he rubbed the lamp again.

The smoke surged out like a predator freed from a cage. It twisted and coiled, forming patterns that faded at the edges. This time, the creature materialized faster, its glowing red eyes locking onto Josh with an intensity that had the impact of a physical force.

Red, piercing eyes stared at Josh, and Josh's determination disappeared. Fear consumed him. He started sweating and rubbing his hands again, but he found courage somewhere deep inside and spoke. "If I am your master, I command you not to overwhelm me ever again!" He pretended to be angry, but his lips and hands were shaking, his voice broken.

"You would mock me and then demand respect. You may command me, but do you not sense that I am evil?" The creature seemed even angrier than before. His being had condensed as if he was ready to burst, his stare at its peak intensity.

"I sense it," replied Josh, showing determination yet again. "And I won't lie, I fear it. But if you want to enjoy the limited freedom you have, remember that it's thanks to me!"

The creature stared at Josh, its red pupils vengeful and dishonest, a hidden motive. But the anger dissipated a bit, replaced with the slightest sense of amusement.

"As you wish, Aaqa," it said calmly. "What is your command?"

Josh exhaled, his body finally relaxing. "Return to the lamp and await my instructions."

The smoke spiraled back into the lamp, leaving Josh alone yet again. He collapsed onto his bed, staring at the ceiling. His thoughts churned with equal parts dread and exhilaration.

What have I gotten myself into?

CHAPTER 2

THE T-TWINS' TREEHOUSE

"What's for dinner?" Josh asked, running a hand through his hair to keep it out of his eyes.

Carol's smile didn't falter, but her tone was firm. "Get a plate and sit if you want to find out."

Nestled within the modest confines of the small kitchen, a medium-sized refrigerator hummed quietly beside an older but impeccably clean oven, while a medium-sized microwave rested atop a small, sturdy table. A silver toaster sat on the counter near the fridge, but it didn't work. The object appeared ancient, and it was plausible that it had once belonged to someone of significance within this family's history. The kitchen was next to a small living area that was furnished with a television and a sofa designed for two people. Although showing signs of age, everything in the place was surprisingly spotless and precisely positioned.

Josh and Carol's mother-son dinner was quiet at first, the kind of silence that comes when there's too much to say but no easy way to start. Carol, ever the doting mother, was piling food onto Josh's plate as though it might heal whatever exhaustion had hollowed him out.

During their meal, a silence hung in the air until Carol spoke. "You remember Mr. Beeds, your fifth-grade teacher?"

Josh nodded absentmindedly. "Yeah."

Carol hesitated; sadness overtook her expression. "He passed away."

Josh stopped mid-motion, his fork hovering over his plate. He looked at his mother, a wide-eyed expression of disbelief on his face. "How?"

Carol swallowed hard, the sadness clear in her voice. "A wild animal entered his backyard. It attacked him the other night. Tore his arm clean off and… and went for his chest. Paramedics rushed him to the hospital, but he didn't survive."

Josh stared at his plate, his appetite draining completely. A knot formed in his stomach as a memory—a dream—crept into his mind. He saw flashes of a beast ripping into someone, tearing through flesh and bone. His chest tightened as a chill overcame him.

"Josh?" Carol's voice was soft, almost apologetic. "I'm sorry. I shouldn't have brought it up during dinner. And you just got home…"

Josh shook his head, forcing himself to take a deep breath. "No, it's fine. I just…he was a good man. It's terrible."

Carol nodded, her eyes glistening. Using her sleeve, she swiftly cleaned them before changing the topic. "How's your sister? Did you like her?"

At the mention of Samantha, Josh's expression softened. A small smile tugged at his lips. "She's adorable. I mean, what's not to like?"

"And your dad?" Carol pressed gently. "Were things…civil?"

Josh shrugged, keeping his eyes on his plate. "More or less."

Carol hesitated, then carefully remarked, "He called me. Said he's missing some lamp. He told me to ask you about it. You didn't take it, did you?"

Josh froze. His fork clattered onto his plate as he tried to come up with a response.

"Joshua Robert Cox," Carol stated sternly, a narrowing of her expression. "We talked about this. You didn't, did you?"

Josh sighed. "It's not stealing. He's my dad."

"It is stealing, Josh," Carol said firmly, her voice breaking a bit. The gentleness in her gaze vanished instantly. While she pretended to be angry, it seemed she was more annoyed and frustrated. "I raised you better than this."

"Fine," Josh muttered. "I'll return it."

Before the conversation could go any further, the front door slammed open, bouncing off the wall with a thud. Kevin strolled in as though he owned the place.

"Yo, bro! I'm here!" Kevin called, his grin wide and unapologetic.

"Kevin," Carol said with a weary smile. "Come and join us for dinner."

Kevin smiled at Josh, happy to see him back. "Maybe later, Ms. J. I'm just grabbing your boy."

Josh, eager to escape, grabbed his jacket and followed Kevin to the door. "Don't wait up, Ma!"

"Be careful, you two!" Carol called after them, worry clear in her voice.

They both yelled, "Okay," as if it were a mere formality.

Outside, Kevin smirked as they climbed into his car. "You're gonna love this party, man. Everyone's gonna be there. And guess who else is coming?"

Josh rolled his eyeballs. "Don't start, Kevin."

"Lily Higgins," Kevin announced in a sing-song voice, poking Josh's shoulder.

"Oh, come on, not this again," Josh groaned, his face already heating up.

Josh, typically reserved, deliberately concealed his feelings for Lily Higgins from Kevin. But Kevin was Josh's best friend and knew more about him than probably anyone else. And he knew back in third grade that Josh liked Lily and has been teasing him ever since, a few times around Lily, which made her smile and embarrassed Josh.

As Kevin and Josh drove to the party, the car filled with the easy rhythm of their laughter and conversation. They pointed out things along the way—cool cars, terrible drivers, odd sights —each comment a thread that wove their friendship tighter.

It was what made them work so well together: a shared love for cars, a similar sense of humor, and a thousand inside jokes.

But their differences were just as important.

Josh was the quieter one, guarded, thoughtful. Kevin, on the other hand, was an open book—loud, mischievous, never afraid to say what he was thinking.

Somehow, it balanced perfectly.

Kevin grinned like a Cheshire cat. "You've been dodging her since graduation. Admit it, you're still into her."

Josh turned to glare at his best friend. "Can we not do this right now?"

But Kevin just laughed, the teasing never-ending as they pulled up to the Sombats' mansion. The T-Twins were outside, their usual energetic demeanor replaced by a state close to panic.

The T-house, fondly nicknamed by the gang, was a treehouse nestled behind the sprawling Sombat mansion. It wasn't just any treehouse—it was the T-Twins' Treehouse—a name that rolled off the tongue in a way that dared you to say it faster every time. Frank and Frederick Sombat, the mischievous twins whose parents hailed from Thailand, had built it with the help of their dad years ago. The name was equal parts tribute and teasing. Josh, the quieter one in their group, had christened them the "T-Twins" after being dubbed "the gloomed" for his reclusive nature. The name stuck, as did their treehouse legacy.

The mansion itself was a fortress of grandeur, surrounded by wrought-iron fencing and guarded by an imposing iron gate that creaked open that evening to welcome guests. Past the gate, two fountains framed the long, winding driveway. Beds of colorful flowers bordered the lawn, and the scent of fresh-cut grass mingled with the faint hum of music coming from inside the house. The three-story mansion loomed ahead, its lights glowing like a beacon of teenage rebellion.

Josh and Kevin stepped out of Kevin's battered car, the sounds of laughter and music echoing through the property. Their destination wasn't the party just yet—it was the small crowd gathered near a large, locked garage. Frank and Frederick were there, along with their friend, Anthony, who stood with his arms crossed and a dubious expression.

The twins, dressed in casual polos and jeans, were having their usual animated debate. The garage loomed behind them, its heavy, locked doors taunting them.

"Yo, what's going on?" Kevin called, hopping out of the car.

Frederick glanced at Kevin and then walked up to his brother, who was staring at the garage, seemingly lost.

"Man, we are never getting those cars," lamented Frank sadly.

Frederick was deep in thought. "Unless we get them and put them back with no one knowing."

"Na, it won't work this time. Dad's got spies everywhere. I wonder why he went so strict," Frank replied.

Anthony, one of their friends from high school, stood fixated on the garage. Without looking away, he said solemnly, "Probably cause you hit Mrs. Lester's house."

"That house was falling apart, just like the Lesters," quipped Frederick.

Frank chuckled.

"Didn't you guys crash your dad's brand-new Buick?" Kevin interjected.

"We are no longer the sad pathetic losers we were when we were fifteen," replied Frank.

"Yeah, we are all grown up. We are eighteen now." Fredrick smiled.

Between Kevin, Frederick, and Frank, there was never a dull moment. Chaos seemed to follow them like a loyal dog, whether they were cracking jokes, stirring trouble, or finding some new way to light up the room—or occasionally, tearing it apart.

As guests poured into the Sombats' mansion, the atmosphere grew lively. Even uninvited guests wandered in, knowing the Sombats were too gracious and kind to turn anyone away.

Josh walked up. "Why don't you just try asking your dad for the keys?"

"We did!" proclaimed the boys together.

Fredrick continued, "When we turned eighteen, we had this mature and civilized conversation with him."

"But apparently," continued a sarcastic Frank, "in my family, if you crash enough cars before you turn eighteen, you don't get to drive!"

"And the parents lock the garage!" Frederick finished, annoyed.

Frank put his arms around Anthony and looked straight at him with determination. "We have got to get into that garage!"

"We," Anthony replied while removing Frank's arm, "are going to get a drink." He started walking into the mansion. The rest followed; Frank and Frederick seemed irritated, but they trailed behind their guests.

Inside, the mansion was alive with energy. The spacious living room held many people, laughing and dancing. A grand chandelier sparkled overhead, reflecting light off the polished floors.

Dual staircases curved upward on either side, and photos of Mr. Sombat Senior lined the walls—hunting, shaking hands with diplomats, posing with athletes, always with an air of command.

Josh stuck close to Kevin, his nerves suddenly kicking in. And then he saw her…

Lily.

She stood across the room, her red hair falling in soft waves over her shoulders. Her dress was simple but elegant, paired with heels that made her seem taller than Josh remembered. He hadn't seen her since graduation a month ago, and somehow, in that short time, she looked different—exuding confidence and a radiant glow.

Lily noticed but continued her conversation with her friends. She was smiling, though it was hard to say if the smile had anything to do with Josh looking her way.

Kevin noticed Josh freeze and grinned. "Dude, you're staring."

Josh tore his gaze away, pretending to admire a photo on the wall. "I wasn't staring."

"You so were," Kevin teased, clapping him on the shoulder.

Before Josh could respond, a familiar voice interrupted. "Hi, Josh."

He turned around and there she was—Lily, standing right in front of him. Her red lipstick made her smile even brighter, and Josh found himself fumbling for words. His vocal cords cracked as he tried to speak.

"H-hey, Lily. Good to see you."

"Good to see you too," she beamed, her voice warm and friendly. Her facial expression sparkled as she looked into Josh's eyes, exciting him and unnerving him at the same time.

Before the awkwardness could settle in, two other familiar faces appeared—Tracie and Liz. They squealed in unison, pulling Josh into a tight hug.

"The Gloomster!" they shouted, laughing as they let him go.

Josh laughed, genuinely happy to see them. "Tracie! Liz! Wow, it's been forever."

Liz grinned. "How was DC? Steal any more daggers?"

Josh's face flushed. The infamous dagger incident still haunted him, even six years later. At twelve, he'd swiped an ancient Syrian dagger from his dad's collection—a move that had sparked an epic showdown between his parents. His mom was horrified, and his dad called him a thief. It was a mistake he'd vowed never to repeat. At least at that moment, he was sure he wouldn't.

"Very funny, Liz," he muttered, rubbing the back of his neck.

Tracie elbowed him playfully. "Relax. We're just messing with you. It's good to see you."

Josh's smile stretched across his face as he played along. "No, but I did steal a lamp."

Josh smiled, his nerves easing. As the group chatted, Kevin leaned in and whispered, "You're doing great, man. Just...try not to look like you've been hit by a truck whenever Lily talks to you."

Josh glared at him but couldn't help the small grin tugging at his lips. For the first time that night, he sensed things might improve—if only he could endure the chaos that always seemed to follow the T-Twins.

"A lamp?" Tracie exclaimed, throwing both hands to her face as if she were witnessing an impending disaster. "Who will you murder with that?" she quipped, feigning horror while casting a glance at Liz.

With his trademark grin, Kevin cut in before Josh could respond, "Excuse me, ladies, but Josh is trying really hard to ask Lily out, and you two are definitely interrupting."

Josh froze, his palms suddenly growing clammy as his eyes darted to Lily. Her gaze met his, and he began rubbing his hands nervously. A slight smile tugged at Lily's lips, and the tiniest glimmer of amusement danced in her eyes. Josh flushed red. He turned to Kevin with a forced grin. "Do you even think before you speak, Kev?"

Kevin's face contorted in confusion; his expression was almost comical. "What did I do?" he mouthed, clearly oblivious to the chaos he had just unleashed.

Tracie and Liz exchanged a glance, their smiles threatening to break free as they watched the scene unfold.

But just as the awkwardness seemed unbearable, Lily stepped in, her voice soft but confident. "Let me handle this, Josh," she stated, her eyes gleaming.

Turning to Kevin with a playful grin, she said, "Hey, Kev, check out your nine o'clock." She pointed to her left.

The group turned in unison, and there, standing a little too close to each other, were two tall blondes scanning the room. They were unmistakably twins, and they seemed to be searching for something—or someone.

The Sombat twins were quietly observing from a distance before making their move. Now they sauntered closer, with Frank slipping a cigar pipe into his mouth like it was the most natural thing in the world. He looked over at the blondes and spoke in his usual tone of exaggerated disinterest. "Those two, like us, are twins. I call them—" He paused for dramatic effect, "—the 'F-Twins.'"

Kevin raised an eyebrow. "I think I know what the F stands for," he said, glancing at the twins with a mischievous grin.

"No, you pervert, you don't know what the F stands for!" Frank shot back, his voice rising with mock indignation.

"Yeah, you know nothing, KEV-in!" Frederick chimed in, his sass dripping with sarcasm. "Their parents are from Finland."

Lily couldn't help but correct them, a small laugh escaping her. "Their parents didn't migrate from Finland. I work with them at the store."

Frederick narrowed his eyes at her, clearly annoyed at being corrected, but turned back to Frank with a question seeming more like an accusation. "Is this our party?"

Frank, not missing a beat, shot back, "It is our party."

Frederick raised his tone again, pushing the point. "Is this our home?"

Frank's answer came just as firmly. "Of course, it's our home."

Frederick's voice rose even higher, his tone dripping with mock outrage. "Yeah, in our home, we fantasize about where girls come from!"

With that, the twins turned, marching toward the blondes with exaggerated purpose. "They come into our home!" one brother yelled.

"Our home!" shouted the other.

"They drink our booze!" one of them bellowed, his voice echoing through the room.

"Our booze!" the other echoed like a chant.

"And then they have the audacity!" the first brother cried.

"The audacity!" the second screamed, his sound rising as he uttered the word "audacity" like a battle cry.

Everyone around them tried to hold back laughter, though smiles were unavoidable. The twins were goofy, but they had a knack for making everyone around them laugh, and Kevin knew this all too well. He'd seen it enough times to know that sometimes goofiness outshined charm, especially with impressing the ladies.

"I seem to have some competition," Kevin mused, still fixated on the twins. "Wish me luck, folks."

"Oh, and good luck to you, bro," he added with a wink at Josh.

Josh paid little attention to Kevin's teasing as he shifted his focus back to Lily, whose eyes remained locked on him with a calm intensity.

"Hi..." Josh stammered with an odd warmth blooming across his chest. "We didn't get to...um...talk."

Lily's smile widened, her eyes shining with amusement. "Too many twins can be a distraction," she teased, tilting her head.

"Yeah," Josh agreed, the words escaping his mouth without a

second thought. "Among other things," he added with a grin, hoping to make things a little less awkward.

Lily's smile grew brighter still, and her gaze remained fixed. "DC was dull yet fun, as usual, I assume?"

"Yeah, same as usual," Josh replied, his voice steady now. "Except I met my stepsister, Samantha. She was fun."

Lily raised an eyebrow. "That's sweet."

Josh faltered for a moment, then found his voice. "Umm, Lily…" he began, his hands growing clammy again. "There's this nice burger joint at the Freedom Mall. I was thinking of checking it out, and, um…maybe we could visit one day and get a bite to eat if that's okay with you."

Lily looked right into his eyes, her gaze unwavering. "Is this a friendly get-together, or is this a date?"

Josh's heart sprang into his throat. He'd skirted around asking her out for months, always suggesting, "Let's hang out," instead of just saying it. But Lily wasn't letting him get away with that this time. She wanted the truth.

Josh flushed red, the words tumbling out of his mouth before he could second-guess them. "Yeah, it's a casual get-together… date kind of thing."

Lily, still calm and collected, shifted slightly to the side and responded, her voice soft but firm, "It's either a date, or it's not."

"I-it's a date then," Josh stammered, the words coming out with surprising confidence.

Lily's eyes gleamed as she turned back to him, a wide grin

spreading across her face. "Oh, that's too bad then. They shut down that burger shop because of some health violations."

Josh's expression changed, his shoulders sagging. "Oh…" he mumbled as embarrassment overwhelmed him. "You could've started with that."

Lily's laughter was the sweetest sound Josh had heard all night. "I could've," she agreed, still chuckling. "But you should've seen your face."

Josh couldn't help but laugh along with her.

Once the laughter subsided, Lily's tone softened. "Listen, I work at that mall, and there's this nice little coffee shop."

Josh perked up. "Okay, sure. Let's do that tomorrow?"

"No, I work tomorrow. Let's meet on Thursday. I'll have time. I'll text you," she said, putting her hands behind her back as her smile grew almost mischievously.

Josh grinned. "Thursday it is, then."

By now, Kevin was hurriedly heading toward them both and announced to them he was taking the twins home as they had no ride, and he hated people from Finland asking for an Uber.

"They are not from Finland!" said Lily, her tone escalating.

"And this is not your home!" replied Kevin, amplifying his tone.

 "Hey, how am I supposed to get home?" interjected Josh.

"Lily can drive you, can't she?" said Kevin, winking at Josh again.

"Shoo," said Lily. She swatted Kevin away and grabbed Josh's hand. "Come on, I'll drive you home. I can't stay late as I need to be at work early tomorrow."

THE DRIVE HOME WAS EFFORTLESS, THE AIR INSIDE LILY'S OLD Honda Civic buzzing with the familiar comfort of friendship. Her mother had helped her save enough to buy the car, and now it was her lifeline—her escape from the frosty mornings when she used to wait for the bus to work. The radio blasted their favorite songs, and they both found themselves lost in the beat of Linkin Park's *In the End*, the song blasting through the speakers like an anthem to the night.

Josh experienced his chest muscles relaxing as the anxiety that had troubled him all night dissipated. They were no longer in front of their friends or trying to impress anyone. This was just him and Lily. They'd known each other for as long as he could remember, and in moments like this, it was easy to forget the mess of emotions stirring inside him. She was his best friend, his constant in a world that was always changing. And tonight, with the music and the dim streetlights outside the window, she was more beautiful than ever.

But Lily wasn't just beautiful on the outside. She was kind, funny, and so incredibly easy to talk to. Josh sometimes forgot how effortlessly their conversations flowed. It wasn't about trying to impress each other—it was just...them. He thought about their history, how they'd grown up together, how their bond had always been there, unspoken but undeniable.

"So, tell me more about DC," she exclaimed, flashing him that bright, teasing smile that always made Josh's heart beat a little faster. "Did you have fun? Meet anyone interesting? Tell me everything."

Josh chuckled, shifting a little in his seat, his eyes glancing over at Lily as she focused on the road. Her smile reassured him more than at any point that evening. "Well, I mostly hung out at parks, y'know? Didn't want to be home when my dad wasn't around. And my stepmom…well, she's not exactly a bundle of joy."

Lily gave him a soft, sad look, her lips curling up in sympathy. Her eyes were warm, always full of understanding, always giving him the space he needed to open up when he didn't want to. Josh smiled sheepishly, rubbing the back of his neck. "It wasn't too bad, though. The weather was nice, and who doesn't love people-watching? There were tourists everywhere, so…yeah, that was fun."

She let out a soft laugh, and Josh couldn't help but join in. It was pleasant, this uninhibited laughter that came between them.

"It was great to see my half-sister, Samantha," Josh added, a genuine smile spreading across his face. "I loved every second with her."

Lily smiled back, her eyes glistening in the low light of the car. Her gaze made Josh feel seen and understood. The quiet moments like this—these were the ones he treasured most. They didn't need to say everything. Sometimes, just being there for each other is enough.

"Glad to have you back in our…boring small town," Lily teased, her voice light and playful, though there was a softness to it that Josh couldn't ignore.

He looked at her, his heart swelling as he gave her a small but sincere smile. "It was never boring," he said, the words coming out before he could think better of it. "It has you."

Lily turned to him, her eyes widening, a spark of something bright flashing in them. But just as quickly, she turned her attention back to the road, her hands gripping the steering wheel with purpose.

Josh's defense mechanism kicked in. After all, old habits die hard.

"And Kevin, and Liz, and all my friends," he blurted, his cheeks flushing with a mix of warmth and embarrassment. "You know, the usual."

Lily's face turned stern—just a little—as she kept her sight on the road and said nothing. But they had known each other long enough to realize exactly what was happening. Josh was screwing it up again.

The silence in the car stretched on, and Josh realized, with a start, that he had missed his chance. He'd spent so long holding back, afraid of ruining their friendship. But he wasn't that kid anymore. He turned and looked at her affectionately. She was staring at the road, listening to the radio. His defense mechanism faltered. It was impossible to ignore his genuine emotions, what he truly desired, and thus, impulsively, he voiced his thoughts.

"I missed you," he said quietly, the words coming out as a raw confession. "And I'm…really happy to be back in this town, even if it is boring."

Lily glanced at him, and for a moment, their eyes locked. There was no teasing, no laughter. Just the truth in the air between them. Her face softened, and she said nothing, but Josh saw the warmth in her eyes.

She didn't need to say anything. Neither of them did.

Lily turned back to the road, her fingers gently tapping the steering wheel as the soft hum of the engine filled the silence. Josh's heart was still racing, but for the first time in a long while, he didn't mind.

The rest of the ride passed in a comfortable, if bittersweet, silence, with Lily occasionally sharing updates about her job and her plans to save enough to attend a decent college. She talked about the hours she put in and how she didn't want to burden her mom, who was already doing so much. Josh listened carefully, but inside, he couldn't help a slight tug of uncertainty. He wasn't sure if college was for him—at least, not yet. He'd always dreamed of working at Kevin's mechanic shop, fixing up cars, making a living in a way that resonated with him. It differed from what his parents expected, but they had no say anymore. He was over eighteen, and they had little control over his choices.

Lily noticed his silence. "I just think you should at least give college a chance. It's not about throwing everything away. It's still possible to work on cars and get a degree. You don't have to decide now. You could take a year off, save up like me, and go next year."

Josh sighed, his sight trained on the road ahead. "Lil, I'm not sure. I'm just not sure it's for me. I'd rather be doing something real."

Lily gave him a knowing look but didn't push. Instead, she changed the topic to something lighter, and Josh found himself grateful for her understanding. They'd always been able to talk through the tough stuff, and her patience was a constant that grounded him.

As they reached his home, the air hung heavy with unspoken words. Josh reluctantly opened the car door and stood up, pausing to face Lily one last time before heading inside. The moonlight illuminated her face, and for a moment, everything else faded. She was smiling at him, her hazel eyes sparkling in the dim light, and Josh experienced a warmth spread through him—something he couldn't name, but it had always been there, lingering just beneath the surface.

He smiled back, but it appeared too small, too unsure. "Thanks for the ride, Lil…I'll see you Thursday. And, uh…don't forget to text me, okay?"

Lily's lips curled up into a smile, but there was something different in her look—something softer, almost vulnerable. She started the car, and for a split second, Josh thought she was going to drive off. But then she stopped, pulling the car to a slow halt.

She got out of the car and stood by the door, looking at Josh, who stood there, wondering, yearning, hoping. She was not smiling, just looking, and he knew what he wanted but was afraid that something might go wrong. She slowly began walking toward him, and he noticed his blood rush to his cheeks until she stopped before him. Putting her hands on his biceps, she moved closer, then looked up into his eyes.

This was not a fling—not two young people thinking of being with each other. This was love, pure and simple, a feeling that had been years in the making. As they gazed into each other, lost in that moment, Josh pulled her closer, and she gave in willingly. He closed his eyes in anticipation of what was to come as he felt her breath on his cheeks, when she suddenly seemed to pull away, her eyes darting to something behind him. He turned to see a silhouette of a person moving away from the window.

Mom, he thought, a bit annoyed.

Lily had her hands in his. She smiled awkwardly…the moment was gone.

Lily gave him one last look, a flash of something unspoken passing between them, before she got back into the car and drove off. Josh stood there for a moment, his mind reeling, his heart pounding in his chest.

He finally trudged inside, his footsteps heavy as he entered the house. Carol was standing near the dinner table, her expression impossible to read. But the grin tugging at the corners of her mouth gave away everything she had seen. Josh tried to ignore it, but it was impossible. He could practically feel her amusement.

"So," Carol said, stretching out the word with a teasing note in her voice. "How was your night?"

Josh sighed, a small, resigned smile forming on his lips as he climbed the stairs. "You know how it was, Ma."

Carol didn't respond. She just stood there, watching him with an expression that said she knew exactly what had happened, and it didn't need to be said aloud.

In his room, Josh changed into his pajamas, the weight of the night settling heavily on his shoulders. He flopped onto his bed, grabbed his phone, and opened his messaging app. His mind was still buzzing, and he needed to talk to someone who could understand—someone who could take the edge off the whirlwind of emotions. He tapped out a quick message to Kevin, hoping for some kind of distraction, something to pull him away from the chaos in his head.

Shadelss143: Yo Kev you up

TintedG564: I have the worst luck

Shadelss143: Let me guess the F twins

TintedG564: Man I thought I was gonna get a double dose of Finland

Shadelss143: Lol and you didnt

TintedG564: Nah they just wanted a ride

TintedG564: Finlands got me messed up bro

Shadelss143: They're not from Finland

TintedG564: Whatever same difference

Shadelss143: Haha sorry bro that's a rough one

Shadelss143: Anyways my night wasnt too bad actually

TintedG564: Let me guess…Lily said yes

Shadelss143: Yeah she did

TintedG564: I knew it man! Night bro. Talk tomorrow

Shadelss143: Night

CHAPTER 3

THE FIRST FUNERAL

Tucked at the edge of the town square, the little white church looked like it had stood there forever, with peeling clapboard siding, a modest steeple that caught the morning sun, and a brass bell that rang out on Sundays like clockwork. Ivy climbed one side of the building, and the wooden sign out front—'St. Luke's Chapel, Est. 1874'—was hand-carved and worn soft by time.

Inside, the sanctuary smelled faintly of old hymnals and beeswax candles. Light filtered in through narrow stained-glass windows, painting quiet rainbows on the scuffed wooden pews. The floor creaked with every step, and the altar was simple: just a white linen cloth, a small wooden cross, and a vase of fresh wildflowers that someone—always anonymously —replaced every week.

It could only fit about a hundred people, yet it appeared full even with only half that many. Folks dressed up for Sunday service, and the pastor knew everyone by name, often pausing the sermon to welcome newcomers or check in on someone's ailing grandmother. It wasn't grand, but it had heart. And in that quiet, creaky space, it was easy to believe that faith didn't need to be loud to be strong.

The air was thick with heavy sorrow as Mr. Beeds's funeral unfolded. The town came together, each person paying their respects to a man who had quietly shaped their lives for nearly two decades. Josh sat silently beside his mother, Carol, his gaze wandering around the room. He could see Kevin and his parents sitting ahead of him, their faces drawn in shared grief. To his right, Lily, the twins, and their families sat together, a tight-knit group of mourners.

The sound of a woman's voice broke the silence. It was Augusta Beeds, the daughter of the deceased, her face pale, and her vision blurred from crying. She stepped up to the podium, trembling as she spoke. Every word she uttered seemed to weigh on her, marked by an unmistakable vulnerability. Her voice quivered, and her handkerchief seemed like her only life-line, wiping away the flood of tears that streaked down her face.

The loss was raw. Her grief was impossible to mask as she recounted memories of a father who had always been there for her, a quiet man whose presence was now nothing but a painful memory. Her sobs seemed to echo through the room, stirring a profound emotion within Josh's chest, a sympathy that tugged at him.

After her emotional speech, Josh and his mother, along with many others, approached Augusta to offer their condolences. People spoke warmly of Mr. Beeds's dedication to the children of this town, and Augusta thanked each one with quiet grace. But when the ceremony ended and most people had left,

Augusta remained. She needed a moment alone with her father —a final goodbye to the man who shaped her world.

In the stillness of the room, with only Augusta standing by his coffin, the air felt as if it shifted. She leaned forward, her fingers trembling as she took her father's cold hand in her own. She whispered, her voice laced with sadness, "I wish we had more time. I wish this didn't happen so suddenly." Her voice cracked, and the tears flowed freely once more. "There's so much I wanted to say. So much I should have said," she sobbed, her body shaking with the weight of her regret.

Suddenly, a deep, chilling voice broke through her cries. "Speak, child. I am here and listening."

Augusta froze. The sound of her father's voice was unmistakable, but an element of it seemed amiss. Something was terribly, terribly wrong. She pulled away from his hand, her heart pounding as fear crept into her bones. She looked up at her father's face, only to see a pair of burning red pupils staring at her. The cold, dead eyes of the man she had known were now alive with an abnormal hunger.

Her breath caught in her throat as her father's lifeless body stirred, one hand lifting to grab her. He reached for her with unnatural strength, his grip tightening around her shirt as he pulled her closer. Augusta struggled to break free, but his hold was like iron. Her legs trembled beneath her as she tried to push him away, but she couldn't escape. The coffin toppled over, crashing to the floor with a deafening noise.

In sheer panic, Augusta turned to run, but before she could reach the door, she stopped in her tracks. Her father's voice, tender yet filled with a terrifying bitterness, called out to her, "Augie."

It was the name he had always used for her when she was little. The sweetness of that nickname now twisted with a malevolence.

She turned slowly, and the sight that greeted her was enough to freeze her blood. Her father was no longer the man she had loved, but something else entirely. His eyes glowed with an unnatural fury as he crawled toward her, his movements jerky and uncoordinated like a creature of nightmares.

As she turned to run toward the exit, her father magically appeared in front of her. He grabbed her by the throat and started walking back toward the coffin.

"You said you wanted to say so much to me, but then you ran away," he spoke. "Just like when you were a child, you wanted one thing, but ran after something else."

Augusta struggled harder now, her heart pounding in her chest as his grip tightened, lifting her off the ground by the throat. She gasped for air, her hands clawing at his stiff fingers, but it was no use. His strength was overwhelming. He dragged her back toward the coffin, his words dripping with anger and despair.

"You wanted me to be with you, but I can't. Don't you understand? I am dead!" he spat, his voice now twisted with something dark and malicious. "But you, my sweet child." He paused, lifting her higher, his face inches from hers. "My sweet, selfish child. You could be with me."

He grinned. "All you need to do is make the ultimate sacrifice."

His words were a death sentence. He pulled her even closer, suffocating her with each passing second. Augusta's vision blurred, her breaths shallow and weak, but she refused to give in. Her heart, though nearly crushed, still beat, hoping someone would come to her rescue.

And, as if summoned by some distant prayer, men rushed into the hall. They saw what was happening, and without hesitation, tackled Mr. Beeds to the floor. The hold on Augusta loosened, and she crumpled to the ground, gasping for air. Her lungs burned as she struggled to breathe, her throat raw from his grip.

The moment Mr. Beeds hit the floor, whatever force that had taken hold of him was apparently gone. His body lay still, lifeless once more. No longer a threat. But the damage had been done. Rushed to the hospital, Augusta clung precariously to life, almost unconscious.

Word of the event spread like wildfire, yet its meaning remained elusive. How could it be possible? A dead man rising, attacking his daughter? It was beyond comprehension. There were witnesses, plenty of them. And Augusta, bruised and broken, lay in a hospital bed, struggling to find words for the nightmare she experienced.

In the aftermath, Augusta made a decision that no one could blame her for. The family, because of their religious convictions, had always buried their dead, no matter what. But after this incident, Mr. Beeds's body was to be cremated, his remains scattered. Mr. Beeds, the kind, gentle teacher, was now much more as exaggerated stories of the man started spreading through town.

Josh saw Carol leave for work the next day. He promised her that he would look into colleges, though secretly, he was thinking about getting a job and making money. His thoughts lingered on his moment with Lily the other night, and he was eagerly looking forward to their date. He imagined taking Lily to a nice, fancy restaurant in an exquisite car, treating her like royalty, and giving her the night of her life. But he had no money, and while he considered looking for a job again, subconsciously, he was thinking about the lamp.

He considered sharing his newfound secret with her but decided against it. The idea of introducing her to this made him uncomfortable. Things were going well with her, and he didn't want to ruin it. But...he needed to tell someone. He thought about his mother but immediately shot it down. She would panic and throw massive tantrums, making the situation worse. He thought about his friends, the twins, and Anthony. The twins were too goofy, and the others were reliable friends, but this wasn't something he would trust them with. All this while, he knew exactly who he wanted to talk to. He fired up his chat program and reached out to Kevin.

Shadelss143: Yo Kev you there

TintedG564: Some of us work

Shadelss143: Seriously I need to see you ASAP!

TintedG564: I'll stop by after work

Shadelss143: Fine! But don't complain if you aren't the first to know

TintedG564: It's like that Fine I'm coming

Shadelss143: Cool

Fifteen minutes later, there was the sound of a car stopping, and Josh was already at the door. Kevin walked in, throwing his jacket on the chair. "What's the big news?"

"Follow me," replied Josh as he headed into his room.

They both stood in Josh's bedroom, and Kevin widened his eyes and stared at Josh. "Okay, so?"

Josh looked at his friend, but his mind was somewhere else. He knew Kevin, he also knew this was a bad idea. But he was way over his head and needed someone, and he trusted Kevin above anyone else.

"Keep an open mind, and please, try to keep your mouth shut!" pleaded Josh.

Josh rubbed the lamp and blurred smoke poured out of its opening. Kevin's jaw dropped as he stood there staring at the blurred image of a creature staring back at them both.

"Bud…" Kevin stated.

"Yeah," said Josh, looking at Kevin excitedly.

"It's kinda hard to keep my mouth shut," whispered Kevin.

"You summoned me, Aaqa!" boomed the creature.

"Whoa!" Kevin squealed. "This thing is freaky, man! Just look at my arms." Every hair was standing on his arm. "Is this thing, like, trying to enter me? I feel as if something has crept inside my body?"

Kevin was squirming uncomfortably. He experienced fascination, annoyance, and fear simultaneously. He was sweating a little and holding tightly to Josh's arm as he tried to process the incident, but it confused him even more.

"Yeah, that's the side effect of bringing him out," mumbled Josh.

"Okay, so what's the deal? Does it do anything, or is it just freaky?" Kevin asked, his voice laced with forced sarcasm, trying to mask the unease settling deep in his gut.

He kept glancing at the creature, struggling to keep his eyes on its face. There was something wrong about it—something ancient, twisted, and far beyond human comprehension. It wasn't just disturbing—it seemed wrong in the very fabric of reality.

The creature hadn't moved since they arrived. It just stood there, still as stone, its eyes locked on them as if it was watching with amusement…or hunger.

Kevin swallowed hard and looked back at Josh. "I hope he won't eat us."

"No." Josh's voice was low, steady—cold. "He's bound to me until I die."

Kevin blinked. "What the hell does that even mean?"

Josh didn't flinch. "It means this creature—this thing—is bound to serve me. Until the day I die."

Kevin stepped back, glancing between Josh and the entity. "No… no, man. We need to send it back. Seal it. Bury it. I don't care how. I'm seriously creeped out right now."

"It told me I can wish for things," Josh said, his voice tinged with both excitement and unease. "At least…that's what I understood."

Kevin's eyes widened, his curiosity momentarily pushing aside the fear. "Seriously? Like actual wishes?" He paused. "How many? I mean, it's usually three, right? That's what all the stories say."

Josh opened his mouth to answer, but Kevin jumped in, unable to hold back.

"Just be careful, man. You don't want to accidentally utter something like—oh, I don't know—God, Kevin, I wish you weren't here, and poof, I'm gone. That'd be a real waste of a wish."

Josh rolled his eyes. "Gee, thanks, Kevin." His tone was dripping with sarcasm.

Kevin smirked. "I'm just saying—don't be a dufus. You usually are, so I figured I'd remind you."

He glanced at the creature, half-hoping it would crack a smile at the joke, but it didn't even blink.

Josh just shook his head, more tired than amused, and looked back at his friend. "He didn't say how many wishes. Just that... he owes me."

"What?!" said Kevin. "Infinite wishes?" He turned toward the thing and ordered, "Creature, get us some excellent coffee, pronto." Kevin turned to Josh and smiled.

All of a sudden, the room darkened, and the creature turned toward Kevin and glared in absolute hatred. He then started moving toward him as his words resonated to where it seemed like the walls were screaming. "Filthy insect of dirt, scum of the known and unknown universe, you would dare command us..."

Kevin was on his knees, trying to breathe, when Josh stepped in. "Creature, return to the lamp!"

The smoke started returning to the lamp. Kevin was on the floor, lying on his back, trying to breathe.

"I told you to keep your mouth shut," Josh uttered calmly.

"Let's never," he coughed, "do that again," Kevin responded, still trying to catch his breath.

Kevin lay on the floor, thinking and panting, as Josh went to get him a glass of water.

After he managed a few sips, Kevin's condition improved and he got back on his feet and started wiping the sweat off his face. "So, this thing is like your slave or something? You just tell it what to do?" he asked.

Josh sighed, rubbing his hands together as if trying to warm something that had gone cold inside him. "It's more complicated than that. What it did to you—it did to me too. I almost didn't make it back. This isn't as simple as it sounds, Kev."

Kevin chuckled awkwardly, brushing off the weight of Josh's words with a smirk. "Sure it is," he remarked, clearly trying to lighten the mood. "Just don't piss the thing off like I did." He sprang to his feet, a spark of excitement brightening his expression.

"C'mon, let's see what it can do. Bring it out again and ask for something."

Josh stared at him, his expression equal parts regret and disappointment. He was afraid that this would happen.

"Like what?" he asked quietly.

Kevin didn't pause. Didn't notice the shift in Josh's tone…or if he did, he didn't care. The thrill and possibility absorbed him.

"He says, 'Like what'," Kevin laughed. "Honestly, man, what do we want, huh? What do we want?"

Josh didn't move. He just watched him, sensing that familiar pull in his gut—that quiet, uneasy voice that always whispered too late.

"Money?"

"Yes, bro! *MONEY!*" Kevin shouted, throwing his arms up as if they'd already won the lottery.

Josh perceived that inner voice intensify, alarm bells tolling like sirens. But this excited him. All his life, he had been short of one thing, and here it was, ready for the taking.

"Okay, you ready? And remember, don't talk to it. It hates us, all of us. I am the only one it will talk to because I freed it."

"*It will only talk to me,*" Kevin mocked, crossing his arms and smirking at Josh. "Wait—don't just ask for money."

"Why not?" Josh whined, frowning at his friend's sudden change in tone.

"Be-CAUSE," Kevin said, dragging out the word with exaggerated sass, "that thing is going to drop ten million dollars' worth of money bags in your bedroom, and good luck explaining that to your mom."

Josh paused, blinking at the absurd visual. "Good point. Wait… ten million?"

"Less?" Kevin asked, raising an eyebrow. "All right, ten billion." He grinned mischievously.

Josh's eyes widened. "I am not asking for ten billion or even ten million!"

"If you ask for one million, I am going to kill you," Kevin shot back, half-joking, half-serious. "Here's exactly what you're going to do. You rub that lamp. The creepy smoke monster comes out. You pull up your bank app and tell him to deposit ten million dollars into that account. THE. END!" He threw his hands up for dramatic effect.

Josh sighed. "Please say nothing," he muttered as he rubbed the lamp.

The room darkened, and the creature appeared in a swirl of smoke. Its glowing eyes burned with disdain.

Josh swallowed nervously. "I want ten million dollars added to my bank account, please," he said in a small voice, glancing at Kevin for reassurance.

The thing disappeared in a flash and returned just as quickly, its voice low and venomous. "Your wish is my command, Aaqa."

Josh whipped out his phone, quickly opening his banking app. Kevin leaned over his shoulder. "Hurry, bro, se—OH MY GOD!" Kevin shouted, his voice cracking. "YESSSSSSS!"

Josh stared in disbelief, his account now showing the impossible. He turned to Kevin, and both of them erupted into cheers, yelling at the top of their lungs. Kevin grabbed him in a bear hug, jumping up and down like a kid on Christmas morning. "We are freaking rich! RICH!" he yelled.

Josh, still grinning ear to ear, turned to the creature. "Please go back into the lamp, and…thank you," he added politely.

The creature's smoky form dissolved back into the lamp, and the room returned to normal.

"Ten million freaking dollars, man. I don't believe this!" Kevin exclaimed, pacing in excitement. "Dude, you are freaking awesome!"

Josh smiled, shaking his head. "We need to come up with a name for this thing."

"You didn't ask him his name?" Kevin asked, raising an eyebrow.

"I did, but apparently, we're not worthy of knowing it."

"Well, let's just call him…Bob," Kevin suggested.

"Bob? He doesn't look like a Bob," Josh said, his face scrunched in disbelief.

Kevin tilted his head thoughtfully. "I wonder if he can take human form?"

Josh hesitated. "I don't know…hmm, human form." He thought for a moment, then added, "I don't know if I should ask. He hates us."

Kevin frowned. "Why?"

"Why?" Josh repeated. "Well, I'm pretty sure we—or humans— are responsible for him being locked up in a tiny lamp for thousands of years."

"Oh." Kevin blinked, lost in thought. "Bring him out and ask if he can take human form. We might need him, like, in public."

"In public? Are you out of your mind?!"

Kevin shrugged. "Dude, I need to go shopping. I need him to follow us. I'll point at things, and he'll make it happen. Easy!"

Josh facepalmed. "He's going to kill you, you idiot. Were you not on the floor begging for air five minutes ago? Or have you already forgotten?"

Kevin pleaded, clasping his hands together dramatically. "Just bring him out. Please!"

Josh groaned but reluctantly rubbed the lamp again. Smoke filled the room as the creature materialized, its presence oppressive and disdainful.

"Your wish, Aaqa," it snarled, glaring at them as if it had far better places to be.

"I have a question," Josh started. "Can you take human form, and is it okay to call you Bob?"

The creature—now a man—fixed its icy stare on Josh, silent and unimpressed. A heavier air hung as if his disdain were a tangible force pressing down on them.

Kevin nudged Josh with his elbow, whispering, "Dude, he's not saying no. I think we're good with Bob."

Josh shot him a side-eye glance, then cautiously addressed the creature again. "So, um, Bob, is that okay with you… you know, something to call you?"

The man's expression didn't change, but his lips tightened somewhat. His voice, low and gravelly, cut through the silence like a blade. "Call me what you will, Aaqa. It matters not."

Kevin smirked, clapping his hands together. "Bob it is! Welcome to the team, Bob."

Josh winced at Kevin's casual tone but decided not to push his luck. "Okay, Bob, thank you for…you know, taking on this form. It's—uh—helpful."

Bob said nothing, his gaze unwavering and sharp. It was as if he were sizing them up and finding them entirely lacking.

Josh cleared his throat awkwardly. "Can I call on you when I want to, or do I always have to rub the lamp?"

The creature grumbled, its voice harsh. The man—Bob—gave a slow, disdainful nod. "I answer Aaqa, no matter where you are."

Kevin grinned, nudging Josh again. "Man, I like him. He's got that whole grumpy-but-loyal vibe going on."

Josh ignored him and nodded toward Bob. "All right, then. Please return to the lamp for now. I'll call on you when I need you."

With a swirl of smoke, Bob's form dissolved into the air, and the lamp glowed faintly before dimming once more.

Kevin let out a low whistle, shaking his head. "I can't believe this is happening. We have a genie—or whatever he is—and his name is Bob. Classic."

Josh sighed, clutching the lamp tightly. "Yeah, and let's not forget, he looks like he'd rather crush us than grant our wishes. Let's not give him a reason."

"Relax, man. What's the worst that could happen?"

Josh gave him a pointed stare. "Famous last words, Kevin. Famous last words." He quickly put the lamp into his bag. "I don't want Mom getting her hands on this and rubbing it by accident," he muttered.

Kevin laughed. "Oh, man, that'd be a sight."

Josh glanced at him, already heading toward the door. "Yeah, let's go."

Kevin followed eagerly. "Dude, we got the money! Let's get a car!"

Josh frowned, unsure of how to deal with that one. "Yeah, and how do I explain that to Mom?"

Kevin's eyes lit up. "We won't explain anything to Mom because the car will be with me," he asserted confidently.

"With you?"

"That's right!" Kevin responded with a grin. "My mind works fast, especially when it comes to women and hot cars."

Josh smirked. "Does it now?"

Ignoring Josh's sarcasm, Kevin laid out his plan. "Here's how this is going to work," he said, shifting into gear as they started driving. "We'll go to the nearest town, talk to a car salesperson, get a certified check from the bank, and buy the car. Simple." Josh was about to speak, but Kevin cut him off. "I'm not done yet. We can't do anything here in this town. You know why? Your mom!"

Josh shot him a glance, but Kevin wasn't finished. "We go to the bank…they call your mom. We go to a car showroom… someone tells your mom. Everybody knows everybody in this town!"

Josh reluctantly agreed, "True." He fell silent for a moment, thinking hard. "Why don't you drive home, Kev?"

"Huh? No, I'm driving to the next town. It's an hour and a half away. They have branches of our bank, so this will be easy!" Kevin was practically bouncing in his seat.

Josh's tone grew serious. "Your home, please, NOW!"

Kevin shot him a quick, annoyed glance. "Fine, fine! But I don't understand why we're wasting time when I have a plan for getting a brand-new car."

Josh didn't back down. "I'm serious. Your home, now."

Kevin rolled his eyes and muttered something under his breath. But he complied, slamming on the brakes and taking a sharp left at the next signal.

The car screeched marginally as he made the sharp turn, his frustration evident in how he gripped the steering wheel. "You're such a buzzkill, man," he grumbled, shaking his head.

Josh crossed his arms, glancing out the window. "I'm trying to think long-term, Kev. We can't just blow through ten million dollars like Monopoly money."

Kevin smirked, tapping his fingers on the steering wheel. "I mean, technically, we *could*. That's the whole point of having ten million dollars, isn't it?"

Josh sighed, pushing his hair back. "Look, I get it—you're excited. I am too, but if we screw this up, we're done for. And we need a solid plan, not some half-baked scheme that will get us in trouble—or worse, caught."

Kevin glanced at him briefly, a mix of irritation and understanding on his face. "Okay, fine. We'll do it your way—for now. But, dude, we have to do something big. I mean, what's the point of having all that money if we're just going to sit on it?"

Josh hesitated before responding, his tone thoughtful. "I have a plan. And we need to make sure no one notices anything unusual. That includes your mom, my mom, and everyone else in this town."

His friend let out a long, dramatic sigh. "Fine. But if I miss out on my dream car because you're overthinking, I'm never letting you live it down."

Josh smirked, his mood lightening. "Deal."

As they pulled into Kevin's driveway, he threw the car into park and turned to Josh. "You're no fun, man. No fun at all."

Josh chuckled, stepping out of the car. "You'll thank me later when the FBI doesn't interrogate us."

"You're lucky I like you. Real lucky."

They both surveyed the area. They wanted this done clean; they weren't just chasing dreams. There was the money, the car, the life that had always appeared distant. The kind of life that turns heads, opens doors, and makes people jealous without knowing why.

But above all, they wanted secrecy. No one could know. Not their families. Not their friends. Not anyone.

And maybe—just maybe—they could actually pull it off.

Because unlike everyone else stuck grinding through life the hard way…they had something no one else did.

Magic.

CHAPTER 4

THE SECOND WISH

Kevin's old Ford Taurus sat in the driveway like a forgotten relic of a simpler time, its faded paint and chipped edges a stark contrast to the anticipation hanging in the air. Kevin and Josh stood side by side, the tension between them as palpable as the evening breeze.

"Okay, what now?" Kevin asked, rocking back on his heels. He conveyed a mix of curiosity and impatience.

Josh's lips curved into a sly smile. "We can't go crazy buying expensive stuff—not yet, anyway. We need to figure out how to make the money legit. You know what they say...follow the money." He paused, then added with a smirk, "But..."

Kevin raised a brow. "But?"

"Bob, I need you," Josh stated, his tone calm but deliberate.

The air seemed to ripple as a swirling shadow appeared, forming into the familiar figure of an old bald man in a flannel shirt. Bob's cold, calculating glance locked onto Josh. "Aaqa," it hissed, voice dripping with disdain.

Josh didn't hesitate. "Bob, I want a brand-new Dodge Challenger Hellcat, red, fully fueled, with a license plate and registration in my name. Put the car in Kevin's garage."

Kevin's eyes widened in disbelief. "Wait, you're serious?"

Josh turned to him with a steady gaze. "Your garage is empty, right?"

Kevin nodded. "Yeah."

Neither of them had a chance to speak further as Bob disappeared in a swirl of air, reappearing seconds later. "Done," it said flatly, the loathing in its tone impossible to miss.

Josh nodded toward the garage. "Kev, open it."

Kevin hesitated, then moved to the garage door. His fingers trembled partly as he pressed the button, the motor whirring to life. Both boys leaned forward, eyes glued to the slowly rising door. As it crept upward, the gleam of an unmistakably red and impossibly shiny object emerged.

"Yes, bro!" Kevin shouted, throwing his arms around Josh in a bear hug. His excitement was almost childlike, pure and unrestrained.

Josh laughed, though his tone carried a warning. "Calm down! People might see us."

The garage door fully opened, revealing the Hellcat in all its glory. Its aggressive stance, gleaming red paint, and pristine condition gave the impression it had just rolled off a showroom floor. Kevin stared, wide-eyed, his hands on his head as he circled the car. "Look at that! That beautiful piece of machinery!" he yelled, his voice echoing in the driveway. He glanced back at Bob, his face alight with gratitude. "Dude, it's got a number plate and everything! I could hug you right now!"

Josh stepped in, his tone firm but not unkind. "Bob, back to the lamp, please."

The creature shot Josh a glare but obeyed, vanishing with a faint swirl of air.

With Bob gone, the boys turned their full attention to the car. They circled it repeatedly, their hands grazing over its smooth surface, admiring every curve and line. Kevin's enthusiasm was infectious, but his attempts to convince Josh to hand over the keys were fruitless. Determined to savor the moment, Josh slipped into the driver's seat, the key fob firm in his hand.

Kevin climbed into the passenger seat, practically bouncing with excitement. "Man, we're driving this thing, right? No destination, no plan—just driving."

Josh grinned, firing up the engine. The roar of the Hellcat echoed through the neighborhood, sending shivers down their spines. "Let's go."

As they tore down the road, the thrill of the ride filled the air, the car's power surging beneath them. Kevin rummaged through the glove compartment, pulling out the car's registration. His eyes scanned the document before he read aloud, "Mr. Joshua Cox."

He glanced at Josh, a grin spreading across his face. "Your name's on the registration, dude. It's official." But then his smile faltered, replaced by a look of concern. "Wait…we forgot insurance."

Josh groaned, his hand briefly leaving the wheel to pinch the bridge of his nose. "Bob!" he called out.

The old man materialized in the back seat, his expression as sour as ever. "Aaqa?"

"Please get me full insurance on this car for a year."

Bob muttered something under his breath, and in an instant, an insurance card appeared in Josh's hand.

"Thanks, Bob," he said, though the gratitude he conveyed was muted. "Back to the lamp."

Bob dissipated as if he was never there.

Kevin was yelling, "You keep this up, and we may have to free you, you wonderfully evil creature!"

The car's engine roared as they picked up speed, the thrill of the drive filling the silence between them. For now, they weren't thinking about the consequences—just the freedom of the moment and the bond between them that made everything else seem insignificant.

The boys took turns behind the wheel, the roar of the Hellcat's engine their only soundtrack as they raced along the highway and wove through the city streets. The car's raw power was intoxicating, and they couldn't resist flooring it more times than they should have. Each burst of speed was met with their uncontrollable laughter, a mix of exhilaration and reckless abandon.

"Man, we're supposed to break it in gently!" Kevin said, gasping between laughs.

Josh grinned, his hands gripping the wheel as the car surged forward. "Who cares? This thing was made to run!"

Their phones buzzed intermittently, disrupting the blissful escape. First came calls from their moms, checking in as usual. Kevin casually lied, saying he was working, while Josh covered with a vague explanation about "helping Kevin out." Then Kevin's boss called, and quick on his feet, he spun a tale about taking Josh to the hospital for some imaginary ailment.

"Your boss bought that?" Josh asked, shaking his head as he switched lanes.

Kevin leaned back in his seat, looking far too pleased with himself. "Of course he did. I'm an artist with words."

Josh rolled his eyes, but a small smile tugged at the corners of his lips.

Their journey took them to the next town and back, with Josh stopping at an ATM to withdraw some cash. The day extended endlessly in the best way, with every minute filled with laughter, banter, and a shared passion for cars. They dove headfirst into discussing the Hellcat in detail—its aggressive design, the guttural growl of its engine, its speed, and how it stacked up against other cars they idolized. They argued over its history and future, comparing notes like lifelong enthusiasts.

Overwhelmed by hunger, they stopped for burgers, laughing about their day. At the mall, they wandered aimlessly, poking fun at strangers' questionable fashion choices. A passing cinema lured them, but neither agreed on whether to stay and watch a movie or return to the car for further driving.

By the time the sun dipped below the horizon, they found themselves parked on a quiet mountain road just outside town. The Hellcat idled softly as they leaned against its hood, watching the fiery hues of the sunset paint the sky. The moment was still, but their thoughts weren't.

Kevin broke the silence first. "I still don't get why you chose a Dodge. I mean, we could've had a Porsche or a Ferrari—something that screams, 'I've made it!'" He gestured dramatically.

Josh smirked, shaking his head. "And how exactly are you going to explain a Ferrari in your junkyard garage, Kev?"

Kevin snapped his fingers. "Easy. I tell them a rich friend gave it to me, Mr. Nunyabiniz."

Josh laughed, but the sound was brief. "You're impossible."

Kevin wasn't done. "Listen, we've got the genie—uh, Bob. Why not go big? Let's get a mansion. Heck, let's move to—"

Josh cut him off, his voice tinged with frustration. "And what do I tell Mom, Kev? How do I explain all of this to her?"

"Oh…yeah. I forgot about your mom." He shifted uneasily, his fingers twitching at his side as if he were trying to keep himself from fidgeting. He paused, biting his lip, then spoke slowly and cautiously. "We could…ask Bob to help us out. Make her believe everything. I mean…he can do that, right?"

Josh's reaction was immediate—volcanic.

"Are you serious right now?" he snapped with a furious expression. "You want that thing messing with my mom's head? And what about the neighbors? Her friends? The dozens of people who'll start asking questions? What then?"

Kevin winced at the tone, his jaw tightening. He hated being wrong—loathed being yelled at. He turned his gaze back to the road, pretending to watch the traffic on the highway.

A moment later, his brow furrowed in thought. Then his face lit up. "Wait—I've got it."

"Do you now?" Josh's tone was heavy with sarcasm.

Kevin ignored it. "We move to a big city. New York, LA, Chicago—somewhere where no one cares how you got your money. We start a business. Anything you want, but I vote for something car-related. We use Bob to help us build it into something legit, and in six months, we bring your mom out to live with us. By then, the money's clean, the business is booming, and no one's asking questions."

Josh turned to him, his expression serious. "You don't get it, Kev. She'd never leave this town. Her parents, her brother—they all died here. This place is her home. She knows everyone here. I can't ask her to give that up. I won't."

Kevin stepped closer, his tone softer now. "She would leave for you, Josh. If it meant giving you a better life, she'd do it. Trust me. This can work. We just have to try."

Josh didn't reply. His gaze remained fixed on the horizon, the golden light of the setting sun reflecting in his eyes. He folded his arms, the weight of Kevin's words pressing down on him. The thought of leaving, of uprooting everything he and his mom had built, seemed impossible. But Kevin's plan lingered in the back of his mind, teasing him with the faintest hint of hope.

The two boys stood in silence, the sound of the Hellcat's engine fading as the sun disappeared below the mountains.

"I never went shopping." Kevin smiled, looking at Josh. "Bob would be an awesome asset at the mall."

"He is going to kill you if you keep annoying him," reminded Josh.

"Nah," responded Kevin. "I am your best bud."

"That is what scares me."

As it was getting dark, Josh returned to the car and declared, "I am starving. Let's go eat."

"Okay." They both jumped in.

Josh wanted to go to their usual burger joint, but Kevin insisted on going to the Freedom Mall.

"Why can't we go where we usually go?" Josh took a left turn at the next signal, a little annoyed. "You know I love the food there."

"Yes, I know!" Kevin said seriously. "Lily works there at a department store. We can pick her up."

Five minutes later, they were parking at the Freedom Mall with no more arguments from Josh. The two of them grabbed a bite to eat and discussed the horrible taste of music on the FM channel. They then checked out a few shops before entering a large department store.

"Hey, look!" expressed Josh. "That little shirt up there. I used to have something like that when I was a kid." He approached the boys' section and started admiring the little T-shirt with a large, friendly dinosaur. Anything his father bought for him when his family was together was valuable to him. It was a reminder of better times and fond memories. He turned around, only to see that Kevin was gone. He probably went to the bathroom, Josh figured.

A few minutes later, the PA system came on.

"Mr. Josh Cox! Please move away from the boys' underwear section." Kevin's voice was booming through the speakers. "Again, Mr. Josh Cox, please move away from the boys' underwear section. The women's lingerie section is right across the aisle."

Josh looked up and shook his head. A few people were looking his way. Kevin stood at the end of the aisle, and Lily was with him, both smiling and laughing.

"You have always been a douchebag!" Josh said with a smile as he approached them.

The store manager walked up. He was thin with spectacles and had a serious look about him, yet he seemed like a kind man. "You again," the manager said, looking at Kevin. He turned to Lily. "I am getting a little frustrated with your boyfriend!"

"He is not my boyfriend," Lily corrected, trying to hold back her smile.

"Public service, sir; he was standing in the boys' section for too long," Kevin said seriously, though he had a smirk.

"Come on." Josh grabbed Kevin and started walking toward the exit.

Lily approached them and whispered, "I will be right out."

A few minutes later, Lily joined the boys, who were waiting by the exit.

Lily, trying to hold back a laugh, nudged Kevin. "You know, one of these days, you're really going to get us kicked out of places."

"Aw, c'mon, we're just getting started," he teased. "There's a whole mall full of people to annoy."

Lily gave him a playful glance. "Just wait until you see the mall security."

Josh rolled his eyes. "Alright, alright. Let's just get out of here before Kevin ends up on some 'wanted' list."

They moved toward the exit, and Kevin slung an arm around Lily's shoulder. "I can tell your boss likes me!" he declared. "See how he personally shows up every time I stop by?"

She laughed, shaking her head. "You'll never change, Kevin."

Josh smiled as they stepped into the parking lot. They may have gotten a few stares inside the mall, but these ridiculous moments with his best friends made everything seem perfect. The chaos, laughter, and annoying stunts were all part of the crazy ride he wouldn't trade for anything.

The parking lot stretched before them, massive and brightly lit, with glowing signs from the surrounding stores casting light over the sea of cars. A freeway ran parallel to the lot, traffic zipping by, making the place vibrant with movement.

Kevin's eyes gleamed with mischief as he looked over at Lily. "Lily, come check out our new ride!"

Josh, already knowing how this would play out, stayed silent. He wasn't in the mood for the inevitable barrage of questions.

"Ride? You got a new car? You?" Lily's voice cracked with disbelief. "You borrowed money from me last week! How the hell do you afford a new car, you scumbag?" she snapped, punching Kevin in the arm.

Kevin laughed and pointed at Josh, his smirk wide. "Not me, doofus! Your boyfriend over there."

Lily's gaze shifted toward Josh as they approached the gleaming, brand-new Dodge Challenger. Her eyebrows shot up in surprise, but her expression showed no trace of admiration—only confusion.

"Josh," she said slowly, concern lacing her words. "I didn't think your dad made that much. How—how did you afford this?"

Kevin nudged Josh with a grin. "Show her," he whispered.

Josh shot him a warning look. "Shut up."

Lily, still unsure, glanced back and forth between them. "Show me what?"

Kevin's grin widened. "Bob!" he shouted.

Lily's head whipped around, startled. Nothing happened.

Kevin called again, louder this time, "Bob!"

Still nothing.

Josh had made up his mind. He wasn't going to tell Lily.

Kevin was easy. Laid-back, quick to go along with things, never one to dig too deep if it meant avoiding a headache. But Lily? Lily was sharp. Too sharp. She saw through half-truths like they were glass.

She wasn't just smart—she was tenacious. Being nice never meant she could be lied to. She wouldn't accept "because I said so" as a reason, and she definitely wouldn't smile and nod while everything inside her screamed that a problem existed.

And Josh knew it. He knew exactly how it would go. She'd ask questions—hard ones. The kind he couldn't answer without unraveling everything. She'd dissect every lie, press every soft spot until it bled.

And the worst part? He knew he'd lose. Before she even opened her mouth, before the first challenge left her lips, he already knew—he couldn't out-argue her.

"Stop it, Kev," Josh muttered, his unease creeping in.

Kevin ignored him and shouted one more time, "BOB!" His sounds echoed through the empty spaces of the parking lot.

Josh realized the questions were coming; she will ask, and he will have to lie. Or tell her the truth…

"FINE!" Josh snapped, exasperated. His shoulders stiffened, and he muttered, "Bob."

Suddenly, a figure appeared in front of them, seemingly from nowhere. The old, bald man in the flannel shirt stood there, unmoving. Lily recoiled in shock, her body going rigid. She stepped back, her breath catching as she bumped into the side of the car. Her skin prickled, the hairs on her arms standing up. Something was unsettling about how Bob stared at her—too intensely and hungrily.

Her chest tightened, and she glanced left, then right, trying to find something—anything—to anchor her. But the air was heavy, almost suffocating.

Kevin's smirk returned, his voice low and teasing. "Is something wrong, Lily?"

"Where did he come from, Josh?" she asked, her voice shaky as she looked at him, still trying to process what was happening.

Josh rubbed his hands together, visibly nervous. "I should've never told you about him," he muttered, his discomfort becoming palpable.

Kevin, clearly enjoying the discomfort, looked back at Bob. "Relax, Josh. Lily, check this out." He turned to the creature, his voice growing louder. "Hey, Bob, do something!"

But as Bob slowly turned his gaze toward Kevin, the air seemed to freeze. Kevin's breath caught in his throat, and he dropped to one knee, gasping for air.

Josh stepped forward, instinctively placing himself between Kevin and the creature. "STOP!" he yelled, his voice firm and desperate. "Bob, stop!"

The creature's eyes flickered at Josh, dark and unreadable. Kevin, still kneeling, gasped for breath, his face pale. "Make him promise," he whimpered, his voice weak.

"Shut up, Kev!" Josh barked, his frustration rising.

Lily stood frozen, torn between fear and confusion. Her fists clenched at her sides, her breath shallow. She looked down at her hands, pressing one into the other, trying to ground herself. But it wasn't working. Her heart raced and tears pricked at the corners of her eyes as the weight of the situation crushed down on her. This was her life now—this terrifying, strange new world of threats she couldn't understand.

Still on his knees, Kevin gasped, "Make him promise, Josh. Please. Make him promise never to hurt us."

Josh stood tall, facing Bob, his voice hardening with resolve. "Bob!" he commanded, his stare never leaving the creature. "I command you never to hurt me, my friends, or anyone I care about. I command you never to hurt anyone."

For a moment, everything seemed to stop. The world held its breath. Cars zoomed past on the freeway, but the area was deathly still, as if time itself had paused, waiting for Bob's response.

The creature stood motionless, staring at Josh, eyes calculating, weighing the command. The silence was heavy, extending until it seemed the entire world anticipated Bob's action.

But Bob's promise had to wait. The sudden silence shattered when four familiar figures emerged from the shadows, their voices ringing in unison.

"Well, well, well…" the twins said, their words synchronized. "Nice wheels."

Josh barely noticed Frank, Frederick, Tracie, and Liz approaching from behind. Having just parked, they were on their way to say hello. As Frank and Frederick circled the car, pretending to inspect it, Kevin groaned and rolled his eyes.

"Where did you steal it from?" asked Frank.

"We didn't steal it!" Kevin shot back, clearly frustrated by their teasing.

"No, no, you misunderstand," Frederick said, giving a nod of approval.

"Yes, we approve and admire your talent." Frank smirked.

Meanwhile, Bob lingered like a shadow—always there, never quite seen. Josh's friends remained oblivious to his presence, caught up in their laughter and careless banter. But Lily… Lily wasn't laughing.

Her expression had changed. No longer the confident girl with the sharp tongue and fearless eyes, she looked…lost. Frightened. Like a child stumbling through a nightmare she couldn't wake from. She kept sneaking glances at Bob, quick flicks of her eyes that darted away the moment they met his. Then she'd force a smile—tight, unnatural—pretending her friends' jokes weren't hollow echoes in her ears.

She was the only one who truly sensed it. The shift. The danger. The thing crawling just beneath the surface of this entire charade.

Bob had his eyes glued to her. A predator eyeing prey, his fixation unsettling, obsessive. One part of him craved her in the way a man might long for something forbidden. Another part…wanted to devour her. Not metaphorically. Literally.

There was something grotesque in his stare, something that blurred the line between sadistic stalker and feral beast. And Lily sensed it pressing in on her, inch by inch. Her hands clenched into the Hellcat's, seeking comfort, grounding herself —but her senses had already begun to betray her.

Reality was warping, sliding sideways.

And Lily was slipping with it.

Oblivious to what was awaiting, Frederick continued, his utterance dripping with sarcasm. "Bro, don't we have the same car locked away in the garage?"

"Yes," Frank replied, adjusting his pipe as he strutted like a smug business executive. "I suggest—"

Frederick cut him off. "We suggest," he corrected, a wicked grin spreading across his face.

"Correct. We suggest," Frank repeated, "that you break into our garage."

Frederick jumped in again. "Like you broke and stole this car and steal the white Bentley."

"For us, of course," Frank added.

"Of course," Frederick agreed. "And all will be forgiven."

Clearly uninterested in the back and forth, Liz crossed her arms and glanced at the group. "Are we going in or staring at the car? I'm freezing," she complained.

"Well, boys, we are off," Frederick remarked, pulling a shiny red card from his pocket. "It's time to see if Daddy dearest knows we also have this credit card."

"We got busted on the last two cards," Frank muttered.

"Dad canceled the cards," Frederick replied dramatically, placing a hand over his chest as though wounded. "What kind of dad does that?"

"Our kind," Frank answered solemnly, shaking his head in mock disapproval.

As the twins continued to banter, their eyes inevitably landed on Bob, who stood nearby, eerily still. Frank froze, his expression faltering. He quickly shoved both hands in his pockets, but his gaze kept drifting back to the old man. Bob, sensing Frank's unease, locked eyes with him, and Frank couldn't look away.

"Is he with you?" Frank asked, his voice low and uncertain.

"This is my dad's friend, Bob," Josh replied awkwardly, his discomfort growing as everyone turned their attention to Bob.

Frederick stepped forward, extending his hand toward Bob. "Hello, Bob, nice to meet you," he said, trying to appear polite. But Bob showed no interest in Frederick and continued staring at Frank, who awkwardly withdrew his hand and stuffed it into his pocket.

The tension was thick. Liz, visibly uncomfortable, spoke up. "Can we go in, please?" Her face reflected a mix of fear and anxiety.

"Yeah," Tracie added, her voice quieter but equally strained.

Frederick, ever the instigator, grinned and turned to Frank. "Is Grandpa going to hang around with us?" he asked, smirking.

But Frank was visibly shaking, his body tense. His gaze remained fixed on Bob, and despite his best efforts, he couldn't look away. Frank fell to his knees, saliva dripping from his mouth. Frederick, noticing his brother's discomfort, stopped smirking. His face shifted with concern as he approached Frank, kneeling beside him.

"You all right, bro?" Frederick asked, his voice laced with worry.

"I don't feel well," Frank gasped.

Lily was trembling now—subtly at first, but enough that everyone noticed. The laughter died down. The smiles faded. A hush fell over the group like a sudden drop in temperature.

They all experienced it. That tightening in the chest. That twist in the gut. Something was wrong.

This so-called 'friend'…this Bob—he didn't fit. He wasn't just odd or awkward, or eccentric. He was unreal.

Josh's heart pounded, the sound of blood rushing into his ears like a crashing tide. The weight of it hit him—this was a mistake. A huge, irreversible mistake. Creatures pulled from myths and nightmares weren't meant to linger under fluorescent lights in a parking lot.

They weren't supposed to stand next to your friends, breathe the same air, or wear someone else's borrowed face.

A sick sense of dread coiled in Josh's stomach. He wanted to take it all back, undo whatever door he'd opened, but wishing it away would only draw more eyes and raise more questions.

"Stop it!" Josh hissed at Bob, his voice full of frustration.

"I'm not doing anything," Bob replied, a smug sense of satisfaction in his voice. "That pile of garbage senses my greatness."

At last, Frederick understood Bob frightened Frank, his vision narrowing in understanding. He turned toward Bob, studying him with suspicion and wariness. Kevin was tending to Frank, trying to help him. Josh took a step toward them but hesitated, glancing at Bob and realizing he couldn't leave the creature alone. There were too many eyes on them now, and he didn't want anyone to know what Bob truly was.

"Let's just go," Liz said, her voice edging impatiently.

Trembling, Frank at last looked away from Bob, rising slowly to walk toward the mall. Frederick and the others followed him, their glances darting nervously toward Bob as they tried to hurry, not wanting to be near the creature for a moment longer.

Josh turned to Bob after they were gone, frustration bubbling inside him. "You enjoyed that, didn't you?"

Bob didn't respond, his eyes unreadable. Josh sighed, staring at the road ahead, a deep regret settling in his chest. He realized that taking the lamp had been a colossal mistake—especially with Kevin's reckless antics adding fuel to the fire.

"Please return to the lamp," Josh muttered under his breath, his voice laced with frustration.

Bob vanished with a whoosh.

The unease in Lily's expression betrayed her feelings. Her unease revealed her disgust. Turning to Josh, she asked softly, "What is that thing?"

He looked at her, his gaze weary. "Remember that lamp I told you about?"

"The one you got—sorry, stole—from your dad?" Lily asked, her voice tinged with disbelief as she met his gaze, her eyes filled with confusion and concern.

"Yeah, that one," he replied. "Turns out there's a real-life genie in the lamp."

Kevin, ever the optimist, piped up with a grin. "Yeah! And Josh has ten million in his bank account."

Josh shook his head, the weight of the situation sinking in. Lily's eyes widened as she stared at him, her expression serious.

"What?" Kevin asked, his face full of excitement. "You guys should be happy! Your boyfriend is rich!"

Lily stepped closer to Josh. "Is this true? Is all of this true? A genie?" Her beautiful face was sad as she stared into his eyes for answers. "I wouldn't have believed it if I hadn't sensed what I did when that thing popped out of nowhere. Josh, you're smart enough to know there's a catch. There always is. And there will be consequences."

"Pfft," Kevin interjected, clearly not grasping the gravity of the situation. "We're moving to New York, and you're not invited!"

"This is not a joke, Kev!" Josh snapped, his anger flaring. "She's right. Something's wrong with all of this."

Kevin threw his hands up in frustration. "What's wrong? What are you talking about? It's the genie-in-a-bottle story, except we've got infinite wishes!"

Josh's voice rose, a mix of fear and frustration. "Except we never read those stories where the genie turns someone's insides out. That didn't happen because it was a *story*!"

Suddenly, Josh's phone rang, cutting through the tension. The three of them exchanged glances as he answered it, the quiet hum of traffic filling the air.

"Hi, Mom," Josh said, his tone shifting to something more neutral. "Yeah, I'm with Kev," he added, trying to calm his mother's concerns. He half-listened as Carol spoke on the other end. "No, it's fine. We ate," he said, trying to wrap up the conversation. "You can go to sleep. I'll see you tomorrow." He paused, his frustration mounting as Carol continued talking. "I did check out colleges, Mom. Can we talk tomorrow?"

"Finally," Josh sighed, hanging up the phone. "Drop me off, and then take the car," he muttered, exhausted.

Lily raised an eyebrow. "I thought this was Josh's car?"

"Mom," Josh replied curtly.

"Ah!" Lily said in realization.

Kevin grinned, clearly enjoying the moment. "Want a ride, Lily? Seats are brand new, too."

Lily, her expression unchanged, shook her head. "I have my car, but thanks."

Josh's frustration was evident as he climbed back into the car with Kevin. Without a word, they drove off, the weight of everything weighing heavily on Josh.

CHAPTER 5
THE RECKONING

When Lily got home, it was 11:00 PM. She had to stop over at the Anderson's home to babysit their two-year-old daughter so they could go on their wedding anniversary date.

Lily lived in a two-story condo with her mom. The homes in her neighborhood mainly had two bedrooms and a single bath. As she entered her house, she saw her mother climbing the stairs. Ms. Rosetta Pierson was just like Lily, only older and chubbier. She worked as a nurse at the local hospital and had to get up very early to make her shift.

"Is that you, Lily?" asked Rosetta as she continued climbing the stairs.

"Yeah, Mom," she answered while closing and locking the main door.

"Good, I'm going to sleep. There is some food on the table," Rosetta continued.

"Okay, thanks, Mom. I'll put the food away before I go to bed," Lily said as she entered the kitchen.

"Night, honey." Rosetta proceeded upstairs.

The living room was small, almost too small as if the walls had crept inward. The furniture looked like it had been chosen by someone long gone—a dusty armchair slumped in one corner, its fabric torn just enough to hint at a hidden item beneath. A crooked coffee table sat in the center, its surface warped, stained by rings that never faded. The air was heavy, faintly metallic, and the dim light from a flickering lamp in the corner cast long, twitching shadows that never quite stayed still. Family portraits lined the walls; however, their faces had faded, and their eyes were too dark and focused.

It didn't have an abandoned impression. It seemed busy... by something that didn't want to be seen.

Lily picked at a leftover slice of cold pizza, her appetite dulled by the uneasy stillness in the air. She flicked on the TV in the living room, trying to distract herself, and mindlessly scrolled through the channels. The open layout of the kitchen let her monitor the screen from the counter, but even her favorite show —a rerun she'd seen a dozen times—didn't feel comforting. Five minutes in, the lights flickered. She froze, clutching the crust of her pizza as the TV screen blinked and distorted before settling on a different channel entirely.

Her stomach twisted. She reached for the remote and switched back to her show, but it was off. Feeling uneasy, she clicked the power button. Nothing. The TV stayed off, no matter how hard she pressed. Frustration bubbled up and she couldn't mask the creeping sense of dread. She shoved the pizza back into the fridge, trying to shake it off, and headed toward the stairs.

Two steps up, she froze. Her breath caught in her throat as the fine hairs on her arms rose like needles. Something wasn't right. Grimacing, she forced herself to keep climbing, but a faint sound—soft and insidious—stopped her in her tracks. A faint rustling. In the walls. Slowly, she turned her head to the right, her eyes scanning the blank surface. There was nothing. Nothing visible, at least. She swallowed hard, her throat dry, and kept climbing, the sound prickling her nerves.

At the top of the stairs, her mother's door loomed ahead. Safe. Familiar. But Lily's instincts tugged her left toward her room. Her footsteps quickened, the rhythmic noise in the walls following her. It wasn't constant—it stopped whenever she did. An eerie mirror of her movements. The walls appeared animated, breathing in rhythm with her, and she sensed her heart pounding. In her room, the door slammed shut behind her as her unsteady hands fumbled with the lock. She felt nervous and left the door as is and went to bed.

Her forehead glistened with sweat, a single bead slipping down her temple. The room was her refuge—her sanctuary—but it seemed smaller tonight, the shadows heavier, the silence louder. She lay on her bed, phone in hand, desperate for a distraction. She needed to talk to Josh.

BlushyRed215: Josh we need to talk

Shadelss143: Sure what's up?

BlushyRed215: I'm worried. About you and Kev.

Shadelss143: Don't be we've got it under control.

BlushyRed215: Under control? I recently heard Pastor Jeffrey's lecture. He talked about exorcisms, Josh. About demons.

Shadelss143: Okay…and?

BlushyRed215: And?! Josh, Mr. Beeds is dead, and his daughter is in the hospital! Doesn't that bother you at all?

Shadelss143: That's just a coincidence Lily!

BlushyRed215: Coincidence? Josh these things are evil You don't want to mess with them. You don't know what you're inviting in.

Shadelss143: Look, he's bound to me. It doesn't matter how evil he is. He's locked in the lamp and only comes out when I summon him. That's it.

BlushyRed215: How do you know he's telling the truth?

Shadelss143: He told me so.

BlushyRed215: Are you even hearing yourself? The word of a demon? Josh, how gullible are you?!

Shadelss143: Lily its late and Im exhausted.

BlushyRed215: Please, just think about it. Promise me you'll think it over?

Shadelss143: I promise.

BlushyRed215: Night 😊

Shadelss143: Night 😊

Lily set her phone down, unease settling deep in her chest. She lay back on her bed, eyes flicking to the shadows playing across her ceiling. The rhythmic glow of her screen dimmed as she scrolled absentmindedly. But despite her exhaustion, sleep didn't come easily.

Half an hour later, her breathing slowed, and she finally drifted off, her phone still clutched tightly in her hand.

It was an unnaturally quiet night, a silence so deep it was unsettling. The indigo sky stretched endlessly, unbroken by a single cloud. Last week's relentless rains had left behind shallow puddles, and now, under the crescent moon's glow, those puddles shimmered faintly like ghostly mirrors. The town seemed peaceful, almost serene, but inside Lily's bedroom, the air was charged with something…wrong.

Unseen, something shifted behind the walls, dragging itself with a faint, grating noise. It crawled higher, moving across the ceiling with deliberate slowness. Though nearly inaudible, a low, guttural grumble grew closer with every passing second. Above Lily—fast asleep—a swirling, cloud-like form manifested on the ceiling. It spun counterclockwise, an unnatural vortex of whitish-gray smoke. Then, from within the mist, two massive arms emerged. They were grotesque, claw-like, each hand boasting three elongated, bone-like fingers.

The claws hovered over Lily, trembling as though savoring the moment, before reaching down. They gripped her blanket, slowly peeling it back, inch by inch, as if savoring the act. The swirling face materialized fully now, just above Lily's head. Although blurry and wavering, its expression was undeniably hungry and expectant. The claws reached the floor, anchoring themselves, while the face loomed closer. Its smoky features rippled as it prepared to strike.

Then, the door swung open.

The noise startled the figure, and in the blink of an eye, it was gone, dissipating like smoke in the wind. Lily's eyes shot open, her breath hitching. For a split second, she thought she saw something—a shadow, a movement—but there was nothing. Just the open door and her mother, standing in the frame.

"Mom?" Lily croaked, sitting up, her tone trembling.

Rosetta stood frozen, her hands clutching the doorframe for support. She was shaking, her face pale and drawn. She tried to smile but failed, her lips quivering as she cast her eyes to the floor.

"I don't know why," Rosetta whispered, her voice trembling. "But I felt like I had to check on you. I couldn't...shake the feeling."

Lily swung her legs out of bed, clutching her phone and pillow tightly. She could see it—her mother was scared. "Come on," Lily murmured softly, walking toward her. "I'll sleep in your room tonight. I've been having trouble sleeping, too."

Rosetta nodded weakly, looking almost ashamed. "Yes," she murmured, rubbing her left arm nervously with her right hand. She seemed rattled, her unease radiating like a cold wind.

Together, they left the room, retreating to Rosetta's bedroom. But the silence in the house now felt heavier, as if the shadows themselves were watching.

Josh lay in bed, tossing and turning, his mind a swirling mess of frustration and unease. Sleep eluded him, and the day's events gnawed at his thoughts. Feeling a growing sense of desperation, he reached for the lamp and summoned Bob.

The room grew heavy as the air thickened, a faint hum echoing as the creature emerged. Bob's glowing eyes locked onto Josh, and his lips curled into a snarl.

"You summoned, *Aaqa...*" he growled, his voice low and venomous.

"I want answers," Josh replied firmly, his speech steady despite the knot in his stomach.

Bob's gaze darkened, the flickering light from his form casting long, sharp shadows across the room. "Answers? About what?"

Josh didn't flinch. "Who put you in the lamp?"

The creature drew back slightly, his expression twisting with a mix of fury and resentment. "Evil men!" Bob spat the words out like poison.

Josh leaned forward, determined. "How?"

Bob's head dipped, his burning eyes narrowing as if the memory caused him pain—or rage. "There is magic powerful enough to bind beings like me to objects. Normally, it's used on lesser jinns. But these men...they dared to use it on an *ifrit*."

Josh's brows furrowed, his mind racing. "What happened to those men?"

A slow, sadistic grin spread across Bob's face, his fangs glinting in the dim light. "They died."

Josh's throat tightened, but he pressed on. "How?"

"I killed them," Bob said, his voice dripping with malice. His grin grew wider and twisted, his face alight with malevolent pride as though reliving a glorious victory. "They trapped me, three of them, and dared to bind me. But their lives were the price for their arrogance."

Josh's hand instinctively rose to his chin, his index finger tapping thoughtfully as he processed the information. "So, there were three of them, and you killed them…but only *after* they trapped you?"

"Yes," Bob hissed, his voice tinged with scorn as if the answer was obvious.

The boy's expression hardened. He hugged his legs and stared at the wall in front of him, contemplating. Then he turned to Bob and spoke.

"I understand they wronged you. What they did was cruel, but I am not them, Bob. I'm nothing like them. Can't we—" he hesitated, trying to gauge the creature's unreadable face. "Can't we have a more civil relationship? One built on mutual respect?"

Bob laughed—a harsh, guttural sound that sent a chill through Josh's spine. "Civil?" The creature leaned closer, its smoldering presence oppressive. "You are human. Dirt of the Earth. Filth." His voice grew cold and sharp. "*I* am an ifrit-nafrit. My kind dances among the stars and the skies, far above your petty existence. You are nothing to me."

The words hit like a blow, but Josh didn't falter. His jaw tightened, his eyes narrowing as he stared at the creature.

"Fine," he said through gritted teeth, his voice steady but hard as steel. Whatever hope he'd had of reason faded, replaced by resolve. If there was no way to find common ground with Bob, then he'd have to find another way to gain control.

Josh sent Bob back to the lamp and went to sleep.

The next day drifted by in a haze as Josh lay in bed, trying to smother his thoughts beneath the blankets. He woke with a gnawing sense of dread in his chest—a heaviness that hadn't lifted with sleep. Each new day seemed harder than the last, like he was walking deeper into something he couldn't name.

He had money, a sleek car, and Lily—*the* girl—was his. On paper, everything looked perfect. But his heart wouldn't settle. It beat with the quiet panic of a man who knew the floor beneath him was starting to crack.

After a half-hearted breakfast, he flipped through the newspaper, pretending to look for jobs. But the words blurred, and the silence in the apartment pressed in too close. His mind buzzed with static.

He couldn't take it.

Reaching for his phone, he sent a message to Kevin.

Shadelss143: Yo You at work or home?

Shadelss143: Dude! Are you gonna leave me hanging like this?

Shadelss143: I guess you're busy. Hook up when you're free.

Realizing that Kevin wouldn't always just be available whenever he wanted him, Josh had to make the best of his time. He spent most of his day anxiously scrolling through job listings, his eyes scanning the screen until the words blurred together. Now that he finally had the money to cover his tuition, an additional weight settled on his shoulders—figuring out where to spend it. Colleges, degrees…it all felt overwhelming, but he knew he needed to decide. Business administration seemed like the right path, which could help him when he finally took the leap and started his own company.

But the longer he searched, the more restless he became. A quiet frustration built in his chest. He needed a distraction, someone to break the monotony of his thoughts. His first instinct was to reach out to Lily, but something held him back. Instead, he hesitated for a moment before trying Kevin again, hoping this time he'd pick up.

Shadelss143: Not cool bro. Where you at?

Having gotten no response, Josh called Joe's Mechanic shop where Kevin worked and asked if Kevin was there. The receptionist, Kimberly, told Josh they hadn't heard from Kevin all day.

"This is unusual even for him because Kevin calls and makes stupid excuses when he doesn't want to come in. But at least he calls," she told Josh.

"All right, thanks." He hung up the phone.

Josh looked around and called, "Bob!"

"Aaqa," replied an old bald man.

"Can you please transport me to Kevin's driveway?" asked Josh.

THE AIR SHIMMERED FAINTLY, AND A MOMENT LATER, JOSH STOOD in Kevin's driveway. He exhaled sharply, his nerves already prickling with unease. A thin layer of dust covered Kevin's Mustang Cobra, sitting in its usual spot as if untouched for days.

"Thanks," Josh muttered, dismissing Bob back into the lamp before turning to the house.

His knock echoed through the quiet neighborhood.

"Kev, open up!" he called out, his voice betraying a hint of nervousness.

There was no response.

Josh rang the doorbell and knocked again, louder this time— still nothing. A strange sense of dread crept over him.

He hesitated momentarily before trying the doorknob, half-expecting it to be locked. To his surprise—and growing discomfort—it turned easily in his hand. The door creaked open.

"Kevin?" Josh called out cautiously, stepping inside.

The air inside the house was stale, carrying the faint but unmistakable scent of leftover food. Josh glanced around. The living room was a typical bachelor's mess—chips scattered on the couch, a half-eaten pizza sitting on the coffee table—but something was off about the silence. It was too quiet, as though the house was holding its breath.

"Kev, it's me, Josh! You here?" he called again, louder this time, trying to shake off the unease clawing at his chest.

He moved toward the hallway, his footsteps slow and deliberate. Each step grew more burdensome than the last as his instincts screamed at him to turn back, to leave. But he pressed on, heading for Kevin's bedroom.

"Kevin?" Josh's voice cracked slightly as he reached the door.

He pushed it open—and froze.

The room appeared to have been violently lifted, shaken, and thrown back down by some unseen force. Shattered glass and splintered wood covered the floor, furniture remains scattered like a crime scene frozen in chaos. The closet had been ripped from its place, lying helplessly on its side. The bed, once a place of comfort, was now nothing more than torn fabric and broken wood, crushed against the corner as if trying to escape. A small TV, smashed beyond repair, rested among discarded clothes without an owner to pick them up.

And then, in the center of it all, lay Kevin.

Or at least, what remained of him.

Josh's breath hitched as he stared at the stretched-out, hollow form of his best friend. His body was there, but something was horrifyingly wrong—there was no skeleton. No bones to give him shape. Just skin, organs, and a gaping absence where structure should have been. As if something had stripped him from the inside out.

Josh's legs gave out beneath him and he collapsed, kneeling before Kevin's disfigured face. His tears hit the bloodstained floorboards—silent at first, then growing heavier, his entire body trembling as he choked on his grief.

"Kev...Kev, nooo..." His voice cracked, broken by sobs.

His hands hovered over his friend, but what was there to hold? This wasn't Kevin. It couldn't be Kevin. His mind refused to accept it, but the horror before him wouldn't let him escape.

"Kev..." he whispered again, regret and agony bleeding into his voice.

His chest felt like it was caving in, crushed by the unbearable weight of loss and something even worse—confusion. He couldn't process it. How was this possible? A body without a skeleton. It didn't make sense. His mind searched for a rational answer, but there was none. His best friend was dead.

He forced himself to his feet, stumbling as he wiped his tear-streaked face. There had to be an answer, something in this ruined room that explained the nightmare before him. But the more he looked, the more suffocating the panic became. There was nothing—no sign of what had done this.

A sob ripped from his throat as he fell to his knees again, help-less, drowning in grief.

With shaking hands, he pulled out his phone and pressed Lily's number.

The line barely rang before she answered, her tone tight with worry. "Josh?" She could already hear his choked breath.

"Lily," he gasped, barely able to say her name. His throat burned. "Kevin..."

"Josh, what happened to Kevin?" Her voice sharpened with alarm.

"He's dead. He's *dead!*" His voice cracked, rising in desperation.

Silence.

A long, suffocating silence.

Josh swallowed hard, his fingers tightening around the phone before he ended the call. He slid down against the wall, his vision blurred by endless tears. His chest heaved, his heart pounding against his ribs as his mind spiraled.

And then—sirens.

Faint at first, but growing louder, closing in.

Help was coming.

But no help could fix this.

CHAPTER 6

THE UNEXPLAINABLE EVENT

The wailing sirens shattered the eerie silence of the neighborhood as police cars, ambulances, and even a fire truck swarmed outside Kevin's home. Red and blue lights flashed, reflecting off the windows of terrified neighbors peeking out from behind their curtains.

The first officers on the scene stepped inside cautiously, their boots crunching against the shattered debris on the floor. The second they glanced at Kevin's body, whatever professionalism they carried instantly wavered. Their stomachs churned. Their hands twitched. They had seen bodies before—but nothing like this.

One officer, Kirk, swallowed hard and turned to his partner, Brian. His tone sounded unsteady. "Brian…"

Brian didn't respond at first. He couldn't take his eyes off the thing lying in the center of the room. The stretched-out, boneless corpse, once a person, once Kevin. It appeared an unseen force had scooped out his entire skeleton and left only the sickening remains.

"Yeah?" Brian finally muttered, his sound barely above a whisper.

Kirk tried to form a sentence but failed. His throat felt dry; his brain wouldn't process the sight before him.

"It's…" He trailed off, struggling to find the words.

Brian exhaled shakily and finished the thought for him. "It looks like it's missing a skeleton." His voice held disgust.

The two men exchanged uneasy glances before stepping closer to the body, their instincts screaming at them to turn away. But they had to look. They needed to understand. They crouched down, examining Kevin's remains from different angles, searching for something—anything—that could explain this nightmare. But there were no wounds. No cuts. No signs of struggle. His skeleton hadn't been removed in any logical way. It was just…gone.

"This isn't natural," Brian murmured, standing back up and rubbing his temples. "It makes no damn sense."

Kirk kept staring, his mind reeling. "How do we even register this? Gruesome homicide?"

Brian let out a bitter scoff. "I think it's best if the sheriff decides."

Behind them, a quiet sob broke through the tense air.

Josh.

He was still on all fours, his body trembling violently, his breath coming out in ragged gasps. Blood stained the floor beneath his tightly clenched fists, his tear-stained face hidden by messy hair.

Brian exhaled and straightened up. "Let's get him up and see if we can get a statement."

Josh, weak and unsteady, was gently lifted by them. His legs wobbled beneath him, and his sobs hadn't stopped. He was still drowning in the horror of it all. One officer guided him to the kitchen and sat him down.

Kirk kneeled beside him, his tone gentle. "Sir…do you have any idea what happened here?"

Josh shook his head weakly, unable to form words.

The paramedics arrived, their faces tight and apprehensive as they stepped inside. "Where's the patient?" one asked.

Kirk pointed toward the bedroom. "In there."

The paramedics hesitated before stepping forward. They had no idea what awaited them on the other side of that door.

Turning his attention back to Josh, Kirk began asking routine questions—his name, address, phone number, and relationship to Kevin. Josh answered in a broken, shaky voice, barely holding himself together.

"We'll need you to come down to the precinct to give an official statement," Kirk informed him.

Josh nodded, hollow and numb.

The front door creaked open again, and heavy boots stomped inside. A man in his late fifties, tall with a goatee and mustache, stepped into the room. A silver star gleamed on his chest.

Sheriff Bill Sanders.

Kirk immediately straightened. "Sheriff."

Bill gave him a nod and headed straight for the bedroom.

Meanwhile, Lily picked up Carol and told her that there was some trouble at Kevin's place and Josh was there as well. Lily wasn't sure what happened and didn't think it wise to worsen a bad situation. The two women hurried toward the house, dread settling deep in their bones.

Minutes later, Bill returned from the bedroom, his face grim. He glanced at Kirk before shifting his gaze toward Josh. "Did we get a statement?"

"Not yet, sir," Kirk replied.

Bill's expression hardened. "Take him to the station."

"Yes, sir." Kirk nodded, then addressed Josh. "Come on, kid."

Josh moved mechanically as if he weren't fully present. Josh barely missed Lily and Carol, who drove in as the police car departed.

Carol immediately faced the sheriff, desperation in her voice. "Bill, what happened here? Are Josh and Kevin okay?"

The sheriff hesitated. He saw Carol eyeing the bedroom, affected by all the commotion. He took a deep breath, his vision flitting between Carol and Lily, both women already unraveling. "Carol...it's best if you don't go in there," he said gently, but firmly. "It's...pretty bad."

Carol's face contorted with fear. Lily stepped forward, gripping Carol's trembling hand.

Carol's breath hitched. "Is Kevin...?" She couldn't finish the sentence. She didn't want to.

Sheriff Sanders clenched his jaw, his voice low and steady, though it wavered ever so slightly. "I'm afraid Kevin is dead."

Carol staggered back as if the words had physically struck her. Lily reached for her, gripping her arm as tears spilled down their faces.

"Dead?" Carol whispered, her voice cracking. Her body shook as grief sank its claws into her. She stared at the floor, hands trembling uncontrollably. "He was like my son. These kids grew up with us…"

Lily sobbed quietly beside her, unable to find the words to ease the pain.

"How could this have happened?" Carol's speech broke, desperation creeping in.

Bill exhaled slowly, his expression unreadable. "We don't have all the facts yet," he admitted. "But…it looks like the work of some sick cultists. They mutilated the body." Even the sheriff, a man who had seen his fair share of horrors, couldn't hide the slight tremor in his voice. Because, deep down, he knew.

This wasn't the work of any cult.

This was something else.

A tall, handsome man with sharp features and a striking resemblance to Kevin—only older and weathered by time—stepped through the front door. His expression showed tension, a blend of worry and bewilderment, yet also included something else— embarrassment.

He locked eyes with Bill. "Hey, Bill. I was on my walk when I heard the sirens. Kevin didn't do a foolish thing again, did he?"

Carol's face crumpled at the sound of his voice. She pressed her hands against her tear-streaked cheeks, struggling to hold herself together.

Michael Morris, Kevin's father, frowned at her reaction. "Why are you crying, Carol?" His utterance showed growing unease.

She took a shaky step forward, reaching out to embrace him, but he instinctively pulled away, his confusion turning into something much darker—a gnawing dread.

Then he saw the open bedroom door.

And he ran.

"Kevin? Kevin!" Michael's voice cracked as he rushed inside. Bill took a step forward, his mouth opening to stop him, but it was too late. The second Michael stepped into the room, he froze. His knees buckled. His wide, disbelieving eyes took in the horror sprawled before him, wrenching the breath from his lungs.

"What?" His words barely left his throat.

His son. His only son.

Michael staggered forward, staring at the grotesque remains on the floor. His lips parted, but the words failed him. His hands trembled as if reaching out would somehow make it unreal.

Tears spilled from his eyes as his face twisted in anguish. "My son," he whispered. His voice shattered like glass.

The room fell still.

Paramedics and officers who had been moving, working, now stood frozen, shifting uncomfortably as if the presence of a grieving father made the horror in front of them even more unbearable.

Michael turned, his grief giving way to rage. His vision darted to the officers, searching for an answer, for a reason, for someone to blame. His breath hitched as the sobs overtook him, but beneath the devastation was a building fury. "He was a sweet boy," he choked out. "Why? Why would someone do this to him?"

A few officers hesitantly stepped forward, placing gentle hands on Michael's shoulders and guiding him away from the gruesome scene. He wanted to grab and hug his only son. But there was nothing—no structure. There was just a gruesome pile of skin and organs. And so he didn't resist. He just kept crying, his body trembling violently.

Bill and Carol approached cautiously. The grief etched on Michael's face deepened, making him look years older in a matter of minutes. His speech was all scratchy when he talked. "His mother needs to know." His jaw clenched, his entire body rigid with suppressed rage. Then he turned to Bill, his expression darkening. "And we need to know who did this."

The anger in his voice was suffocating. His fists clenched at his sides, his tear-streaked face contorted in a mixture of devastation and fury.

Bill swallowed hard, placing a firm hand on Michael's shoulder. His voice was softer now, but there was steel beneath it. "Mike, I will not rest until we find this monster. I promise you."

Michael looked up at him, desperate for something to hold on to, but there was no comfort in Bill's words—only grim determination.

"I'm so very sorry, Mike," Bill added, his voice barely above a whisper.

Before anything else could be said, one deputy walked out of the bedroom, his face pale and tight with unease.

Bill turned to him, his posture straightening. "What?"

The deputy hesitated. For a moment, he glanced at Michael and Carol before focusing on Bill, who walked over to the deputy.

"Sir, the boy's entire skeleton…teeth, bones, skull…everything. It's gone."

Bill's eyes darkened. "Filthy cultists," he muttered, his mind already spinning with rage.

But the deputy shook his head. He looked scared.

"I don't think so, sir," the deputy admitted, swallowing hard. "There's no incision. No cuts. No bruises. The blood—it only came from his nose, mouth, and eyes. There's no place for the skeleton to have been pulled out. It's like… like it just…" He hesitated, forcing the words out. "Disappeared."

A heavy silence settled between them.

Bill's expression hardened. His disbelief clashed with growing, unspoken terror. "You hear yourself, son?" His voice was low, laced with restrained fury. "None of what you're saying makes any damn sense."

The deputy didn't argue. He simply nodded, his lips pressing into a thin, uneasy line. "Once the autopsy is done, maybe we'll have some answers," he said, though even he didn't seem to believe it.

Bill exhaled slowly, his gaze flickering back toward Michael, who was still silently weeping. He clenched his jaw, his fingers twitching at his sides.

Answers. That's what they needed. But in his gut, Bill knew that whatever had happened to Kevin wasn't a matter they were prepared to understand.

The sheriff shook his head in acknowledgment and turned toward the body. "Make sure you look for all evidence, check all the rooms, including the garage and the surrounding area, and seal off this area," he said affirmatively.

"Of course, sir," replied the deputy.

Josh entered his bedroom, exhausted, hollow, and numb. The interrogation at the precinct had drained him, and the grief clawing at his chest only grew heavier. His best friend was gone, and the weight of that reality pressed down on him like an unbearable force.

He reached into his bag with trembling hands and pulled out the lamp. His bloodshot eyes locked onto it, his breath uneven.

"Bob."

The word left his lips like a command, a curse, an accusation.

A dark shimmer flickered in the air beside him, and in an instant, the creature appeared. Bob stood there, towering and malevolent, his presence filling the room with an unnatural cold. His black eyes gleamed with their usual detachment as if the world around him was nothing more than a dull, meaningless stage.

Josh turned to face him, his expression raw—pain, betrayal, and mourning battling for dominance. "Kevin is dead!" His voice sounded hoarse; his fists clenched so tightly that his knuckles turned white.

Bob hardly blinked. His expression remained empty, indifferent. "How very sad," he replied flatly.

Josh's breathing hitched. That tone. That absolute lack of care. His grief morphed into rage. "You did this!" he spat, taking a step forward, his entire body shaking.

Bob sighed, bored. "I wish I could have," he said, meeting Josh's glare without a trace of remorse. "But, as you well know, I am bound to this lamp unless you call me. I was with you all night."

Rapidly, Josh's chest rose and fell. He wanted to believe Bob was lying—needed to believe it. "You're lying!" His voice cracked, fury rising like a tidal wave. "I don't believe you!"

Bob tilted his head slightly. It was hard to tell whether he was amused or angry. "Why would I lie?" he said, his voice eerily calm. "I have made no secret of my disdain for your kind or my desire to see you all eradicated. I am only disappointed that it wasn't me who reduced that pathetic sack of flesh to...whatever remains of him."

Josh's stomach twisted. His rage faltered briefly, giving way to something far more sinister—dread. His hands trembled as he forced himself to ask, "K-Kevin's entire skeleton was removed...who would do s-something like that?"

Bob's expression finally shifted. His gaze drifted for a moment as if searching his mind for something long forgotten. "Is that what happened?" he murmured, almost to himself. Then his lips curled into a knowing smirk. "Ah. Of course. Your kind is a delicacy in our world," he said, his tone matter of fact. "We are…particularly interested in the bones."

Josh felt his stomach churning. "Delicacy?" he echoed in horror. "We're like…goats and pigs to you?"

Bob scoffed, shaking his head. "Not at all." His voice was cold and condescending. "Goats and pigs are merely food. You, however, are a delicacy."

Josh's entire body tensed with disgust and fury. His fists clenched as he took a step closer. "Who did this?!" he demanded. "Explain!" His voice wavered, thick with emotion—anger, pain, remorse.

Bob merely stared at him, unmoving.

Josh shuddered. No matter how furious or grief-stricken he was, the weight of the creature's pure, undiluted hatred was suffocating. It was like staring into the abyss—an abyss that stared back, relishing his suffering.

At last, Bob spoke.

"Your kind knows very little about our existence," he mused. "Most deny it, while others confuse us with myths, folklore, and lesser spirits. And what you fail to understand is that we are a most vengeful species. Our animosities have existed not for centuries, but for thousands of years. While we hate and despise your kind, we also have quarrels within our kind."

Silence filled the room briefly. Josh listened intently, hoping to find some sanity in this chaos. Bob seemed to show some emotion, which was rare, but there seemed to be sadness in his tone.

"Thousands of years ago, my influence and power were significant. I held the position of commander of the southern armies. Southern armies are a location on a map for you, but for us, they may be part of a universe. Three other ifrits, brothers, wanted to usurp me. They made their move."

"One ended up dead, one escaped to the north, and the whereabouts of the third remain unknown. Then, just like that, I disappeared. I am partially aware of what they did to my descendants, which enrages me. I know also that the descendants of these ifrits can sense me when I visit you. I do not doubt that they plan to seek their revenge."

Josh swallowed hard.

Bob seemed lost in his own words and continued. "But even the least powerful ifrit is a force to be reckoned with, so I would not doubt that they are careful. They are playing games with me, attempting to assess my continued status as the brilliant commander I once held. Your friend and you have been around me long enough for my enemies to pick up the scent. They can best test me through you and those close to you." The creature seemed sincere, a fleeting sadness present, then gone.

"Why us? What did we do to them?" asked Josh.

"Why not? Is it likely a great commander will mind if some humans die under his command? Do you believe every species has a similar mind and similar views on morality as you?"

The flicker of sadness that had briefly crossed Bob's face was gone now, like a shadow chased away by the sun. He had slipped back into his old self: confident and commanding.

"Enough chaos can do wonders for those desperately looking for a way to inflict pain. And sometimes," the creature was again glowing with hatred, "hurting the innocent can create great opportunities for a seasoned general."

Josh's eyes locked onto Bob like a blade drawn and ready. His chest heaved; he was on the verge of exploding. Every inch of his body was tense, trembling with a mixture of grief and fury, but it was his eyes that spoke loudest—eyes that screamed of betrayal, sorrow, and a rage so deep it could shatter walls.

"You think my friend's death is a joke?" he growled, his voice low and cracking under the weight of everything he was holding in.

But Bob was unimpressed and chuckled darkly. "I do."

Josh's stomach churned in disgust.

"If you command me to stop, I will," Bob added mockingly. "But I strongly suggest you don't. I'm thoroughly enjoying this moment."

Josh turned away, his skin crawling. He knew Bob was telling the truth. The creature was reveling in his pain. Josh whipped back around, his eyes burning. "Then find these 'enemies' and destroy them! I command you!" His voice was fierce and desperate.

Bob didn't even blink. "I cannot," he said, his tone flat.

Josh's nostrils flared. "You serve me!" he hissed.

Bob smirked. "No," he corrected. "I am bound by ancient magic. And that magic has chained me to you, not to your friends, not to your enemies. You. I will fetch you riches and toys, but I will save no one at your request."

Josh was seething. "So your stupid quarrels got my best friend killed, and now you won't do a damn thing about it?"

Bob stepped forward, and in that moment, Josh felt something twist in the air—something wrong. "No, my master," Bob murmured, his voice like silk and venom. "The day you stole me from your father's showcase...was the day you got your friend killed."

Josh flinched.

Bob grinned.

Before Josh could react, a knock at his door shattered the moment. His breath hitched. "Back in the lamp," he whispered.

Bob vanished.

Josh, breathless, crammed the lamp into his backpack and then turned to the door. "C-come in," he stammered.

The door creaked open, and Lily stepped inside. She looked pale and shaken. "Josh," she whispered. "You need to come outside. Now."

As they exited the house, Lily turned to Josh and said, "What are you doing here?"

"I live here, remember?" replied Josh, trying to compose himself. He wiped his red, puffy eyes, blinking away his remaining tears.

Lily stopped...something was brewing inside her as she stared at the ground.

"You don't think that creature killed Kevin?" She redirected her gaze to Josh, angry and hurt. "You don't think he is going to kill you, and you come back here all by yourself?"

Josh tried to answer, but she wasn't in the mood.

"Josh, please get in the car," Lily said sternly, her voice agitated.

Lily told Josh that Kevin's parents were at Kevin's house as they drove off. "It was painful. I don't need to tell you what they are going through," she sorrowfully explained.

Josh gave a small nod, remaining silent.

"I sent your mom with Mrs. Morris to give her some support. My mom will probably stay with her tonight as well. They should stay together," Lily informed Josh with concern.

"Good," said Josh. "I don't want Mom back in our house."

Lily glanced at him and said, "You shouldn't be there either."

Josh was quiet again. Lily usually gets upset when there is a cause, and Josh knows she has a cause.

The drive was short, and they talked little. Besides the immense loss, other problems troubled them. The horrific way Kevin was killed left no doubt that the supernatural was at play here, and they needed information if they were to face this problem head-on.

"Where are we going?" he asked.

"To get some information," replied Lily as she pulled next to a church.

THE CHURCH WAS QUIET, ITS EMPTINESS AMPLIFYING THE WEIGHT OF Josh and Lily's footsteps as they stepped inside. The scent of old wood and burning candles lingered in the air, mixing with the faint echo of distant footsteps.

A man was cleaning near the altar, his movements slow and deliberate. Lily took a deep breath and approached.

"Pastor Jeffrey," she called gently.

The man straightened, wiping his hands on a cloth before turning to face her. He looked to be in his early forties, with golden hair, sharp features, and a slender build. His piercing blue eyes studied her for a moment before recognition sparked in them.

"You must be Rosetta's daughter," he said softly. "You look just like her."

Lily smiled back, a slight, familiar warmth spreading in her chest. "Yes, I am. I'm Lily."

The pastor nodded, a hint of fondness in his expression. "Your mother is a kind woman. She was a great help when my brother was in the hospital." He gestured toward one of the pews. "Please, sit."

They sat down, but Lily wasted no time.

"Pastor Jeffrey," she began, her voice steady but urgent, "have you ever performed an exorcism?"

The pastor blinked, surprised. His gaze flickered between her and Josh, taking in their solemn faces. Something had happened—something bad. He had seen this look before, but years of guiding people through their darkest moments taught him when to ask questions and when to listen.

Lily hesitated, then continued, "I remember you discussing demons and exorcisms in one of your sermons. I wondered if you could provide some understanding.

Pastor Jeffrey studied them for a long moment before answering.

"I have never performed an exorcism myself," he admitted. "But I have been involved in two." He leaned forward slightly. "Is there something specific you need to know?"

Josh, who had been silent until now, finally spoke. "Do you know if there are…levels to these demons? Like, are some ordinary and others…worse?"

The pastor considered this. "Well," he said thoughtfully, "that notion exists in all species, doesn't it? Some are stronger, more cunning, more ruthless. I believe the same applies to them. But I don't have specifics."

Josh frowned, clearly dissatisfied with the vague answer.

The church was old but well-maintained. The wooden pews gleamed from regular polishing, and the stained-glass windows, though weathered, had recently been restored. The silence was peaceful, almost deceptive, until the sound of the front doors creaking open broke it. A man entered, glancing around before settling onto a pew to wait for the pastor.

Pastor Jeffrey acknowledged him with a gentle nod before turning back to Lily. "Although," he murmured, "I could direct you to an expert on this topic."

Josh leaned in slightly, his tension palpable.

The pastor continued, "Now, mind you, I do not vouch for her beliefs—only for her character. She struck me as honest and courageous. If anyone can give you deeper insight, it's her."

Josh and Lily exchanged glances.

"Where can we find her?" Josh asked quickly.

Lily placed a hand on his arm, sensing his urgency. "Thank

you, Pastor," she interjected, trying to keep the conversation steady. "We could use all the help we can get."

Pastor Jeffrey nodded. "She runs a mystique shop in the state's capital. It's about a two-hour drive, but if you're willing to make the trip, she may be able to help."

Lily hastily wrote the address; meanwhile, Josh watched the man waiting to talk to the pastor. There was an unspoken urgency between all of them, like time was slipping through their fingers.

Pastor Jeffrey finally broke his silence. His voice was softer this time. "Did something happen again?"

Josh tensed. The question felt loaded—almost like the pastor wasn't just asking about this. Maybe he was referring to Mr. Beeds. Maybe he was referring to something worse.

Lily stood up, forcing a polite smile. "Thank you for your time, Pastor Jeffrey."

Josh hesitated for a moment, but when Lily turned to leave, he followed.

They stepped out into the crisp evening air, the church doors closing softly behind them. Within minutes, they were back in the car. Neither of them spoke as they pulled onto the highway.

CHAPTER 7

150 CENTRAL DRIVE

Back at the precinct, the investigation into Kevin Morris's murder was in full swing—but the deeper they dug, the more lost they became. No one knew how to proceed. There was no protocol for a situation like this. This wasn't just another homicide in a small town where the worst crimes usually involved drunken bar fights or petty theft. This was something else. Something very wrong.

The air in the precinct was thick with unease. Deputies sat hunched over their desks, their vision scanning through case files, old crime reports, and forensic databases, searching for anything that might resemble what they had seen in Kevin's bedroom.

But there was nothing.

They expanded their search, reaching out to other precincts, looking for similar cases, similar horrors. As they combed through records of gruesome murders, they found disturbing things—ritualistic killings, bodies left in unspeakable conditions, and scenes so violent they made even seasoned officers queasy.

But none of them matched this. None of them described a body without a skeleton. None of them sensed such complete unnaturalness.

The quiet hum of the station received occasional interruptions from muttered curses or the sound of a deputy pushing away from their desk, rubbing tired eyes, trying to make sense of the impossible.

And yet, deep down, they all knew the truth.

This wasn't the work of a cult. It wasn't the work of a man. This was something else. Something that belonged in the dark corners of childhood nightmares. Something they had all stopped believing in.

Several officers occupied the main area. The door to the sheriff's office remained closed. The sheriff stood in his office before his two seated deputies.

"What's the update on the Morris boy?" asked Bill.

"Sir, the body is with the coroner. They are running an autopsy on it," Brian replied immediately.

"The family is pretty shaken; they want to bury him as soon as possible. The horrible condition of the body…" Kirk stopped talking, his face turning sad.

Bill ran his hands through his hair and sank into the chair, his body heavy with the weight of a reality he didn't want to face. He shook his head slowly, disbelief etched deep into every line of his face.

Pain sat with him—raw, relentless—the silent torment, thinking about the parents who were now enduring this nightmare that no one should ever have to endure. His eyes were distant and glassy, as if experiencing the proximity of loss.

"To have your young son taken away in his prime and mutilated. I don't think this town has ever seen anything like it. Did you guys thoroughly sweep the house?"

Kirk looked at Brian for a second before answering.

We only found prints belonging to the deceased and his friend, Josh. There is no murder weapon, and I doubt the coroners are going to find anything."

"Well," interrupted Brian. "There was that car in the garage."

"What about the car?" inquired Bill interestingly.

"Well, sir, it was a brand-new Dodge Challenger Hellcat. That car costs over one hundred thousand," continued Brian.

The mood shifted—subtle but undeniable. A flicker of energy stirred in the air as their instincts began to spark to life. The detective in them, dulled by exhaustion and grief, started to awaken.

It wasn't much—just a hint, a thread—but it represented something. A possible clue. And with it came a glimmer of hope, fragile but real.

"Hmm," Bill remarked, stroking his chin. "Where does an eighteen-year-old boy get that kind of money? I understand Michael is grieving but check with him when you can.

"That's the thing, sir. The deceased did not own the car. It belonged to his friend, Joshua Cox," advised Brian.

"Carol's boy?" said Bill. I am acquainted with that family—good people, but I don't think they can afford that much unless her ex ran into a gold mine.

"Well, sir," continued Brian, "the license plate and registration check out under his name. But when I called the office to confirm, they didn't know its registration status.

"Say what?" Bill's face contorted into one of disbelief and slight annoyance. "What do you mean they didn't know?"

Brian glanced at Kirk, uncertainty flickering in his eyes. He remained silent, yet uncertainty hung heavy in the quiet shared between them.

Kirk briefly met his gaze, giving a subtle nod afterward. As the more senior officer, the weight of the moment naturally shifted to him. He stepped forward, calm and composed, ready to take the lead.

Across from them, Bill adjusted in his chair, sitting upright now, bracing himself. His gaze moved between the two men, guarded and wary, as if already preparing for answers he had no desire to hear.

Kirk spoke, "For a person to end up in one of our prison cells, they must commit a crime punishable by law. Someone must file a report, and we need to make the arrest and add the necessary information to our system. Say one day you walk in, and someone is in one of our jails, but there is no paperwork, and no one knows how they got there."

"That's looney. The DMV needs to get their act together," Bill muttered in frustration.

"There is more, sir," suggested Brian.

Bill sighed, looking at Brian, anticipating some more crazy talk.

"We ran a check on the car's VIN to see if we can dig up any more info," Brian added, looking straight at Bill.

"And…?" Bill said, looking back at Brian and gesturing for him to continue.

"Yesterday, our local Dodge dealer reported a theft of the car," interjected Kirk.

Bill leaned back in his chair, exhaling slowly as he pressed his index fingers to his lips, deep in thought. His eyes darted to the floor, then back up, and he shook his head—half in disbelief, half in surrender to the sheer madness of it all. Across from him, the two officers exchanged a glance—brief, uncertain. Then their gaze returned to Bill, searching for something, anything, that might make sense of what they were dealing with.

A look of bemusement came on Bill's face. He crossed his arms, raising an eyebrow. "A stolen car gets its registration and license plates made in under a day. Tell me, doesn't it take at least two weeks to get a new plate and registration card?"

"Sometimes even longer," added Brian.

"Get a search warrant on Josh," ordered Bill.

"Well, sir, after we found out the car was stolen and registered to Joshua Cox, we got the search warrant right away. John is running the search on Cox," Brian replied.

Bill got up and looked outside the large window in his office, thinking. "We have a kid whose entire skeleton is missing, with no cuts on the body." He paused briefly.

"A stolen car with proper registration and a license plate." He paused again.

"A DMV that seems clueless." He turned back to face his officers.

"If the press gets a hold of this, we'll all look like clowns."

An officer knocked on the door. Brian opened the door, took a note from the officer, and then closed the door.

"What is it?" inquired the sheriff.

Brian looked at Kirk and then at Bill. "Sir, we were checking out Josh Cox as a person of interest…"

"Carol's boy," interjected Bill.

"Yes, sir," continued Brian. "It turns out he has…uh…" Brian pulled up the note given to him. "Oh, gosh…h-he has nine million, nine hundred and ninety-nine thousand…" he tried to say it correctly, calculating all the zeros on the paper, "…thirty-two dollars in his bank account."

"What? How? Where did he get this money?" Bill seemed confused and anxious. He glanced at Kirk. "The car was reported stolen yesterday?" Bill asked.

"Correct, sir," replied Kirk.

"And the license plate and registration showed up yesterday as well?" Bill continued.

"Yes, sir," Brian answered. "And the ten million additional sums of money were also added to his bank account yesterday."

"By whom? Who gave him the money?" asked Bill.

"Hmm." Brian opened the door and yelled, "Hey, John, you want to come here for a second?"

A young black man in his twenties, short and stocky, walked into the office.

"You ran this check on Joshua Cox?" Brian asked.

"Yes, sir," John replied.

"I brought the manifest with me." He handed a document to Brian.

Brian browsed through the document. "Thirty-two dollars two days ago, ten million and thirty-two dollars yesterday. He then withdrew a thousand dollars yesterday."

"Let me guess," interrupted the sheriff. "There is no information on how or who deposited the ten million."

"No, sir," Brian replied, still reviewing the document. Then he looked up and ordered John to go to the bank and ask them for an explanation. "Where did the ten million come from?"

"Do that," affirmed the sheriff. "But I have a feeling we won't find anything."

After the officer left, Bill looked at his deputies.

"This boy, Cox, knows something he is not telling us. These two probably got mixed up in some cultist rituals, and one of them got himself killed," Bill suggested, pacing up and down, rubbing his hands on his chin.

The sheriff stopped pacing and looked at his deputies. "I will have a talk with Josh and see if he can remember anything else. You two continue working on this case and see if you can find more leads."

The officers nodded and left his office.

ON THE HIGHWAY, LILY AND JOSH HAD SORROWFUL EXPRESSIONS. They looked at, but did not enjoy, the beauty of the summer mountain scene.

The summer landscape was breathtaking, with towering mountains rising against a crisp, cloud-dappled sky, their slopes cloaked in a fiery tapestry of summer foliage—green leaves fluttering in the wind. The air was cool and sharp, carrying the earthy scent of leaves and distant pine. Streams ran clearer, colder, murmuring through rocky beds as if whispering forgotten stories. The world felt quieter here, suspended between the vibrant life of summer and the stillness of winter—peaceful, yet tinged with the melancholy beauty of change.

"Please call Carol and make sure she stays with Kevin's mom tonight. Make some excuse, but don't let her go back home," Lily suggested.

Josh nodded, and he rang his mother.

"Josh, sweetie, are you okay?" was Carol's first question.

"I am fine, Mom. How is Sybil?"

"She is…" Carol started to cry.

Kevin meant a great deal to her. Josh and Kevin played together, fought, and grew up in front of her. His absence now left her feeling incomplete.

"It will take time; there is a lot she will have to come to terms with. I am glad Rosetta is here," Carol said between sobs.

"Mom, please stay with her. Don't go home," advised Josh.

"What about you? I am worried for you and Lily," Carol said anxiously.

"I'm with Lily. She's fine," he stated, though his voice wavered, cracking slightly. He cleared his throat, striving for a steadier voice than his emotional state. "We'll probably figure something out. It's best to stay together…you could use the company."

On the other end of the line, Carol's quiet sniffles turned back into full sobs. Sitting beside Josh, Lily wiped her eyes, struggling to hold back her tears. "It's like I've lost my son," Carol choked out.

Josh clenched his jaw, his grip tightening on the phone. He stared down at the floor, willing himself not to break. "He was like my brother, Mom," he whispered. His lips pressed into a thin line, his chest tightening with grief. He wanted to cry, but he understood that doing so would distress his mother further.

Shortly, he collapsed; losing his closest companion became unendurable. Hearing him, Lily started sobbing but tried to concentrate on the road.

"…I'll call you later," Josh finally said, inhaling sharply. "Please take care of yourself… and Sybil."

Carol couldn't form words—only soft cries came through the phone.

Josh hung up and exhaled, staring blankly ahead. Lily looked at him, her eyes full of unspoken sympathy, but she said nothing.

For the next ten minutes, the car was silent. The low hum of the engine and the weight of their grief pressing down on them like an anchor comprised all the sound.

Then Lily turned to Josh and spoke. "I expected this from Kevin; he would never think things through. But you?" Anger and disappointment marked her tone. "You, Josh! I believed you to be smarter, more careful," she huffed, her eyes narrowing.

Josh stared at his shoes, his face sad, his eyes teary.

Lily continued without restraint. "How could you be so naïve to think you'll have a genie grant you wishes? Did you not think WHY?" Her voice raised, and Josh winced at her tone.

He turned to his right and sadly stared at the mountains. Things were quiet again before he turned to Lily and started talking. "I didn't know something was inside the lamp; how could I? I was playing around with it, and this thing came out. And…" He stopped briefly to muster the courage, taking a deep breath, "I…am not sure he killed Kevin…"

Lily shot Josh a piercing glare, which caused him to look back at his feet.

"Think about it," he continued. "He makes no secret of the fact that he despises us, has expressed a desire to kill us, and yet takes no responsibility for Kevin's death. Why would he do that? He seems to have nothing to lose. If he killed Kevin, why wouldn't he confess? He seems to revel in my agony and pain," Josh finished and turned his attention to Lily.

Lily met his gaze and softened a little, but her frustration remained clear. "Is it possible that you could punish him?"

"I wouldn't even know where to begin," he replied, pain and sadness resonating from his tone. "This creature can bring people to their knees just by looking at them. He suffocated both me and Kevin to near death." Josh shuddered at the memory, slumping slightly.

"And yet you asked that creature for favors," Lily huffed, her eyes narrowing further at the road ahead, her hands gripping the steering wheel until her knuckles paled to white.

"B-but I tried to stop Kevin, you know how he gets...er...g-got..." whimpered Josh, hanging his head low.

Lily glanced at him, a slight growl tucked away in her glare. "Don't you dare blame him!"

"I...that's not what I meant to do..." mumbled Josh.

Things were quiet again except for the whoosh of the car speeding on the highway. Lily turned to him. "You want to drive? It's a long drive."

She seemed to have calmed down a bit, which relaxed Josh.

"Sure, I'll drive..." he mumbled back, nodding slightly. They stopped and switched seats, staying silent.

As the journey continued, Lily fell asleep. Josh drove for the next hour, trying to keep his attention on the road. He eventually looked at Lily and sensed relief, knowing she appeared safe and all right. He glanced at the rearview mirror and saw Bob sitting in the back seat, smirking with his arms crossed. Josh gasped sharply and jumped as he turned his head to the rear, causing the car to swerve from left to right and right to left. A car from the other side started blowing its horn as Josh turned toward the road and took control of it.

He looked in the rearview mirror again. The back seat held no one, sending chills down his spine. Lily had awoken and gazed at Josh, her brows furrowed and eyes crinkled as she studied his expression.

Did I summon Bob and forget? Josh thought. *Did he just appear on his own? But he can't! He can't leave the lamp unless I ask for him. So, what did I see in the back seat?*

"You saw something, didn't you?" Lily said, staring at him.

He looked at Lily, still shaken, and answered, "Ah…er, perhaps my imagination."

She gave Josh a stern expression. "Perhaps not…" she continued. "By the way, I saw something last night."

"Something?" asked Josh.

"Something hovered above me while I slept. I awoke, and Mom appeared; she was all spooked. Something was in our house last night," explained Lily. "Do you think it was Bob?"

Josh remained silent for a while before speaking. "I'm uncertain what to trust, or how to stop this. He says he has to stay in the lamp unless I call him."

"And you trust him?" she asked in a skeptical tone.

"I don't trust him, but if he is lying, why doesn't he do away with me? Why does he obey?"

"And this is why we are here," Lily said with confidence. "To get answers and hopefully figure this out."

Josh offered no words. He just nodded.

The mountains disappeared. Josh parked the car after they reached their destination. Lily and Josh walked into a marketplace with a large mall, a cinema, business offices, a few burger joints, a cafe, and a mini theme park. The location bustled, and a large store stood out as they turned a corner.

"This is it…" Josh muttered, gathering his courage as he looked up at the building towering over the two.

CHAPTER 8

THE MAGIC BEAN

The store exterior felt cozy and tidy. An ancient-looking sign spelled out "THE MAGIC BEAN" in bold fantasy font. A few mystical books, plus magic cards, appeared on display. As Josh and Lily entered the store, they immediately realized it was far bigger than its outward appearance. The space stretched far beyond what the modest entrance suggested, with aisles branching into various sections.

Directly in front of them stood a circular counter with a single cash register beneath a hanging sign that read **"PAYMENT."** Three employees remained at the counter, each occupied with a different task.

At the center, a man engaged in conversation with a woman, explaining something about her credit card. To his right, a woman with dark, curly hair sat in a swivel chair, her sharp eyes flicking toward Josh and Lily with what seemed like curiosity—or suspicion. To her left stood an older man with rectangular glasses, exuding a quiet, knowledgeable air. He conversed with a younger customer, who seemed to need help with a book related to his college thesis.

Around the counter, seven signs pointed in different directions, each leading to a specific part of the store. The signs, shaped like road markers but adorned with an elegant, almost fantastical font, read:

Exit
Ancient Books
Magical Books
Brooms and Rugs
Administration
Magical Items
Confectionary

Josh and Lily stood near the exit sign, taking it all in.

Lily noticed the young woman in the swivel chair, still watching them. Taking the initiative, she stepped forward, with Josh trailing behind.

"Hi," Lily greeted.

The woman straightened slightly; her expression polite but measured. "Hello, how can I help you?" Her voice was smooth and professional. She wore a long green dress, her curly hair neatly pulled into a tight bun. A small name tag pinned to the right side of her dress read "Sheila Adisa."

Lily smiled. "We're looking for Alvira Adisa."

Sheila's expression remained neutral. "Do you have an appointment?"

"No, but Pastor Jeffrey sent us. It's urgent," Lily said, keeping her tone warm but firm. "We drove two hours to get here. Please—we need to see her."

As the conversation unfolded, Josh let his sight wander. His attention drifted toward a shelf displaying magic trick boxes meant for sleight-of-hand illusions. The temptation to pick one up was strong, but he remained beside Lily, half-listening to the conversation.

Sheila hesitated for a moment, then sighed. "She rarely meets people without an appointment, but hold on—I'll check with her." With that, she rose and disappeared down the hallway marked "Administration".

Now that they had a moment to take everything in, the true scale of the store became apparent. It seemed small and unremarkable from the entrance, but standing here, they could see its vastness and activity. Every section bustled with activity. Employees assisted customers, guiding them through shelves filled with rare and peculiar books. Some visitors appeared lost, searching for specific items, while others engaged in hushed conversations with the staff.

It wasn't just a store. It was something more.

A few minutes later, Sheila returned. "She'll see you. Take the stairs behind me."

Lily and Josh exchanged glances before following her instructions. They climbed a narrow wooden staircase that creaked under their steps. At the top, they reached a door. Lily knocked.

From the other side, a calm, muffled voice followed the sound of shuffling papers. "Come in."

Lily pushed the door open.

The room smelled of herbs and dried flowers, their scents blending into something both soothing and slightly pungent. Dim lighting filled the space, the air thick with an almost tangible presence. Against the walls, bookshelves overflowed with tomes, glass jars filled with unknown substances, and small wooden boxes. Some shelves held ointments and strange trinkets, which seemed old—older than the room itself.

Lily turned her head and found the source of the voice.

An older black woman with dark, curly hair sat at a desk to the left, her features strikingly resembling Sheila's. She wore round spectacles perched on her nose and a black dress that contrasted with her deep brown skin. Around her neck hung a peculiar necklace strung with beads and a small, intricately carved pendant resembling a miniature statue.

Her presence was calming, yet something about her radiated authority.

She smiled, gesturing for them to sit on a wooden bench across from her.

"How is Jeffrey?" she asked, speaking with deliberate slowness, as if weighing each word before releasing it.

Lily and Josh sat. Lily returned her smile. "He's doing well. He spoke highly of you and sends his regards."

Alvira's expression softened slightly, though her sharp eyes never wavered.

Despite her amiable manner, the room itself had a strange atmosphere. Something about it was subtly uninviting. It wasn't cold, but it wasn't warm either. There was a presence here, lingering in the air, something unseen but undeniably there.

Josh felt it. Lily did too. But neither of them spoke about it. Not yet.

Alvira studied them both, her sharp eyes scanning their faces as if reading the thoughts behind them. The silence between them stretched uncomfortably, thick with unspoken words.

Josh cleared his throat, shifting in his seat. He hated awkward silences, so he spoke first. "Uh, we were wondering…are there levels to demons? Like, do some outrank others?"

As soon as the words left his mouth, he regretted them. *Stupid question,* he thought. He scratched the back of his head and gave a sheepish smile, waiting for Alvira's reaction.

To his relief, she smiled. "First, introductions," she said, her accent carrying a soft but unmistakable Jamaican lilt.

"Oh! Of course," Lily declared hastily. "I'm Lily Higgins, and this is Joshua Cox."

Alvira nodded, still watching them with quiet amusement. "And what brings you to me? Demons?"

Josh exhaled, realizing his first question had probably given that away. "I, uh…yeah, I'm sorry for blurting that out earlier. You see, we—"

Alvira raised her hand, stopping him. "Son," she said, her delivery steady and knowing, "people don't come to me with these questions unless they—or someone close to them—are in trouble. And I've heard whispers of strange events in your town. If you want my help, you need to start from the begin-ning. Leave nothing out. Otherwise, you'll only get pieces of the truth from me."

Josh hesitated, glancing at Lily. She gave him a slight nod. So, he told her everything.

From stealing the lamp to the eerie presence that emerged from it. From the cryptic words the entity had spoken to him to the nightmares that followed. And finally, to the worst part—Kevin's death. His voice wavered, cracking slightly, and he clenched his hands to keep them from shaking.

When he finished, Alvira sat back in her chair, her expression unreadable.

"Hmm." She exhaled, tapping a finger against the armrest. Then, after a pause, she spoke again. "This…is…" she trailed off, her eyes locking onto Josh's. "You said he called himself an ifrit-nafrit?"

Josh nodded. "Yeah. That's what he told me."

Alvira's face darkened. "Are you familiar with an ifrit?"

Josh thought back to his conversations with the entity. "From what I understand, they're like…a more powerful version of a genie?"

At that, Alvira's lips pressed into a thin line, her eyes flashing with irritation. "Genie?" she repeated, her voice sharp. "Whatever stories you've heard about 'genies in bottles,' I strongly suggest you forget them. There are no genies—only jinns! And jinns do not grant wishes."

Josh swallowed.

Then, after a moment, she leaned forward, her fingers interlocking. "Now…I don't know if it has ever been possible to capture an ifrit-nafrit. Jinn, yes. But an ifrit-nafrit?" She shook her head, deep in thought. "We wouldn't even know how to summon one."

Josh listened intently. He wanted answers, explanations. And he wanted to find who did this to Kevin and really hurt them. And deep down, he felt Bob wasn't being completely honest.

"So, he's lying," Josh muttered, frustration creeping into his voice.

Alvira looked at him calmly. "Oh no, I don't think so."

Josh blinked. "But you just said—"

"Only the most foolish jinn would claim to be something they are not," Alvira interrupted. "Their social order is rigid. Lying about rank is not just forbidden—it is dangerous. If he truly called himself an ifrit-nafrit, then he is one." She let the words sink in before asking, "Was he chained when you first saw him?"

Josh frowned. "Chained? He's made of smoke. How would he even have chains?"

"Captured jinn bear restraints," she explained. "Not physical, but magical." She paused; her gaze was distant. "Then again… ifrit are different. Perhaps my question does not apply to them."

Lily had been quiet, absorbing every word. But she needed to ask so many things, and she feared she'd forget the most important ones. "Should we summon him here?" she suggested. "Josh can call him."

Alvira's entire posture changed. She remained still, yet a subtle change occurred with her shoulders tensing ever so slightly, fingers tightening around the armrest. "I don't think that would be wise," she said carefully.

Lily hadn't expected that response. Surely, the creature coming before Alvira would give her a lot more insight. And, given her experience and expertise, she may dissect the lies from the truth. Even so, Lily decided to press on. "Then…how do we defeat this thing?"

Alvira let out a small chuckle, shaking her head. "Defeat?" she repeated, amused. "Lily, dealing with a common jinn takes years of study. And you're asking about an ifrit-nafrit?"

Lily and Josh exchanged a glance. Fear flickered in their eyes. Josh cleared his throat. "Okay, then…earlier, you said you wouldn't even know how to summon one. So, how do you call a jinn?"

"By its name." Alvira tilted her head. "Let me guess—you're unfamiliar with his name."

Josh sighed. "He's evasive whenever I ask."

Alvira smirked. "Of course he is. Names hold power—especially in their world."

She adjusted herself in her chair before continuing. "Has he told you anything about his world?"

Josh shook his head. "Very little. Only what I ask."

Alvira nodded, then took a slow breath. "Listen closely. Maybe my words will help you." She leaned forward awkwardly, looking at Josh, demanding his full attention.

"Our universe exists on two very separate planes. We, the biological bodies, live on one plane; those who are not biological live on another. These planes share a commonality: they coexist, but some boundaries separate us while others allow inter-action between the two planes. For example, we do not know how to get to the other plane, even when walking or occupying the same area of Earth or the universe as them. But there are focal points that bring the two planes together. We can magi-cally create these focal points, or we can find them in nature. A good example of a natural focal point would be a graveyard."

Alvira stopped, reached for a thermos, and drank from it. Then she wiped her lips with her tongue, looked at her guests, and continued. Lily and Josh sat glued to their chairs, watching Alvira intently.

"Sometimes, you hear of a single house being haunted in a neighborhood. Whatever is haunting it, why doesn't it just walk over to the other houses? It's a reasonable question, isn't it?"

"Because," Alvira answered, "it is bound to something in that one house, and it can't leave that place. In other instances, we see entire neighborhoods haunted, though this is rare. This usually happens when people build homes on old graveyards."

Lily looked at Josh, wondering if he understood what she meant and saw the same connections she did. There had to be a solution buried in all of this, some hidden path through the chaos. Part of her still clung to the idea of summoning Bob. Risky, but having Alvira confront him directly felt like the sole method of exposing the truth. Alvira was sharper, harder to deceive. If anyone could hold their ground against that thing, it was her.

Lily shifted her focus back to Alvira as she spoke, trying to quiet the voice in her head.

"But then, some fools try to break the barrier on purpose. Summoning rituals, dark magic, reckless curiosity…these all create openings where there should be none. The jinn do not cross into our world on their own."

Lily frowned. "They don't?"

"No, if they could break the barrier, we would probably have stopped existing as a species. Only humans are arrogant enough to break the barrier. We have that knowledge, for example, your friend," Alvira pointed at Josh, "broke the barrier when he rubbed the lamp."

Josh stiffened. "I...I didn't know."

"That doesn't change the facts," Alvira replied.

He didn't need another reminder, he knew he was responsible for this mess.

Kevin's death weighed on him like a chain around his chest, tightening with every breath. And Mr. Beeds...caught in the ripple of choices Josh could never take back. His heart sank, dragged down by guilt and the crushing need to fix it all. His thoughts raced, looping over the same hopeless questions. What could he do now? How could he stop this? Was there any way to bring justice—or at least some shred of peace—to the people he cared about? The anxiety coiled tighter. He didn't want riddles or vague warnings. He wanted answers. Clear. Direct. Now.

"He says he didn't kill my friend...can I trust him?"

Alvira answered with a cautious look about her. "No, you can never trust him. These creatures tend to lie, and even when forced to tell the truth, that truth is usually surrounded by lies." After another sip of her tonic, Alvira continued, "The ifrit-nafrit says he didn't kill your friend, and you believe him?"

"Yes, maybe…I am not sure." Josh was uncomfortable with this line of questioning.

"Why would you believe him?" asked Alvira.

"He stated he is bound to me."

"Besides," continued Josh. "He has shown no remorse for Kevin's death. The ifrit cherishes his death and says he wishes he had killed Kevin. Why would he deny the killing if he was truthful about his feelings and his desire to see Kevin dead?"

Alvira's eyes narrowed.

"Because," she said, her voice barely above a whisper, "the best lies are the ones wrapped in truth."

"To what end?" Josh's voice wavered. "What can I possibly offer him?"

Alvira didn't answer right away. A heavy silence stretched between them before she finally spoke.

"Did he explain how your friend died?"

Josh swallowed hard. The memory of Kevin—his face pale and twisted in terror—haunted and pained him. "Yes," he admitted. "He told me his kind carries a hatred that never dies. Generations of blood feuds, always looking for a way to strike, to kill. He said Kevin was just…collateral damage. His enemies wanted to hurt the ifrit or humiliate the ifrit by killing those under his protection." His voice cracked.

Alvira exhaled slowly. "His story holds up. Not necessarily the part about your friend's death, but what he says about his species. They are vengeful. That much is certain."

Josh clenched his fists. "So, what am I supposed to do?"

"Understand this," Alvira said, her voice firm. "You will never get the full truth from them. They twist it, mold it, wrap it in riddles until you can't tell what's real and what's not." She pondered for a second, then continued, "The key isn't just knowing that they lie. It's understanding how they perceive truth itself."

Josh's irritation was clear. Under normal circumstances, this lecture might have been great. But he was no closer to understanding how to tell the lies from the truth. Who killed Kevin? And why? If he is getting half-truths from Bob, where is the rest of it? Who is going to give that to him? Where does he turn? What does he do?

Lily, who had been silent for some time, finally spoke, "What do you mean?"

Alvira leaned forward. "Think of a fifteen-year-old boy," she began. "His father asks him if he's done his homework. What does the boy do?"

Lily frowned. "He probably answers."

"And if a stranger asked the same question?"

Lily shook her head. "He might ignore them. Or lie."

Alvira nodded. "Because his truth is bound to his father. The stranger has no claim over him, so truth becomes…optional."

Josh was getting restless. "How does this relate to me?"

Alvira turned to Josh. "If this creature is truly under your control, then, by his logic, he must obey you. But even then, he will twist his words to trick you."

Lily's voice dropped to a whisper. "And if he's not under Josh's control?"

Alvira's expression grew grim. "Then you are in more danger than you realize."

Josh's blood ran cold. "If he's not bound to me, why hasn't he just killed me?"

"I do not know. What I know is that these creatures weave webs of lies and deceit. They don't just strike—they toy, they manipulate. And by the time you realize you've been played, it's already too late."

Lily's posture slouched slightly, giving the illusion that she was relaxing into the chair, but her face told a different story. Her jaw was tight, eyes restless as they scanned the room as if trying to spot something—anything—that made sense. There was a flicker of defeat in her expression, a quiet crack in her usual resolve. She glanced at Josh, just for a second, as if hoping he might speak up, offer a solution—an answer, a plan, a miracle. She turned back to Alvira, her gaze steady but heavy, and spoke.

"How do we stop him?"

Alvira looked weary. "I don't know if you can. No human has ever successfully defeated an ifrit-nafrit."

Josh's stomach dropped. "Then what do we do?"

Alvira exhaled sharply. "You can try to banish him. If he's truly bound to you, it might work."

Josh's mind reeled. "And if he's telling the truth about his enemies coming after us?"

Alvira's voice remained barely above a whisper. "Then you're already doomed. If he leaves and his enemies still want you dead...nothing will stop them."

A heavy silence filled the room. Alvira closed her eyes; she seemed to doze off. Lily and Josh were thinking and feeling. There didn't seem to be a way out. Who else could they ask? Who else would know?

The air shifted—heavy, electric—carrying with it a presence that hadn't been there before. Lily couldn't see it or hear it, but every instinct in her screamed. The hair on the back of her neck stood rigid, her breath catching in her throat. There were no windows open, no cracks or doors open, yet a chilling breeze curled around them like icy fingers. She whipped her head toward Josh. His face had gone pale, his eyes wide and locked on her, mirroring her terror. He felt it too.

Without a word, Alvira pushed back her chair—the sudden screeching sound cutting through the silence like a knife. She stood slowly, stiffly, her body trembling. But she wasn't looking at them. She stared ahead, fixed on something neither Lily nor Josh could see. For the first time, genuine fear contorted Alvira's features, raw and unhidden, and it sent a deeper, sharper dread clawing through Lily's chest.

"Something is here," Alvira whispered.

Lily shot to her feet. Her hands trembling. "I felt him last night. It's him."

Josh turned in panic. "No. It can't be. He only comes when I call."

The room exploded into chaos.

Two massive shelves wrenched themselves from the walls, spinning violently through the air before crashing through the window onto the main floor. The glass shattered. Screams echoed from the shop below as people ran for their lives.

In the center of the room, two glowing orbs—smoldering like embers—stared directly at Alvira.

A cabinet flung open, and three glass jars rose into the air. The tops burst open. Thick white smoke poured out, twisting, writhing—taking shape.

Three figures emerged. Their bodies were shapeless wisps of blackened mist, but their eyes were sunken, hollow, hungry.

Magical chains ran around them as they looked at Alvira and whispered, "Our mistress commands us, and we obey."

"Our mistress commands us, and we obey."

Alvira's face was pale. "Your mistress commands you to destroy him!" She pointed at the glowing eyes. The smoke thickened, swirling with malice.

A loud pounding sounded on the door. "Mother!" Sheila's voice.

"I'm fine! Close the shop and go home!" Alvira's voice wavered.

"Mother, open the door!" Sheila pleaded.

Lily was frozen in place. If the events at the parking lot had unsettled her, this was on another level entirely. All the talk about jinns, ifrit, had her spooked, but nothing could've prepared her for this.

The air was alive with menace, objects tearing themselves from the walls, flying through the room with a violent force that made no sense. It was a nightmare made real, and Lily stood caught in it, eyes wide, breath shallow, as if her mind was still catching up to what her body already knew—this was real, and it was dangerous.

Josh, in contrast, moved with purpose. He wasn't calm, but he was focused. His instincts kicked in, staying close to Lily and Alvira, placing himself between them and whatever chaos was being unleashed. If something came flying their way, he'd take the hit. Because if there was one thing he could do, it was to protect them.

Suddenly, the shelves hurled themselves at the door, splintering the wood. The impact sent Sheila flying down the stairs with a sickening thud.

"Sheila," whispered Alvira with a show of concern. But she immediately regained control, realizing there were bigger things to worry about.

The menacing eyes turned toward the three jinns, and the stare intensified.

Alvira gasped. The chains on the jinns shattered.

The smoldering eyes narrowed, lips curling into a wicked grin.

Alvira started chanting, first in murmurs and then yelling with all her might. Josh and Lily stood frozen, unable to fully comprehend the death staring at them all.

The air thickened. The room spoke. "Foolish woman."

The jinns, now free, turned toward Alvira.

Alvira stopped chanting for a moment and turned to Josh and Lily, her face aged and fearful. "Run!"

Lily and Josh looked at each other and started searching for an exit. They tried to move, but their feet felt frozen. Panic had completely sunk in.

Alvira started chanting even louder, with all her concentration. But there was something in that room negating her magic.

Lily screamed. "Stop him!"

"It's not him!" Josh shouted, staring at the eyes.

The voice laughed. "You imprisoned my kind...and now you will pay the price!"

The smoke collapsed onto Alvira. She shrieked—the sound, raw and agonized, sent shivers down Josh's spine.

Lily grabbed Josh's arm. "Call him!"

Josh's hands shook. "BOB!"

The air trembled.

A towering figure appeared in the room, eyes burning with fury. Bob was seething.

The other creature—a mere shadow in comparison—shrank back, flickering for a moment before vanishing. The three jinns, smoke only, writhed and screamed in pain at Bob's feet until the fire consumed them.

Josh's voice cracked. "Save her!"

Bob glanced down at Alvira, her body mangled, her insides exposed. His face twisted in disgust.

"Filthy human," he spat. "You enslave my kind and expect mercy?"

Josh's heart pounded. "I told you to save her!"

Bob slowly turned to Josh. "You would protect her? Knowing what she does to my kind, knowing what they did to me?!"

Josh swallowed. He forced himself to stand tall, though his knees trembled. "Back into the lamp. Please."

For a moment, Bob stared and said nothing. But he whispered in anger before disappearing. "And you asked why we can't have a civil relationship?"

A worker stumbled into the room. "Is it over?"

Another gasped. "Alvira!"

Josh didn't want to look. He didn't want to see the aftermath. The floor was slick with blood. The shop—once neat and orderly—was now a wreckage of shattered glass, overturned shelves, and bodies.

Lily grabbed his hand. "We should go."

Josh hesitated. "We should help."

Lily's tone was distant and hollow. "We will only bring more misery."

And with that, they left.

CHAPTER 9
THE DREAM

Lily looked at Josh and said, "We are taking a longer route home. There is this scenic area that people talk about, and I want to see it since we are here."

"I don't know if I feel like taking a scenic route," Josh said sadly.

"Enjoy it while you can," Lily added firmly. "I feel we may deal with a lot more pain."

Josh nodded. Lily was headstrong and practical. She was hurting as much as Josh, but she worried about him. He didn't need to go through this again after he had just lost his best friend. They crossed a long bridge with a swooshing large river under it. Vibrant green mountains appeared in front. The peaks were sharp as swords, towering over the horizon, their bright colors contrasting well with the soft and pale sky. Twenty minutes later, they were on top of one of these mountains.

"I don't know about you, but I am hungry. Let's eat," Lily said.

Food stalls and other shops were in the scenic area, so they stopped by one and got a sandwich. Josh put his hands in his pockets to pull out some money. Lily immediately grabbed his hands. "You are not touching that money, you hear me?!" she yelled, and people started looking at them. "Sorry." She smiled and paid for the sandwiches.

The view was spectacular. They stood near the top of one of the larger mountains; around them were other mountains, varying in shape and size, but looked breathtaking. About thirty miles from them was the state capital, separated by a calm, running river with crystal-clear water. The sun was setting, and the weather was pleasantly warm, with calm and chilly breezes flowing often. They stood there, admiring the view, and started eating their sandwiches.

"What do you think will happen now?" asked Lily.

"What do you mean?" asked Josh.

"Bob didn't seem too happy."

"He is never happy. But I feel like his anger is justified. To see his kind imprisoned after what he went through," Josh added.

Lily took a bite and looked at Josh, hoping he had some answers. Josh seemed equally lost while he chewed away at his sandwich.

"You think that other creature killed Kevin?" asked Lily.

"Probably!"

"So, send him after the other creature. Finish him," Lily demanded with a firm look.

"I tried, he refused," Josh replied, looking at the city skyline.

Lily had a confused look on her face. She stared at the running water, wondering if there was something wrong with her. The things she had to process today made little to no sense. She turned to Josh and asked him seriously, "Wait! I thought he obeys you?"

Josh shook his head. Words didn't need to be spoken. He knew exactly how Lily felt; he was feeling no different.

"It's complicated, but it seems like Bob may be telling the truth. If it weren't for him, we would both be dead, too."

"Maybe," Lily replied while eating her sandwich. "But remember what Alvira told us; we will only get half-truths."

Josh seemed sadder. He stopped eating and momentarily looked at the sky, then turned to the tourists in the area before he spoke.

"I don't know about her. I mean, enslaving those creatures, that was bad."

"Yeah," agreed Lily. "That was not cool. But Father Jeffrey seemed to have a very high opinion of her; there must be a reason."

"No wonder Bob is angry and pissed off at us," Josh observed sadly.

There was silence while they ate. The sun disappeared behind one of the distant mountains. Sunset was not far away.

Lily smiled and then laughed a little.

"What?" asked Josh, looking at her.

"Remember the time Kevin claimed to have fallen from the tree house?" she asked, still smiling.

Josh smiled, looking at the city. He then tried to imitate Kevin and his snarky attitude. "Even though I can sue you for millions of dollars, I suppose I can settle for a thousand dollars."

They both smiled.

For a moment, it was as if the weight of everything vanished.

Josh smiled—genuinely, effortlessly—the tension slipping from his face like it had never been there. Lily felt it too, that rare lightness, like breathing fresh air after being underwater for too long.

Their memories wrapped around them, warm and unshakable. Strong enough to cut through the noise, to dull the ache. In that fleeting pause, pain and fear stepped aside. Just for a moment, the world felt whole again. And so Josh continued.

"Kevin lay on the ground, pretending to have fallen on his left hip. *Someone help me, I think I broke something!*" Josh mimicked Kevin, holding his face in mock dismay.

"I remember seeing Mr. and Mrs. Sombat laughing," said Lily.

"Yeah, they knew Kev was faking it, and he wasn't doing a very good job."

"Why did he want a thousand dollars?" asked Lily.

"Some baseball card for his collection. The one he wanted was costly," answered Josh.

"Mr. Sombat still gave him the money," Josh added.

"Really? Why?" asked Lily.

"I don't know," he replied. "Kev won some company sweepstakes we never heard of, and he received a thousand dollars. But I'm pretty sure Mr. Sombat arranged for it."

"How do you know Mr. Sombat did that?"

"A hunch," replied Josh. "I asked Frank about it, but he immediately turned it around and said, 'Did Kevin really fall off the treehouse?' I wouldn't give Kev away, so I let it go."

Josh put his half-eaten sandwich on one of the stone pedestals. The sun was an hour away from setting, and the scene was breathtaking. Other people stood looking at the beautiful view, some with loved ones, others just taking pictures. Josh was looking at the view. His eyes teared up, and he looked gloomy as he spoke.

"I still can't believe we lost Kevin." He sniffed, trying to hold back tears.

"I feel like he is going to come back any minute and laugh at us for buying into this dreadful joke of his." He looked at Lily longingly. "But he isn't, is he?"

Lily's eyes watered.

"Lily, I am sorry I brought all of this upon us. I didn't mean to…"

Lily grabbed his hand and stared compassionately into his eyes. "I know," she whispered.

Josh tried to look away, pretending to look at the mountains. He was tired of the gloom and sadness. "There is so much I didn't get to say to Kevin, what he meant to me and how much I loved him, how much I miss him."

"Oh, Josh," Lily said, moving a little closer to him.

"I don't want the same to happen between us," he continued. "I have been so uptight about everything." Josh looked at Lily, his eyes puffy with pain and regret. "About my feelings. About expressing my emotions. I'm so worried about what I say, I end up screwing things up, failing to appreciate those around me, to treat them the way I should have."

"Kev knew how you felt, and not everything needs to be spoken," Lily whispered.

Josh held Lily's hands gently, his thumbs tracing slow, deliberate circles over her skin. His heart pounded, but he didn't look away. He couldn't. "I have loved you, Lily, since the ninth grade," he confessed, his voice barely above a whisper. When he finally lifted his gaze to meet hers, the weight of years of unspoken words hung between them.

Lily didn't speak. She simply stared at him, her eyes shining with unshed tears before they spilled, trailing softly down her cheeks.

Josh exhaled shakily. "I was afraid of losing you as a friend." His voice cracked, but he pushed forward. "I should have told you sooner, should have treated you better. Shouldn't have waited this long to say what's always been in my heart."

For a moment, Lily remained still, her breath trembling as if she were standing on the edge of something vast and terrifying. Then, without a word, she stepped closer, closing the space between them. She reached up, cupping his face, and pressed her lips to his.

The world around them faded—the chaos, the fear, the lingering shadows of what they had just faced. None of it mattered anymore.

All that remained was this moment, this kiss, this feeling—two souls finding their way back to where they had always belonged.

As the sun melted into the horizon, bathing them in warm, golden light, Josh wrapped his arms around her, pulling her closer, silently vowing never to let her go again.

Lily and Josh felt better on the drive back. The pain was still there, but sharing it helped them both. Lily drove, and Josh was tired and fell asleep. The sun had gone down, and nightfall had taken over. It was a two-lane highway with barely any traffic.

"HEY BUDDY, NICE OF YOU TO DROP BY. I HAVEN'T SEEN YOU forever," said Kevin, looking at Josh. Josh was in Kevin's home, sitting on Kevin's bed, and Kevin was smiling.

"Have you seen my baseball card collection? I think I gave those up and am more interested in cars now?" Kevin looked at Josh as if hoping for acknowledgment, then staggered to his feet, his movements slow and unsteady. He turned to Josh, his face pale and drenched in sweat.

"I don't feel too good… I feel sick."

Josh stiffened. Something was wrong—very wrong. Kevin's face appeared different, as if years had passed in mere seconds. Wrinkles etched across his skin, deep cracks forming like fractured stone. His once-thick hair thinned rapidly, strands falling to the floor like dead leaves.

Josh's stomach churned. An overwhelming urge to flee surged through him, but his body wouldn't move. His muscles felt leaden, like an unseen force had shackled him.

Kevin groaned, his voice shifting—deeper, heavier, unnatural. "See what you did to me, buddy? I thought you were my best friend!" His eyes, once familiar, now burned with something grotesque. Thick, dark blood oozed from the cracks in his skin, turning to pus as it dripped down his hollowing cheeks.

Josh's breath hitched. This isn't real. It can't be real.

"We were friends! Best friends!" Kevin's voice cracked with anger, but his body was no longer his own. His skin stretched unnaturally, pulling away from his bones like melting wax.

Josh's instincts screamed at him to wake up and run. But no matter how much he willed it, he couldn't even blink. His body refused to obey him.

Kevin let out an agonized wail as his limbs jerked violently as though something unseen was twisting and pulling at them. He lifted off the ground, suspended in mid-air, his arms and legs yanked outward by some invisible force. His screams grew sharper, raw with torment.

"Josh, buddy—make it stop! Please!"

His plea was desperate, but Josh could do nothing. He was paralyzed, trapped in this living nightmare.

Something else was looking at Josh through Kevin's eyes. Josh could not see it, but he perceived it. Kevin's eyes were glowing red as he looked at Josh with a sinister smile. "Yes, Josh, buddy!" He laughed in a deep voice. "Make it stop, why don't you?" Kevin's voice was gone; this was a piercing, evil voice, and the room resonated with Kevin's screams and a sinister voice laughing. The voice challenged Josh to help Kevin, but Josh was helpless. He couldn't even stand.

Kevin shrieked again, his body convulsing. And then—the ultimate horror began.

Josh watched helplessly as Kevin's skeleton began to move.

Not from within him—but through him.

Bones slid forward, pushing through his flesh without tearing it. The skull pressed outward from beneath his face as if trying to escape, its hollow sockets bulging against the stretched, thinning skin. His ribcage slithered forward, pressing against his torso like a grotesque parasite forcing its way out.

Josh's breath came in ragged gasps. His heart hammered against his ribs—too fast, too hard. He was going to die.

Kevin's body, or what was left of it, was little more than bloated, pulsing slime. A sickly sack of ruined organs and shredded tissue, twitching in place.

And then the skeleton broke free.

With a sickening, wet sound, Kevin's full, red-dripping skeleton collapsed onto the floor.

Josh choked back a scream.

In the background, Josh heard something chewing away at the skeleton. Kevin's eyes were looking at him in pain.

"Josh!" Kevin yelled. "JOOOSH!" he yelled again.

JOSH SUDDENLY AWOKE, AND LILY STOOD BEFORE HIM, THROWING water at him. Josh was shaking, saliva dripping from his mouth, and drenched in sweat. He tried to position himself to get a better look. It was night, and Lily had pulled over to the side. Another car stopped before them, and a man stood next to Lily.

"Hey, mister, you okay?" the man asked.

Josh did not get a good look at the man. Everything was a little blurry, and he was still trying to understand what was happening.

Lily grabbed Josh's face gently and turned him to her. "Hey, stay awake." The man handed a blanket to Lily, who thanked him, and he left. Lily wrapped the blanket around Josh and stared at him with concern.

"Who was that?" asked Josh.

"Someone who saw me in distress and offered to help," Lily answered. "Josh, you were yelling and screaming and... sweating and waving your hands every which way. No matter what I did, I couldn't get you out of your nightmare."

"I-I knew I was in a dream. I kept telling myself to wake up and open my eyes, but I couldn't. Something was holding me back," Josh muttered shakily as he tried sipping some water.

"Don't go to sleep, I'll, uh...I'll try to get us home soon," she said.

"O-okay," said Josh as he tried to use the tissues in the car to clean himself up as much as possible.

The two of them were back on the road; Lily was exceeding the speed limit by a bit—something she rarely did.

"I don't want to go back home..." Josh whimpered, hugging himself as he shook a little.

Lily looked at Josh. Her face was firm, but anger was getting to her. She was angry at what happened to Kevin and what was happening to Josh. She was angry at how helpless she felt. "Call Frank," she said sternly.

"What?"

"Call him and tell him you want to stay with him," Lily advised.

"Okay," said Josh, and he took out his phone and dialed Frank.

"Hey, Josh," said Frank, who picked up his phone immediately. "Listen, we were going to call you but didn't have the nerve…" Frank said quietly, his voice cracking and straining as he sobbed through the phone.

"Kev was dear to all of us, and I don't know who would want to hurt him." He continued crying, but seemed to have taken some control of his emotions. Josh listened quietly and then said, "Is it okay if Lily and I crash at your place tonight?"

Lily looked at him, staying silent.

"Yeah, sure, anything, Josh, just name it," said Frank.

"Thanks," Josh said, wiping his nose. "We'll see you in an hour."

CHAPTER 10

FINAL PEACE

As they approached, Josh and Lily found the gate to the twins' house open. Frank was standing by the entrance to the house. He walked up and hugged Josh. They remained in that position for a while, and then he hugged Lily. Frank motioned the two to follow him. They went through the house into the backyard. There were a bunch of people sitting around a large tree. A small tree house was resting halfway across the tree with a rope stairway hanging from it. A fire around the area provided some warmth in the chilly evening.

Their friends Liz, Tracie, Anthony, and Frederick walked up to Josh and Lily and the friends started hugging each other. Their faces were gloomy; everyone was crying or holding back tears. There were a few additional people, but these were the house's servants. They stood there quietly with serious expressions on their faces.

Eventually, everybody started settling across the large silver maple tree. The tree's strong roots elevated the nearby ground, showing their firm grip. Someone placed the fire a little away from the tree, and everyone sat around it.

"Josh," Liz began, looking down, "we all loved Kevin. He was family, and we are so sorry for what happened."

"He was a fierce friend," Anthony added, looking straight at Josh. "He was goofy, funny, sometimes annoying, but man, he loved you!"

Josh looked at Anthony, and tears started falling. Lily and a few others tried to fight back tears, but they were crying before long.

There was silence before Tracie, who was looking at the tree, started talking. "Remember the time Kevin fell from this tree?"

A few of the friends started chuckling. Josh said, "He didn't fall."

"Of course he didn't," said Frank, and he had a sad smile on his face.

"He wanted a thousand dollars," said Frederick. "Dad gave it to him."

"He did?" Frank snapped back.

"Yeah, you didn't know?" asked Frederick.

A few of them wiped their tears as the conversation gently shifted.

Lily's eyes found Josh, her heart tightening at the sight of him. She knew him better than most, knew the weight he carried, the guilt he tried to bury. She could see the pain etched into his face, even when he tried to hide it behind a forced smile. This distraction, this momentary lightness, was good for him. As much as she missed Kevin too, she understood—Josh needed healing.

"Your father could never remember any of our names," said Tracie.

And everyone started laughing.

"I was Elle," said Lily.

"I was Jeff," said Josh.

"I was Andrew," said Anthony.

"And he called me You," said Liz.

"Yeah, 'YOU,'" said Tracie. "That was the best." Everyone laughed some more.

"But Kevin, my dad always remembered. Told us this kid has the tenacity to see things through," Frank spoke, staring at the tree.

"Yeah, he liked Kevin," continued Frederick. "He had some made-up company run a raffle, which purposely selected Kevin to pay him the thousand dollars."

Josh jumped in. "Kevin was ecstatic and told me he had never won anything in his life. He was literally glowing with pride and happiness. He got some baseball cards that he wanted. I had never seen him that happy."

There was silence again. The only noise was the burning fire and some insects in the bushes. And then Liz spoke. "Didn't you two get detention once?"

"More than once." Josh smiled. "It almost always involved girls. Remember Suzie Lancaster?"

"Isn't she some hotshot fashion model in New York now?" interjected Frederick.

"Well, she was always a looker," said Josh. "We were in ninth grade, and she was a senior. Kevin was nuts about her and kept calling her WO MAN."

"Well, she was…is," Frank added, seemingly adrift as he stared at the sky, a slight smile on his face.

"So, we were heading to the gym," remembered Josh, "and she and her friends walked out and headed toward the girls' locker room. Kev grabs me and drags me into their locker room because he wants to see her naked. We somehow sneak in, and there she is, and Kevin is bewitched by her. Then we heard Ms. Monroe, the gym teacher, and we both ran out… only, I forgot my water thermos in there."

Josh's friends were listening intently. Josh was a man of few words; he usually kept to himself, and Kevin was the one who told the stories, though with considerable exaggeration.

"So," Josh continued, "I returned and got my thermos. I told Kevin to wait outside, but he wouldn't listen. He went with me, and Ms. Monroe caught us."

"Kevin would do that," Lily quietly whispered. "He was very devoted."

"Yes," said some.

"He was," said others.

"I don't even want to ask what excuse Kevin made," said Liz, laughing.

"Well," said Josh, laughing back, "he raised his left leg and put it down, then raised his right leg and put it down and made a face like he was desperately trying to hold something back." Josh tried to imitate Kevin. "I have to relieve myself, Ms. Monroe, and I can't hold it in anymore; I heard this place has the facilities I need," Josh concluded.

Everyone laughed. They spent the night talking about Kevin, their friendships, and their time together growing up. Frank and Frederick were quieter than usual. They seemed genuinely happy to see Josh with them and tried to make the stay pleasant.

Around 1:00 AM, everyone started heading back into the mansion. The servants received instructions to be most helpful; they scurried between floors, ensuring everyone's contentment. Josh got a room on the third floor, beautifully decorated with a Persian carpet, thick multi-layered curtains by the windows, and a high ceiling holding a small chandelier. The bed was huge and had more pillows than Josh cared to count. He threw a bunch of them on the floor, turned off the lights, and crashed on the bed. He'd had a rough day, but the last few hours had calmed him considerably. Thinking how lucky he was to have friends, the door suddenly opened. A figure stood in a robe with long, wavy hair running down her back.

Lily used to have short hair, but that changed after high school. Since he'd been back, she'd had her hair pulled back or set in a ponytail. But tonight, she seemed very inviting. Even in the darkness, Lily glowed as she moved toward Josh.

"Scoot over," she whispered, and Josh moved a bit to the side as she lay down next to him.

She was radiating. It was as if she was finally next to someone she had wanted to be for a long time. Josh had never seen anything this precious, this perfect in his life, and he thought nothing could feel this wonderful.

But…

He couldn't find the words. There was a lot he wanted to say and a lot he wanted to do, but when it mattered, he seemed to have lost his mojo. He just stared at her, his mouth refusing to open, his hands refusing to move.

"So," she said with a smile.

That smile seemed to have given him the push he needed. He slid closer to her and kissed her. She did not resist and gave in completely. They embraced and spent what felt like an eternity kissing each other. Then she pulled away.

"I don't want us to rush this," she murmured, her voice soft but certain. "And with everything going on, I'd rather we take our time." She gazed into his eyes, and he saw affection, tenderness, and the slightest flicker of caution.

Josh didn't push. He wouldn't. Instead, he let her ease back, his expression warm and understanding. "Of course," he breathed. "I'm just happy you're here." And he smiled at her, a smile that held nothing back—no pretense, no hesitation—just pure, undeniable love.

Lily leaned in, pressing a delicate kiss to his lips before turning away. He moved instinctively, closing the space between them and wrapping an arm around her from behind. She sighed at his touch, her fingers trailing along his forearm before pulling his hand to her chest, holding it there as if grounding herself in his presence.

She kissed his hand softly, a quiet gesture that sent warmth surging through him. Then, turning briefly, she met his lips again slowly, unhurriedly, lingering—before resting her head against his.

Josh swallowed, his heart beating a little faster. For a fleeting moment, temptation stirred in him, the pull to go further, to let the moment sweep them away. But as quickly as the thought came, so did the realization—this wasn't just desire. This was Lily. And with Lily, he wanted no regrets. What they had now, in this moment, was more than enough.

He drew her closer, pressing his forehead gently against her hair. Her floral, sweet scent—a blend of perfumes that made his head light—wrapped around him, soothing and intoxicating. He exhaled slowly, allowing himself to exist with her in this perfect sliver of time. Eyes drifting shut, he felt peace—a rare, beautiful stillness. He was exactly where he was meant to be.

CHAPTER II

THE SECOND FUNERAL

There was a knock on the door. Josh and Lily covered themselves with the blanket, and the door opened.

"The little—" the lady corrected herself. "Young masters are asking that you meet them in the dining room as soon as possible." They both got up, then Lily left, and Josh got dressed. Downstairs, just about everyone was present, and the help was busy serving breakfast. Lily came shortly after with her usual ponytail. Josh noticed, and Lily saw him looking. He smiled at her, and she smiled back.

Fredrick addressed his friends.

"I spoke to Kevin's dad this morning. They want to hold the funeral as soon as possible. Given that..."

Fredrick stopped talking as he searched for both the words and the strength to continue. Tears started dropping on the dining table as he made another attempt to finish his sentence.

"Given that Kev..."

And then he broke. The weight of it all came crashing down and he collapsed into tears—raw, unfiltered, the kind that comes from a place too deep for words.

The impact on Lily, Josh, and everyone else in the room was like a wave. No one could hold it in anymore. Silent tears welled and spilled over. The room filled with the soft sounds of grief—quiet sobs, trembling breaths, the occasional sniffle trying to hold composure that simply wasn't there. It was a moment stripped of pride, of pretense. Just people—hurting, together.

After a few minutes, Frank rose and signaled his brother to sit. He seemed more composed as he spoke.

"Kevin's body was mutilated. That would understandably disturb any parent, so they want to put the body to rest."

He paused briefly, then looked at his friends, clearly trying to stay strong.

"Since this is an ongoing investigation, there is some resistance from the town when it comes to releasing the body. But the parents... well, he was their son. The idea of Kevin in the state that he is, is agony. Basically, as soon as they can get the body back, they want the funeral held."

A heavy silence settled over the room, thick and unmoving. No one spoke. Each person sat with their thoughts, haunted by the weight of Kevin's death and the unimaginable torment his parents were enduring. It was a silence not born from awkwardness, but reverence—a collective mourning that needed no words.

When breakfast ended, the spell slowly lifted. One by one, they rose from their seats, moving quietly, gently—like people walking through a dream they hadn't asked for. Life, as it always did, called them back. So, they gathered their things, exchanged soft nods, and drifted back toward the rhythm of their daily lives, carrying the ache with them.

AFTER TWO LONG DAYS OF PAINFUL WAITING AND COUNTLESS conversations, the authorities finally returned Kevin's body to his parents. With hearts heavy and spirits worn thin, they made the heartbreaking decision to lay him to rest.

They held the funeral at the local church—a place that now felt far too small for the weight of the sorrow it held. The air was thick with grief, and the soft murmur of whispers and quiet sobs filled the space. Kevin's parents sat in the front row, their faces pale and tired, the kind of tiredness that goes beyond sleep. Beside them sat a few unfamiliar faces—relatives, likely, who had come from out of town. People who bore the same pain etched differently across their expressions. Someone had clearly informed them in advance, preparing them for a moment no one is ever truly ready for.

The church hall held a packed crowd. Friends from every corner of Kevin's life had come—co-workers, childhood companions, neighbors, and those who had simply crossed paths with him long enough to feel his absence now. They filled every pew, lined the walls, even stood in the back, shoulder to shoulder in quiet mourning. Kevin had touched more lives than anyone realized. And now, in this last moment, they had all come to say goodbye.

Understandably, they excluded visitation from the ceremony. Pastor Jeffrey expressed some lovely things about how to honor our loved ones. He reminded the congregation that memories are the most precious things we leave behind. So cherish them and honor them, he said.

It was almost unbearable to witness the pain Mr. and Mrs. Morris were enduring. Their grief hung in the air like a tangible presence—thick, suffocating, impossible to escape. Josh and Carol approached quietly, their steps slow, as if afraid to break the fragile moment. Carol wrapped her arms around Sybil, who clung to her, trembling. Josh embraced Michael, who was already crying, and the two held on as if trying to keep each other from falling apart.

Josh couldn't stop shaking. The sorrow coursed through him in relentless waves, crashing again and again with no mercy. It clawed at his insides, deeper than he thought the pain could reach. He wanted it to stop—wanted it to end. And in the darkest corners of his heart, he wished he had never met Kevin at all. Never laughed with him, never shared those moments of joy and brotherhood. Because maybe then… it wouldn't hurt this much. Maybe then… he wouldn't be breaking like this.

Michael gripped Josh, seeing the boy who had once been so full of fire now trembling, his head bowed, tears falling to the floor. He loved Josh like his own, just as he had loved Kevin. And watching him like this tore something open in him. Still, he took a breath and steadied himself. There were others who had come to grieve, others who needed comfort, answers, a kind word. He needed to be strong—for them, for Sybil, for Kevin.

As Michael pivoted to meet with others, Josh let go. His steps were slow, almost uncertain, as he walked toward the door with his mother beside him. And though the room behind him continued to be full of people, still full of love and mourning,

Josh felt like he journeyed through the loneliest place in the world.

Josh and Carol returned home with a heavy heart. After changing, he came down and sat with his mother; he realized she was hurting and wanted to be there for her. They didn't talk much, but Carol was always happy to have Josh around. There was a knock on the door, and Carol opened it. William Sanders, the local sheriff, stood at the door.

"May I come in?" the sheriff asked, speaking low and steady. He didn't smile. One hand rested on the doorframe, the other on his belt near the badge that caught the hallway light. His glance scanned the room as if he knew his objective.

Carol moved and let the sheriff in. He walked over to Josh and sat next to him.

"How are you holding up?" he asked with some anxiety in his voice. "I know you were close to Kevin."

Josh looked at him and smiled sheepishly but said nothing. Bill looked at Carol and then turned to Josh again. He spoke gently but firmly. "You were at Kevin's place before anyone else. Did you see anyone? Do you recall anything you may have missed?"

Carol felt uncomfortable. She should have asked for a warrant before letting Bill in, but it was a little late now.

"Listen, Josh, I need to know what's going on. Otherwise, I can't help you," Bill pleaded.

Carol squared her shoulders as she opened the door, though her grip on the knob betrayed a tremble. "I think you should leave," she said, her voice steadier than her emotions. She didn't meet his eyes; afraid they'd read the hesitation she was trying so hard to hide.

Bill looked at Josh and then got up and walked over to Carol. Bill spoke firmly, but there was a hint of care in his voice.

"He has a stolen car in his name, he has ten million dollars in his bank account, and he was the first to see his friend's dead body. He was also in the capital at a shop called the Magic Bean…the place got ripped to pieces."

Carol's jaw dropped. She simply stared at Bill as he continued.

"You think I can't get a warrant and take him in? He and Lily were present in the capital when the owner died, and they were the only ones with her when this happened."

Carol stood in disbelief, looking at Bill. Her eyes were red, her initial anger turned to fear, and her lips shook. This defeated woman had sacrificed everything for her son's future, which now promised little or no hope.

Bill's firm stance grew softer. Deep down, he knew these were good people thrust into an unpleasant situation. But he also had a job to do. "I am not trying to be a cop, Carol; I grew up here like you. I went to the same school as you. And I want to help, but eventually, this town will demand answers. Please talk to him, talk to me." With that, Bill left.

Carol stood by the door in shock, weeping. Josh got up, went to the door, and closed it. He looked at his mother, and she turned to him. "Is all this true?" she demanded firmly, in intense pain.

Josh's heart bore a simple, undeniable truth: he loved no one more than Carol. Not now, not ever. It went beyond simple affection. Carol had given everything to him—her time, her patience, her heart. She had sacrificed so much, never asking for anything in return. And Josh saw it all. Every little thing she did, every quiet act of love that she thought went unnoticed. He was absolutely certain that there was nothing she wouldn't do for him.

In the moments of hesitation that crossed his mind, he fleetingly thought of perhaps lying to protect her from the truth... but he was unable to. Not while she stood before him, vulnerable, her eyes showing apprehension. The notion of hurting her once more was unbearable. So, he swallowed his doubt and let his heart speak the truth, however unrefined it seemed.

"Yes," he whispered under his breath.

Carol shook her head; the movement slow and heavy as if the burden of everything bore down. Her eyes locked with Josh's, and in that moment, he saw it all—betrayal, hurt, confusion, and a deep, aching sorrow. Josh, his heart breaking, took a step toward her, trying to hug her. Before he reached her, Carol pushed him away, not forcefully, but with a sadness that made each movement feel like an unraveling.

Without another word, she turned and began walking up the stairs.

"Mom," Josh called out to her.

But she didn't stop, she had reached the fourth stair when he called to her again.

"Mom, please."

This time, she stopped and turned to him. "How?" is all she said, looking straight at Josh, her pupils blood-red.

"I am uncertain," Josh said, rubbing his hands, and Carol

noticed. He realized that the price of his truth would replace her pain with absolute fear. And so, he changed his mind.

"We thought it might be a glitch in the bank, we hoped they wouldn't find it. Kevin and I started spending the money without thinking this through."

Carol's stare hardened, and anger supplanted the pain. "You don't even know how to lie."

"Trust me, Mom." Josh's nervousness and desperation showing. "The lie is much more believable than the truth."

Carol stared at Josh briefly before turning and continuing her climb up the stairs, sobbing quietly.

Josh remained standing in the same spot, the weight of it all pressing down on him.

CHAPTER 12
THE DEMONS' WILL

Josh looked at Carol's closed bedroom and heard her weeping. He was in trouble, severely in trouble, and he realized that stealing the lamp had been a terrible decision. He walked into his room, closed the door, and called Bob.

"Aaqa," a sinister voice declared as Bob appeared in his smoke-filled form.

"You tricked me!" said Josh.

"I did?" inquired the creature.

"You stole that car!" continued Josh.

"I did," answered Bob, acceptingly.

Josh stared at Bob, wondering how to handle this. The image of his weeping mother fresh in his mind, the nosy sheriff poking for answers. He sensed things were soon going to spiral out of control. And then there was Bob, impossible to reason, impossible to deal with. Josh was losing his temper.

"I never asked you to steal the car."

"You never asked me not to," replied Bob, his eyes fixated on Josh.

"Why didn't you simply make the car I desired? Why did you have to steal it?"

The creature shifted a bit toward him, and momentarily, Josh forgot his anger. He looked around in desperation, his hairs standing, wondering if he had gone too far.

"If you want things done honorably, free an angel next time." The creature smirked, thoroughly enjoying this moment.

"You are telling me you can't create something I desire? You must steal it?" asked Josh, irritated at Bob's indifference to his problems.

"No, I cannot," replied the creature seriously.

Josh's temper flared—white-hot and unfiltered.

He took a step toward Bob, fists clenched, eyes burning with fury. But just as quickly, he stumbled two steps back. Genuine anger existed, but so did fear. The helplessness clung to him like a second skin, and the weight of it settled thick in the air, pressing down on him. His fury failed to mask the truth: he was outmatched by this creature, a fact he couldn't deny.

"Aren't you the mighty ifrit-nafrit, masters of sky and whatnot?"

"I am that ifrit-nafrit, yes," replied Bob. "But to create something out of nothing… only the master of all universes can do that. I live to serve you, Aaqa. If you desire it, I find and bring it to you. I do not care who it belongs to, even if you do."

Josh stared at Bob in silence, his eyes locked, but his mind in overdrive. He had been sifting through every word, every subtle twist in Bob's tone, trying to untangle the half-truths and buried lies. At the same time, he was desperately mapping out some kind of strategy, some way to get ahead of the chaos he was sinking into. And beneath it all, he was scrambling for the right words—words that wouldn't give too much away and get Bob to actually help him.

"I don't want you anymore. How do I get rid of you?"

The ifrit stared at Josh momentarily, almost with a sense of accomplishment. "You die."

The creature's animated patterns moved through the smoke, and an undeniable little smirk played on what could be called his face. Josh, meanwhile, continued his mental struggle, part of him wishing he had never gone to see his father this summer.

"There has to be another way," Josh exclaimed, annoyed.

The creature studied Josh for a minute before speaking. "You could banish me, but I would advise against that."

"Why would I care?" asked Josh angrily.

"It is an eternity in a world with no beginning or end. It is far worse than the lamp. I will forever roam this world with no purpose and no end. And I will never be free," the creature pleaded with Josh.

Josh was uncomfortable. As much as he despised Bob, he couldn't condemn him to such an end. He looked around, thinking about what to do.

"I may have to reveal you to a few people. I don't know how to explain the money, the car, or the murders. They will eventually take me away and demand an explanation," Josh muttered to himself.

Bob's usual smirk had vanished, replaced by something darker. His expression lacked humor; only a cold, calculating gleam remained. He leaned in slightly, the motion slow, deliberate— like a conspirator about to share a secret too heavy for the room. It did not show deference. It signified intimacy with a purpose. A predator pretending to whisper to its keeper.

"You are impulsive, Aaqa, and you don't think things through."

"Don't try to change the subject," demanded Josh.

"I would dare not," replied Bob calmly. "Did I clarify that my sole purpose is to serve and protect you?"

"You did," he replied, wondering where this was going.

"Let's assume you reveal me to these few people," Bob seemed confident, but there was a slight hint of desperation. "Do you think your kind will accept this truth and leave it at that? Especially after realizing the power that rests in your hands?"

Bob moved a little closer to Josh. "What about your friend who died? You may believe you had nothing to do with it, but they certainly won't see it that way. And what about the next death that happens? Do you think they will not hold you responsible?"

Josh was having difficulty finding flaws in Bob's arguments. "There will be no more deaths!" he uttered aggressively.

Bob paid little attention to Josh and continued, "If the deaths continue and I am revealed as a powerful, magical, evil enti- ty…" Bob stopped for a moment and sneered. "They will blame me and hold you responsible. Their justice will demand your head even though you have no control over this."

Bob seemed to inhale this moment as if he had a prey trapped and was ready to strike. He was patient momentarily, giving Josh enough time to process the argument before continuing.

"And the moment they decide to take any drastic action, which they most certainly will, I will finish half of this town. Thus, I will end up doing the very thing you are trying to prevent."

Josh stared at Bob, seeing reason in his arguments but knowing full well how deceptive he could be. "I asked you to save her in the magic shop…you could have, but you let her die."

Bob remained emotionless, unfazed by the challenge. "She was already dead when I stopped the other jinns. The jinns tore through her, and her heart had stopped. But what surprised me is your intent to defend and protect those imprisoning us," Bob said, deflecting the conversation back to him and looking for a reaction.

"About that," Josh reasoned uncomfortably. "I am sorry for what happened to you and your kind."

Bob interjected. "Your apology doesn't matter. I was imprisoned for thousands of years, and those jinns are now dead. Your apology changes nothing. But you would mourn the death of those who did this to us."

"I didn't ask you to kill the jinns. I only asked you to save her," Josh argued guiltily.

"But I enjoy killing," Bob replied with a smirk. He gently glided back, as was his nature, a creature of immense pride and equal levels of prejudice.

"I don't care about some jinns; they are beneath me. But then, I don't hide what I am...you do!" he confidently stated. "I will tell you I am evil, but you won't admit this about yourself. I will tell you I enjoy death and power, but you won't admit this even when you ask for millions of dollars that you have not earned. And then apologize for my imprisonment, but defend the woman who imprisoned us."

Bob decided to strike while the iron was hot and spoke again. "If you desire, Master, I could fix all of this in a heartbeat. All you have to do is remove the restrictions on me. Let me be... me."

"No more favors from you," shot back Josh.

Bob remained calm. "Come now, Master. I can feel your fear and your agony. You try so hard to protect these insects, and they would lock you up for something you had no control over. Let your inner demon loose, my master. Unleash me! Imagine the power you would wield through me; you would be unstoppable. Not an army of men and jinn could touch you!" Bob radiated with power, overwhelmed by a feeling of triumph.

Josh averted his face from Bob, took a few steps back, and said, "You will do no such thing."

"Is it because of that filthy redheaded bitch?!" snarled Bob.

Josh turned toward Bob, his fists clenched, his face stiff, fury building inside of him.

"Ah, it is," answered Bob wickedly with a sense of satisfaction. Josh turned away again. "My master, there will be many like her that will worship your power. Trust me. Let go of the good and embrace what you are...through me."

"I need this problem solved, and I need these killings to end." Josh glared at Bob. "And I mean it. Find a solution, or I will have to banish you!"

Bob snarled, his face twisting with raw anger. The mask of charm fell away, revealing something colder, older, and infinitely more dangerous. The shift was immediate and jarring —his tone no longer that of a devoted servant, but of a bitter, cornered beast, tired of playing nice.

Josh sensed the change ripple through the room like a sickness —hatred thick in the air, despair creeping in around the edges. A hollow emptiness settled in his chest as if Bob had sucked all the warmth from the space and left only dread behind. This wasn't just a creature acting out. This was something ancient... offended.

"Very well, Aaqa, you win. I will kill as much of my kind as I can to make sure that your kind survives." And with that, Bob vanished.

It might've looked like a minor victory—Bob stepping back, silenced, momentarily contained.

But Josh knew better.

He'd seen enough, heard enough, experienced enough to understand the truth: with an entity like the ifrit, there were no real victories.

Only delays. Only trade-offs.

Because, in the end, you don't win against something like that.

You just survive...if you're lucky.

CHAPTER 13
AN UNHAPPY FAMILY

Josh and Carol sat quietly at the dining table; their plates barely touched. The dinner had passed in near silence, Carol only muttering a few words, picking at her food without actual interest. Josh had so much he wanted to say, pleas, reassurances, even just small talk—but he held it back. They were both too tired, too worn thin. He couldn't handle another argument.

Then came the sound of a car pulling up outside. It cut through the silence like a sudden breath of air, almost welcome. Josh and Carol exchanged a glance—neither of them eager, but both silently relieved for the interruption. They stepped outside into the soft gloom of evening, and there he was—Pastor Jeffrey, emerging slowly from his car.

His face carried a heavy sorrow, his shoulders drawn in as if the weight he bore had finally started to bend him. He said nothing at first, just walked toward Carol with eyes full of something deeper than grief.

"It's so good to see you, Pastor Jeffrey. Please come in and join us for dinner," Carol said with a smile.

The pastor smiled kindly, gave Josh a look, and then turned to Carol.

"If you don't mind, ma'am, I am going to decline, as I must be somewhere else soon. If you can excuse us, I wanted to talk to your son."

Carol turned to Josh and then looked back at the pastor. She felt a bit uncomfortable but decided not to make an issue of it.

"Of course." Carol went inside the house.

Pastor Jeffrey looked at Josh. In those kind eyes, Josh saw pain. He also saw anger as the pastor's eyes started to tear up and he looked away to hide his emotions. Eventually, he turned back to Josh and spoke. "I understand you met Alvira?"

Josh's stomach churned, a cold weight settling in his gut. He didn't know what to say, didn't even know where to start. His thoughts spun in frantic circles, reaching for the right words, the right tone...but nothing came. Just silence and the pounding of his own heartbeat. He turned to the pastor, his expression heavy with the burden of everything he couldn't explain.

"I met her, and I was told that she passed away. And I am very sorry for what happened to her."

"She did not pass away," the pastor replied. His temperament seemed calm, but he failed to hide his anger as he continued. "She was brutally murdered and mutilated."

Jeffrey put both his hands in his pockets. Tears were visible on his face as he fixated on Josh and spoke again. "Alvira was no ordinary woman. She was a uniquely gifted individual, kind and resourceful, who saved me more than once from certain doom. For her to end up like this." A few tears fell from his face. "I hope," continued the pastor, "she could at least give you something to help defeat this monstrosity."

For a fleet second, Josh recalled seeing those imprisoned jinns in Alvira's possession. And he thought whether the pastor knew. But as he saw the pain in his eyes and the reality of a friend lost, he came back to his senses.

"She was of great help. At the risk of her own life, she helped us. I can never truly thank her for her insight and courage." Josh replied.

The pastor nodded. "How are you and your mother doing? These past few days have taken a toll on our community, especially you?" there was kindness in his voice, pain in his tone.

Josh gently nodded his head, looking away from the pastor. Whenever someone asked him how he was doing, Kevin's face flashed before him. And it immediately hurt. The tears started dancing in his eyes and he wished he could go back inside. He was tired of crying.

"We are okay, I mean, as okay as we can be." And a few tears fell.

The pastor put his hand on Josh's shoulder, gently and Josh looked at him, a fatherly figure, caring and kind.

"If I can help, you know you can always talk to me."

"I know I can, and thank you," acknowledged Josh.

Pastor Jeffrey stood there for a moment, sharing this moment with Josh before getting back in his car and driving away.

Carol sat at the dining table near the kitchen, absently stirring what remained of her coffee. When Josh walked in, she looked up, her expression unreadable. "What did the pastor want?" she asked casually, though there was a weight beneath her words.

Josh met her gaze for a moment before shrugging. "Nothing—just checking up on me."

Carol smiled gently. "You know you can talk to me about anything, right?"

"Yeah, Mom," he said quickly, turning toward the stairs, hoping the conversation would end there.

But it didn't.

"Let's assume there was a glitch in the bank, as you mentioned," Carol continued, calm but laced with something sharper. "What about the car? The one you stole?" She took a slow sip of coffee, eyes locked on him.

Josh froze on the first step, his fingers tightening around the banister. Not this again. He inhaled sharply, then shifted to face her. "I didn't steal it. There was some mix-up at the DMV."

Carol set her mug down with a quiet but deliberate clink. "A mix-up at the DMV?" she repeated, her tone almost mocking. "Then tell me, what was that car doing in Kevin's garage, registered under your name? Did the DMV personally deliver it to you?" Her words cut through him like a blade, edged with anger and disappointment. She stood and took a step closer, her presence suddenly overwhelming.

Josh clenched his jaw. He wanted to run—out the exit, down the street, anywhere but here. Instead, he forced his voice to stay even. "Mom, I didn't steal anythi—"

Carol cut him off. "Ten million dollars, Josh." Her voice cracked.

Josh's stomach dropped.

"Where did you get ten million dollars?" Her hands cupped his face, forcing him to look at her. Her eyes, usually warm, now shimmered with unshed tears, a mix of heartbreak and desperation. "I raised you to be better, didn't I?" she whispered.

Josh couldn't speak. Nothing remained to be said.

Carol let go of him, stepping back as if she no longer recognized the boy standing in front of her. She shook her head, her composure breaking. "I tried so hard to raise you right," she said, trembling. "I don't know where I failed."

The words impacted more forcefully than any punishment.

Carol wiped her tears quickly, as if angry at herself for shedding them, then returned to her seat. She reached for her coffee, but it had gone cold. With a small sigh, she pushed it away and sat silently, trying to gather herself.

Josh lingered momentarily, guilt clawing at his insides, but he lacked the right words.

"I'm not hungry," he muttered finally. "I think I'll just go to bed."

Without waiting for a response, he turned and disappeared upstairs, leaving Carol alone with her cold coffee and a broken heart.

BlushyRed215: Josh I have goosebumps. I hope I am wrong. Please tell me she will make it.

Shadelss143: I am sorry Pastor Jeffrey was here and Bill Sanders also told me she passed away.

BlushyRed215: They ripped her open. It was nothing but savagery.

Shadelss143: She kept those things imprisoned. This was expected once they were freed.

BlushyRed215: Really, don't you have something far more powerful imprisoned?

Shadelss143: I didn't imprison him it's not the same.

BlushyRed215: Since that thing came out, bad things have happened. Banish! Banish! Banish! Please!!!!!!

Shadelss143: You're jumping to conclusions he may be the only one protecting us.

BlushyRed215: You mean you! He doesn't care about any of us remember?

Shadelss143: He doesn't care about me either. It's his stupid ancient magic that he cares about. Don't forget he saved us at the Magic shop.

Shadelss143: You know I would never let anything happen to you.

BlushyRed215: REALLY???? I would love to hear how you intend to COMMAND the creature to protect anyone but you.

Shadelss143: We need him. I agree he lies, I agree he is evil, but I don't believe he is killing these people.

BlushyRed215: The next person we care about that dies is entirely on you!

Shadelss143: I don't think it's fair—

BlushyRed215: BYE!

Shadelss143: Bye.

Josh set his phone down, exhaling sharply, frustration tightening his chest. He hadn't expected this.

Lily came off strong—too strong. He knew she was trying to help, but her certainty and conviction rattled him. After Kevin, she was the only person he could turn to who truly knew his predicament. He needed her to see this through with him.

But this idea of banishing the creature forever? It seemed… extreme.

Josh ran a hand through his hair, staring blankly at the wall. He remained unconvinced of Bob's role in Kevin's death. Yes, he presented a danger, practiced deceit, appeared unearthly—yet this did not show his guilt.

Did it? And if there was no proof…, did he deserve a punishment that severe?

The thought gnawed at Josh, leaving him with a sinking sensation in his gut.

THAT EVENING, PASTOR JEFFREY SAT IN HIS STUDY, IMMERSED IN HIS book, the warm glow of the fireplace casting flickering shadows along the walls. A cozy room lined with neatly arranged bookshelves held a mix of theology, philosophy, and history in its contents. A window overlooked his well-kept garden, the moonlight spilling through the glass in soft silver streaks. He lived here with his wife Natasha and his eleven-year-old daughter, Dawn.

He turned his gaze toward the window, a strange sensation prickling at the back of his neck. Was someone out there? Discomfort unsettled him, but he shook it off and returned to his book, determined to finish the chapter before heading to bed. Still, the unease lingered.

His fingers tightened slightly around the pages, his focus wavering. Another glance at the window. Was that movement? He swallowed, walked over, and shut the curtains with a firm tug, blocking out the night. But as he settled back into his chair, the tension only grew.

Then—a book tumbled from the shelf.

Pastor Jeffrey's eyes flicked up, his expression unreadable. He didn't look surprised. He exhaled quietly, lowering his gaze back to the words on the page.

Thud.

Another book hit the floor.

Then another.

Pastor Jeffrey remained still, the firelight casting long shadows across his face. He closed the book in his hands, carefully setting it down, and took a deep breath. "You know I can sense you," the pastor said calmly.

"Can you now?" a voice boomed in the study.

"You do not scare me!" the pastor said, but the hair on his hands stood.

"I do not?" the voice asked, amused.

The door opened, and Dawn walked in. "Dad," she said. "Mom's saying it's late and you should come to bed."

The door behind her closed. Dawn felt startled by the closing door. Her facial expression turned to fear, and she hurriedly turned toward the door and tried to open it, but it wouldn't budge.

"Dawn, I am coming. Please go back to bed," Jeffrey said to his daughter hurriedly.

"How about now?" asked a confident, resonant utterance.

Dawn jumped and turned; her eyes watery as she shook in fear. "Daddy?" she exclaimed, alarmed.

The air in the room felt thick, claustrophobic, as if the walls inched closer with every breath. A sense of crowding filled the room, not with people but with fear. The pastor stood at the center, a man known for his patience, his calm resolve, his unwavering faith. But now, that steady presence was crumbling. His hands trembled slightly. His gaze drifted, unfocused.

His beliefs had carried him through storms, through grief and chaos. But nothing—not scripture, not prayer, not years of quiet strength—had prepared him for this.

Not when it involved his daughter.

This represented no test of faith. This represented heartbreak, raw and relentless.

"Please don't hurt her," he said helplessly.

"Why not?" asked the voice.

"Please let her go. She is just a child," the pastor implored.

Dawn started shaking and crying.

"Why?" the room asked again. "What does that give me?"

"I will give you anything you want," replied the desperate pastor.

"Anything?" asked the voice, as if playing with the pastor. "Will you give me your faith?"

The pastor lovingly held his daughter, who was now shaking. "Look at me, don't be afraid, Dawn," he said, trying to be brave.

"So not anything," said the voice.

An unseen force instantly suspended Pastor Jeffrey mid-air. His limbs flailed, his face contorted in agony as something unseen, something merciless—pulled him in every direction at once.

Dawn's piercing scream shattered the air.

"Dad!"

Her father's mouth opened as if to comfort her, to tell her everything would be okay—but the pain was unbearable beyond anything humans could endure. His body stretched unnaturally, bones cracking, tendons snapping under an unseen force.

And then, in a nightmarish, impossible moment, his ribcage tore through his chest.

Dawn's shrieks grew raw, hysterical. She staggered backward, horrified, her wide, tear-filled vision locked onto the grotesque scene unfolding before her.

"Dad!" she sobbed, her voice breaking. "STOP! PLEASE!"

Upstairs, her mother heard the screams—heard the horror in them. She bolted toward the study, slamming her fists against the locked door. "Jeffrey! Dawn! Open the door!" she cried, her voice frantic. She twisted the knob, yanking desperately, but it wouldn't budge.

"The whole family is here; how entertaining!" the room said. But the screams of the father and the daughter swallowed the words.

Jeffrey's lifeless body crashed to the floor with a sickening thud. For a moment, silence reigned.

Then—the door creaked open.

Natasha burst in, her breath ragged, panic wild in her eyes. She spotted Dawn, still frozen, her face pale, her body trembling. Without hesitation, Natasha pulled her into a tight embrace, shielding her as if her arms alone were sufficient protection from whatever horror had just unfolded. But nothing could have prepared them for what they saw next. Before them stood a skeleton, drenched in blood.

Natasha's breath hitched, her mind screaming to reject what she saw. Dawn had stopped screaming entirely, her wide, unblinking eyes locked onto the grotesque figure that had once been her father.

Then—it moved. The skeleton stepped forward, its bones rattling with each unnatural movement. And as it walked, something began devouring it. The sound proved unbearably sickening—a wet crunch like flesh being torn from bone. But no flesh remained. Something invisible was eating away at the skeleton itself.

Step by step, the bones vanished, as though being consumed by an unseen force. Another sickening crunch. More bones disappeared. And then—only the skull remained.

Floating in mid-air, the skull oriented itself toward Dawn. A voice, distorted, broken, yet unmistakably Pastor Jeffrey's, echoed from the half-dissolved remains. "Look at me, Dawn... don't be afraid." Dawn whimpered, her breath coming in shallow gasps.

It laughed. A shrill, unnatural, maniacal cackle ripped through the air, making Natasha's blood run cold. Her instincts took over. Natasha grabbed the shocked and paralyzed Dawn and ran. But before they could escape,—The door slammed shut.

Dawn bit her mother hard and moved away from her. Natasha let out a squeal. "Are you attempting to keep me away from my father?" Dawn asked, her expression shifting to one of menace. "You can leave," continued Dawn, and the door behind Natasha opened. "But I will not leave father!"

"Please," Natasha said, sobbing, "whatever you are, please let her go."

"Mother!" yelled Dawn wickedly. "Aren't you supposed to turn to God for help?"

Natasha tightened her grip around Dawn, desperation surging through her veins. She had to get her daughter out of here—away from this horror and that thing. The skull watched them silently, hovering mid-air like a twisted spectator enjoying a theatrical performance. Natasha's frantic gaze darted around the room. A way out. She spotted the open window.

That was it.

She pulled Dawn toward it, yanking her arm. "Come on, sweetheart, we need to go!"

But Dawn resisted, digging her heels in. "Didn't I say you could leave?" she hissed. "I won't betray Dad like you!" Her words cut through Natasha like a blade, but she didn't stop.

"Your dad is gone, sweetheart." Her voice cracked, but she kept pulling. "Please—snap out of it!" For a fleeting moment, Natasha felt relief as Dawn's body softened, her resistance fading. But then—a dagger materialized in Dawn's hand. And before Natasha could react, the blade plunged into her throat.

Dawn's eyes were burning, rage and hatred all visible as she backed away from her dying mother. "You can never take me away from Dad!"

Natasha stared at Dawn, her eyes wide—not with anger, but fear. Worry. Natasha's knees buckled. She collapsed to the floor, choking, gasping—dying.

The skull stared with amusement, and it glided in front of Dawn. Whatever was holding her faded, and she came back to her senses. She looked around in fear and then saw her dead mother in front of her, as if seeing it for the very first time.

Dawn fell to her knees, her face contorted in horror, grief, and disbelief. "Mom... no—no, no, no!" she wailed, her body shaking violently as she clutched Natasha's lifeless form. Her sobs filled the room, raw, broken.

And then—the voice spoke. "I came to kill your father," it mused, cold and amused. "But then you came along…and made this much more entertaining." Dawn's bloodshot eyes lifted, her face streaked with tears, her whole body trembling. "And for that," the voice continued, mockingly sweetly, "I will bestow one favor upon you."

Without warning, Dawn's head detached from her body. It hit the floor with a sickening thud, rolling slightly before coming to a stop. Her wide, unblinking eyes still held the last flicker of terror.

And as the room fell silent, the voice boomed one final time, "Let no one say that I am without mercy."

CHAPTER 14
FRIENDSHIP

The following day, Josh sat in the kitchen eating breakfast. He was chewing on some cereal with milk and reading the morning paper when he heard sirens in the distance. The sirens started growing louder and louder. Some sounded like police cars, while others sounded like ambulances and fire trucks. He put down the newspaper and spoon, walked over to the window to see if he could catch the commotion. The neighborhood hid the engines and cars, but he could see red, blue, orange, and yellow flashes in the distance as they crossed the intersections.

Josh picked up his jacket and walked out of the house. Other concerned citizens were also standing, some walking and running toward the noise and commotion. Josh followed them, and he eventually found himself outside Pastor Jeffrey's home. The neighborhood was laden with small houses; everything was nice and neat, with religious figures and signs outside many homes.

There were police lines outside Pastor Jeffrey's home as they walked out with two and a half bodies covered in white sheets. Officer Brian was standing by a patrol car, staring at Josh. Josh saw him looking at him and felt very uncomfortable. Josh put his hands in his pocket and headed back home. He had seen enough and figured out what had happened without the need to see anymore.

Josh was drowning in helplessness.

The sickness in his gut wouldn't fade, an unbearable mix of guilt, frustration, and grief.

This was his fault, maybe not directly, but his actions had set something in motion that had spiraled beyond his control. He wanted to fix things, to make it right, but the more he tried, the worse it got.

And now, the entire community was suffering because of his stupidity.

He wanted it to end. All of it. He wanted a way to stop the madness, to take control of the nightmare he had unleashed. But deep down, he knew the truth—this was bigger than him. He had tried to blame Bob, but the more he thought about it, the less it made sense. Bob had killed no one. Neither of them had. And yet, the bodies kept piling up, and all roads seemed to lead back to them.

Josh exhaled sharply, running a hand through his hair. Bob was right about one thing: the longer this continued, the more people would start looking for someone to blame. And right now, Josh was the easiest target. A glance across the street confirmed his fears. Some officers were still watching him. And the stares spoke about what they were thinking. That Josh had something to do with all of this, at the very least he knew, but wasn't telling. He walked lost in his thoughts and worries until he was standing at the entrance to his home.

Josh sat in the kitchen trying to watch TV. Guilt churned within him. He felt anger, sadness, desperation, and defeat. The story about the beloved pastor was all over the news within an hour. It wasn't that he died, but he was murdered, and it wasn't that he was murdered; he was barbarically mutilated. His skeleton is missing; this is a new breed of evil that the world may have never seen, or so spoke the newscaster. They didn't spare the teenage girl and her mother, deprived of their future, the newscaster continued.

The report also mentioned a young man murdered similarly a few days earlier. References to the similarity between Kevin's and Pastor Jeffrey's death were being made. Josh was in agony. He picked up a plate on the kitchen table and threw it at the TV. Luckily, it missed and shattered when it crashed into the wall. He trembled miserably, his gaze fixed on the wall beside the television. He was utterly powerless, rested his arm on the kitchen table, and cried.

After a while, he walked over to the broken dish and started sweeping the broken pieces when he heard a car outside. A knock sounded on the door, and the door opened. It was Frank Sombat.

"Hey man," Frank said as he saw Josh walking with pieces of a broken plate.

"Hey," said Josh gloomily.

Someone pushed Frank into the house. Frank looked at his brother, annoyed. "Move in already," Frederick exclaimed. He looked at Josh and asked, "Let's go get something to eat."

"You guys go ahead, thanks, but I am not really hungry," Josh replied.

Frank walked up to him, removed the broom and garbage can from his hand, and pulled him toward the door. "Sorry. No is not an option."

Frederick walked up to Josh, put his hands on his shoulder, and said, "Dude, you've stayed cooped up in here all day. Come with us; we are not leaving without you."

Frank looked at Josh and smiled. "We aren't."

Josh realized what the twins were trying to do. He tried to smile, then turned around, put on his jacket, and left with them. He didn't feel like it, but didn't want to say no to them either.

As they started the drive, Frederick spoke. "Pastor Jeffrey was a good man, kind, and always there for anyone who needed help."

"He was. What happened to him and his family is unfortunate. I am sure he is in a better place now," Frank commented sadly.

"Amen," said Frederick.

"Amen," Josh whispered.

"The best thing we can do is remember Pastor Jeffrey through kindness toward others," advised Frank.

"Yeah, that is what he taught us and stood for," finished Frederick.

A wave of emotion crashed over Josh, heavy and unexpected.

For all the chaos, the regret, the moments where life felt like it was unraveling, there had always been something else waiting —a new chapter, a second chance, and, most importantly, people who refused to let him fall alone. No matter how dark things got, someone always showed up—sometimes at the strangest hours, in the most unexpected ways—to remind him he wasn't alone.

And now, as everything threatened to crush him, he realized how lucky he was. He had friends. Friends who stood by him. Friends who saw him at his worst and never walked away. Friends he loved—and who loved him back. And that kindness—that pure, unwavering kindness—mattered. Because, in the end, that was all they were trying to show him. And maybe…just maybe, it was enough to keep him going.

"Maybe we could pick up Lily?" Josh asked.

"We tried, dude," Frank said, turning to Josh.

"Yeah, she seemed upset and angry," Frederick smirked.

"You guys didn't try the 'we won't take no for an answer on her'?" Josh inquired.

"Of course we did," replied Frederick.

"But you are a wuss!" said Frank, looking at Josh again.

"Yeah, exactly, and she is not," added Frederick.

"So, we had to leave without her," continued Frederick.

The road eventually merged into a busy freeway, where the landscape shifted into a sprawl of commercial properties. Buildings of all shapes and sizes lined the route—some sleek and modern, others worn with time.

Bright, welcoming signs beckoned from storefronts, while bold advertisements screamed from billboards above, promising everything from luxury cars to late-night diners.

It was a stretch of relentless noise and color, the kind of place designed to distract, to sell, to never stop moving.

Josh turned to Frank, who was driving, and said, "Is this a Bentley?"

Frederick, seated in the back, put his arms behind his head and said, "Apparently so."

"I thought you couldn't get these cars because they were locked up?" asked Josh.

"Nothing's beyond our reach." Frank grinned.

They were driving on the freeway at about thirty-five miles per hour. The car was gliding over a well-placed road. Passers-by in other cars were slowing down or speeding up, trying to take pictures of the vehicle. The boys certainly did not mind and occasionally smiled at some prettier faces.

"Where are we going?" asked Josh.

Frank looked at his brother in the rearview mirror again, and both brothers smiled.

"Pizza Hurt?" said Frank with a goofy face.

"Just stop…" moaned Josh as he ran his hands down his face, a little annoyed. The brothers never stopped with their jokes, and this certainly didn't feel like the right time.

"He doesn't like Pizza Hurt Frank," Frederick remarked.

A few years ago, Josh got hurt while leaving a pizza restaurant, and Frank and Frederick came up with the name 'Pizza Hurt.'

The name caught on and drove up sales for the pizza place. The manager thanked Josh, realizing the joke of Pizza Hurt indirectly helped their sales because the name started trending. When Josh tried to correct the manager, Kevin interjected and not so humbly took credit. The restaurant started giving Josh and Kevin free or discounted pizzas.

Frank and Frederick didn't care about the free pizza but were unhappy they didn't get credit for their brilliance. So, they took their business elsewhere. They told another pizza chain that if they changed to 'Nominoes,' it would trend better. When that didn't work, they suggested 'Baba Johns' at another chain to bring in Mediterranean customers. Except there were barely any Mediterranean customers. They soon realized they were just too talented for this measly little town and would have to wait until they moved to a bigger city to shine.

Back at 'Pizza Hurt,' as the boys called it, they met Anthony, an assistant manager at a nearby store, who joined them at the table. Frank and Frederick tried to keep the conversation away from local events. Their goal was to get Josh's mind off the things that would depress him. They were their goofy self, trying to make silly and sometimes not-so-silly jokes. Anthony would laugh at times and shake his head at others. Josh forgot, at least for a bit, the troubles that had been haunting him for the past few days. After enjoying their meal, it was time to pay the bill.

"Let's split the bill, guys, please," pleaded Josh.

"No, no," said Frank. "He will handle the bill."

Josh looked at Frederick and then asked Frank, "Who will?"

"The Benefactor!" the twins uttered together.

Half-eaten pizzas sat on scattered plates, greasy crusts abandoned in favor of laughter and inside jokes. Empty dishes and half-filled glasses—sodas, iced teas, something suspiciously neon—crowded the table, a chaotic mosaic of a time well spent.

The place wasn't packed, but a few familiar faces glanced their way—some with a nod, others offering a smile or a quick hello, as if watching a memory unfold in real-time.

"You mean your dad," interjected Anthony, shaking his head.

"Do not call him that," said Frederick.

"For he is so much more," added Frank. "He is this," said Frank, throwing a red credit card on the table like a playing card. "And also, this," he continued proudly as he put a shiny black credit card on the table. "As well as this." Frank now threw a blue credit card onto the table, grinning smugly.

"Let's not forget these!" interrupted Frederick, throwing all sorts of credit cards onto the table. Josh couldn't even count all of them.

Anthony chuckled, shaking his head. "So, you guys finally broke in and stole your dad's car and credit cards."

While sipping his soda, Frank seriously stated, "We were inspired."

"You see," Frederick interjected excitedly. "We were watching 'Home Alone.' Those two clowns were trying so hard to break into the house. We realized we were already in the house!"

"Yeah, after that, not stealing felt wrong," Frank finished.

Josh looked bewildered. "Isn't your dad going to flip when he finds out?"

"We are betting on it." Frank smiled.

Frederick took a sip of his soda and made a serious face. "Last time he flipped, we went on vacation to Europe."

Anthony looked at Josh in disbelief.

"It's called guilt; he gets angry, says things, then takes things away from us," explained Frank.

"We sulk in a corner, talk all sad and gloomy. Mom says *I think they have learned their lesson*," continued Frederick.

Frank relaxed on the sofa. "We will have a new car by next week."

"Or a vacation," finished Frederick with a smile.

The manager stopped by, looked at Josh, and offered his condolences for Kevin's untimely departure. He sat for a few minutes and expressed his regret at the early demise of, as he put it, such a talented young man. He reminded everyone how Kevin masterfully manipulated the restaurant's name and how it started trending and helped sales. Frank and Frederick exchanged glances. They wanted to say so much, but because this discussion was about Kevin, it would have been too insensitive. Anthony, moved by the manager's respect for Kevin, offered the credit cards on the table as payment and told the manager that he wouldn't mind if the manager charged all of them.

Frank snatched the credit cards, fake-smiled at the manager, and offered him the black credit card for payment.

Anthony returned to work while Frank, Frederick, and Josh got back in the Bentley.

On the way back, things were quieter, probably because everyone was full and a little lazy.

"Did Lily say anything?" asked Josh.

"She was upset about the pastor. We all are," Frank answered.

Fredrick was driving. He turned left to get back on the freeway. "Yeah, it's best to give her some space,"

Josh noticed the brothers were trying to hide something, but he didn't push it.

"You know you can stay with us; you don't have to go home," Frank smiled at Josh hopefully.

"I don't want to leave Mom alone," said Josh.

Frederick let out a burp. "Yeah, totally understandable, though it may not be a bad idea for her to stay with someone or have someone over. Everybody is hurting and being alone makes it worse."

Josh adjusted on the seat. It was one of the more comfortable seats he had been on. "I will see if she wants that, otherwise, I think it's best…"

"Of course, just call us for anything, all right," Frank advised, looking at Josh.

"Yeah, thanks." Josh smiled at Frank.

The twins left Josh at his place and headed home. Three blocks down, they stopped at a signal and waited for it to turn green. "This is messed up," Frederick said, who had moved to the passenger's seat after Josh left.

"You think Josh knows what's going on?" asked Frank.

"Definitely!" replied Frederick.

Frank looked at Frederick, and someone honked from behind. The light turned green, and Frank started driving. "What do you mean, definitely?" asked Frank.

"Let's see," said Frederick. "Josh comes back, and Kevin dies. Then, some lady dies the same way as Kevin in another town. And now Pastor Jeffrey and his family."

"You are crazy," said Frank. "Josh wouldn't know how to kill someone even if he wanted to; he is too…what's the word?"

But Frederick interrupted him. "You asked me if Josh knows. I never said Josh killed them."

"So, what exactly are you saying?" asked Frank, puzzled.

"I'm saying," replied Frederick in a brotherly way, "that we should probably drop it unless we want to end up dead. Whatever's going on, Josh's insides turned upside down. Didn't you see it on his face?"

"And that friend of his, that creepy old man," Frederick shuddered.

"Please don't speak of him," Frank begged, his face contorting at the mention of Bob.

The afternoon sun hung low and pale, casting a sickly golden light that seemed to stretch shadows into unnatural shapes. The road wound through a forgotten stretch of countryside—cracked pavement, overgrown shoulders, and trees that leaned too close, their branches clawing at the sky like brittle fingers.

The radio crackled now and then, fading in and out with static like an unknown presence didn't want you to hear what was playing. Every so often, a lone mailbox or rusted-out sign would appear, half-swallowed by weeds, hinting at lives long abandoned.

Inside the car, the air felt thick, the silence between songs heavy with something unspoken. Even the breeze seemed wrong—cool and dry, carrying the faint scent of dust, metal, and decay.

FRANK WAS QUIETER THAN USUAL FOR THE REST OF THE DAY. Something felt…off.

As the sun dipped toward the horizon, he stepped onto his balcony, leaning against the railing, his gaze drifting over the view. Warm hues of orange and pink painted the sky, but its beauty did little to ease his unease.

Later, he took a shower, letting the hot water soothe him. Steam filled the small space when he stepped out, curling against the mirror. He wrapped a towel around his waist and entered his bedroom—only to stop cold.

His dirty clothes were on the bed.

Frank frowned. That wasn't right. By nature, he was neat and meticulous. He distinctly remembered tossing those clothes into the laundry bin before his shower. His first thought was that he'd been distracted, maybe absentmindedly, left them there. But that didn't sit right.

Still, he didn't dwell on it. He gathered the clothes and tossed them back in the bin, brushing off the strange feeling creeping up his spine.

Standing before his dresser, he reached for his comb and dragged it through his damp hair. The rhythmic strokes were familiar and grounding. But then his hand stilled. In the mirror, he saw his pillow. On the floor. His brows knitted together. How did that happen? He turned to pick it up.

But it was exactly where it was supposed to be, on the bed.

A chill ran down his spine. What the hell was going on?

A loud noise erupted behind him, sharp and sudden. Frank spun around, his breath catching. The mirror had moved. Something had tilted the mirror to the right; this shouldn't have been possible. The metal rods securing it to the dresser had been manually turned. A feat impossible for human hands.

Frank took two steps back, his breath uneven, a cold sweat forming at the back of his neck. He needed to get out of this room. Now. As he hurried toward the door, a shadow caught his eye. Someone was standing near the stairs. Frank's pulse hammered.

It was his mother. She just stood there, unmoving. Watching.

"Mom?" Frank inquired. "Is Dad with you?"

Mrs. Sombat did not answer. She kept looking at him. Frank started walking toward her and realized something was off. His mother was glaring at him. She looked like his mother, but clearly, this was not his mother.

"Mom? You okay?" asked a puzzled Frank.

"Who are you talking to?" asked a voice from behind.

Frank turned and saw Frederick standing there. Frank turned back to face his mother, but nobody was there. Frank closed his fists, kept staring at where his mother was standing, and asked, "Can I sleep in your room tonight?"

"Why?" questioned a perplexed Frederick.

"Please," Frank said, turning to Frederick. Frederick saw something was off but didn't push it.

"Okay," replied Frederick, "but you are sleeping on the couch."

Frank and Frederick spent time in the gym, watched a little TV, and then turned in. Frank seemed spooked and uncomfortable, and Frederick figured a good night's rest should fix him up. Frederick tried to open a discussion, but Frank shot him down.

Frank crashed on the couch in Frederick's room, seeking comfort in his presence. But comfort didn't come easily. The couch was stiff and unfamiliar, and every small sound in the house made his skin prickle. Still, exhaustion eventually won, and he drifted into a restless sleep.

SOMETIME DEEP IN THE NIGHT, HIS EYES SNAPPED OPEN.

A heavy unease settled over him, the kind that made his breath shallow and his heartbeat quicken. He wished he hadn't woken up. And he knew he wouldn't be able to sleep.

Something was wrong.

He could feel a tension in the air, an unshakable sense that he was waiting for something. Or worse…something was waiting for him. He squeezed his eyes shut, willing himself to sleep. But it was useless—his mind was too alert, his nerves too on edge. And then, the soft creak of a door.

His body stiffened. Slowly, cautiously, he opened his eyes and looked toward the doorway. She was there. Standing perfectly still in the entrance, staring straight at him. His mother. But no —not his mother.

Frank's chest tightened as a cold sweat broke across his skin. By now, he knew the difference. The thing in the doorway wore his mother's face, but its eyes were all wrong.

Red.

Burning.

Unblinking.

It watched him, its presence crackling with something unnatural. Frank tried to move and turn away, but his body wouldn't cooperate. He was paralyzed with terror; his breath hitched in his throat. He forced himself to look toward Frederick, silently begging him to wake up. But Frederick was asleep, oblivious to the nightmare unfolding beside him.

Frank turned back to the doorway, his pulse hammering. She hadn't moved. She just stood there. Watching. Menacing. His mind screamed at him to do something, but he could only squeeze his lids tight and pray.

Please. Let it be gone. Let it be gone.

Minutes passed. Maybe seconds. Maybe hours.

Finally, he risked a peek.

The doorway was empty. The door was closed. And yet, the room still felt wrong. Like something had been there. Like something still was.

Frank tried to steady his breathing, to convince himself that it was over, that whatever he had seen in the doorway was just a trick of his exhausted mind. But his body knew better. A deep, primal instinct clawed at him, screaming that something was still wrong.

He swallowed hard and turned toward Frederick again, and his heart stopped. His mother was sitting on Frederick's bed. Her fingers moved slowly, almost lovingly, through Frederick's hair, stroking it in a rhythmic motion. But her eyes…

They weren't warm. They weren't kind.

They were on him.

Red.

Burning.

Unblinking.

Frank's stomach plummeted.

The air in the room felt thicker, heavier—like the walls were closing in, like something unseen was pressing down on him. His hands clenched into fists, his body rigid with terror. How the hell was he supposed to handle this? How was he supposed to reason with something that wasn't real—wasn't human?

But this was real.

He had pinched himself enough times to know he wasn't dreaming. His breath came faster, his pulse hammering in his ears. He forced himself to blink, rub his eyes, look away just for a second, and snap himself out of whatever this was. But when he looked back.

She was still there. Still stroking Frederick's hair. Still watching him.

Frank shoved his face into the pillow, his breath coming in short, shaky gasps. If I don't see it, it isn't real. He squeezed his eyes shut, wishing—praying—for whatever this was to just go away.

Fingers ran through his hair.

Soft.

Gentle.

Cold.

His entire body locked up. A wave of pure terror crashed through him, every hair on his body standing on end. His heart stuttered, missed a few beats, and slammed violently against his ribs. Then the grip tightened. His scalp burned as the hand yanked his head back. Frank gasped, eyes flying open, staring directly into her face.

His mother. But not his mother.

Her red, glowing eyes bored into his soul, filled with something unnatural, inhuman, hungry. Paralyzed. He couldn't scream. Couldn't move. Couldn't think.

He was sitting upright now, the cold leather of the couch beneath him. His hands trembled, and his breaths were sharp and uneven. And in his right hand.

A butcher's knife.

He stared, his mind scrambling to process it. Where had it come from? He hadn't reached for it. He hadn't even seen it before.

Her voice. Soft. Sweet. Dripping with a sickly and wrong quality. *"You know what to do, my love."*

The voice coiled around his brain, seeping into his thoughts like poison. Frank's grip on the knife tightened. And deep inside, a part of him begged to resist. Frank walked up to where

Frederick was sleeping. He raised his hands to deliver the knife, and Frederick awoke. As Frank drove his knife, Frederick moved away.

"Frank?!" yelled Frederick. "What are you doing?!"

"I am doing what Mother asked me," Frank replied, now chasing Frederick.

"Mother says that you must die," said Frank as he lunged at Frederick. Frederick tried to wrestle Frank, something Frank always lost at, but Frederick was no match as Frank threw him halfway across the room with little difficulty. All the while, he kept talking to someone who seemed to be seated on the couch, someone Frederick could not see.

Frederick looked around and yelled, "Frank, snap out of it! There is no one here."

Frank was closing in fast with his knife drawn. Frederick tried to find something to use against the knife in Frank's hands. He pulled the curtains hard and grabbed the rod after wrapping Frank in the curtains.

Frederick's survival instincts kicked in. His heart hammered as he swiveled and bolted for the door, sprinting out of the room, his voice raw with desperation. "HELP! SOMEBODY HELP ME!"

He flew down the stairs, two at a time, his only thought: *Get out, get out, GET OUT.* But as he reached the main entrance, he skidded to a stop, hands slamming against the wood, yanking at the handle. Locked. His breath came out in frantic gasps. He turned, trying another door—locked. Another—locked.

A creak.

Frederick's blood ran cold.

He turned slowly, his entire body tensing. Frank was standing at the top of the stairs. Staring. A butcher's knife glinted in his hand. His chest rose and fell steadily, but his eyes…

They weren't Frank's eyes anymore.

They were empty. Cold. Not human.

Frederick's stomach dropped.

He turned again, desperately trying another door, and this one opened and he darted inside and slammed it shut, his fingers shaking as he turned the lock. He took a shaky breath, trying to gather his thoughts and think. Then he spotted it—a phone.

911. He could call 911.

He lunged for the receiver, his last shred of hope. The second his fingers wrapped around it.

It shattered.

Frederick yelped, his hands stinging from the splintered remains. He stared, wide-eyed, at the broken pieces. *No. No, no, no.* His breathing became ragged.

Through the window, he saw her. Seated on a garden bench. Watching. His mother. Frederick's blood turned to ice.

She raised her hand slowly—index finger up—and wagged it once. A silent, chilling "No."

Frederick's entire body locked up.

BANG!

The door shook violently.

Frederick spun, his pulse exploding. Frank was pounding against the door.

BANG! BANG!

"DIE, FREDERICK! DIE!"

Frederick swallowed a scream. His eyes darted around the room, looking for anything—any way out. The window. It was his only chance. He turned and ran toward it, but before he could touch it, it sealed shut. Like it had never been open in the first place.

Frederick gasped. He turned toward the garden and saw his mother. She was still there. And once again, she raised her finger. Another silent "No."

Frederick's mind was spiraling into pure panic.

CRACK!

The door splintered. Frank was almost through. Frederick grabbed a chair and hurled it at the window.

SMASH!

The glass exploded outward. The night air rushed in. He didn't hesitate—he ran for it.

But as he tried to climb out, something grabbed his legs. A force ripped Frederick backward and threw him across the room, making him scream. Pain shot through his body as he hit the floor hard, and the wind knocked from his lungs. He looked up, gasping.

Frank stood over him, knife in hand. And he wasn't stopping.

Frederick barely heard it, a whisper buried beneath the

madness. *"Run, Fred, please."* For a fraction of a second, it was Frank's voice. The real Frank.

Then a violent swing of the knife.

Frederick dodged, his breath coming in short, desperate gasps. He bolted across the room, but Frank, whatever was inside him, was relentless. The creature tore through furniture, sending splintered wood flying as it lunged for him. Then the voice. Low. Twisted. Not human. *"We are sorry."* It sneered, mockingly cruel. *"But Frank is not here anymore. And soon, neither will you."* A grotesque, maniacal laugh followed before Frank launched himself at Frederick.

The lights flickered—and Frederick finally saw it.

Frank's face was ruined.

Deep, festering scars and gashes covered his skin, oozing a vile mix of blood and pus. His eyes bulged unnaturally as if trying to free themselves from his skull. Frederick's stomach churned with horror. This wasn't his brother anymore. It couldn't be.

Panic surged through him. He turned and sprinted for the door, yelling for help. But the house was too big. The servants' quarters were outside. No one would hear him. He leaped for the shattered doorway.

But Frank's hands caught him mid-air.

A force ripped Frederick backward and threw him to the ground, making him scream. His ribs ached from the impact, but there was no time to recover—Frank was already on top of him. Frederick struggled, thrashing wildly. His hands found the knife in Frank's grip. Pain exploded through his right hand as the blade sliced deep into his flesh—but he pried it free.

For a split second, he had the advantage. But Frank—or the thing inside him—didn't care. His fingers wrapped around Frederick's throat and squeezed. Frederick gasped, his vision blurring, black spots forming at the edges. He couldn't hurt Frank. Not his brother.

Not until the very end.

With the last of his fading strength, he plunged the knife into Frank's leg. But Frank didn't even flinch. The pressure on his throat increased. Frederick's lungs burned. His hands scratched weakly at Frank's grip, but the strength was leaving him. His body felt heavy. Slow. Distant.

His eyes rolled to the side, where the couch sat against the far wall. She was there. His mother. Watching. She sat calmly, a slow, sinister smile curling her lips. And her eyes…

That red glint.

Frederick wanted to scream. To demand why, to plead, to fight. But darkness swallowed him first.

The room was silent for an instant. Frank fell to his knees. Whatever hold was on him was gone. His hands were shaking as he cradled Frederick's lifeless body.

"Frederick…no." His voice cracked, barely above a whisper.

Tears streamed down his ruined face, mingling with the filth and rot seeping from his wounds. His whole body trembled as he rocked back and forth, gripping his brother.

"Frederick, please…"

The lights flickered back on. Frank's breath hitched. His mother sat across from him, perched on a chair, her face alight with satisfaction. She was smiling. Frank's grief twisted into rage. He lifted his head, his ruined eyes burning with fury.

"He was my brother!" he screamed, his voice raw. "He was your son!"

The smile never wavered. Instead, it grew. Her expression darkened, twisted, and stretched into a monstrous visage.

Frank felt something shift inside him.

He gasped—a sharp, sudden intake of air that wasn't his own. His body stiffened. His head snapped back violently. And from somewhere deep inside him, a voice, not his own, erupted from his throat.

"FREDERICK! FREDERICK!" he yelled.

Frank's body convulsed, his laugh turning hysterical, unhinged, dripping with madness. His hand trembled. The knife rose. And then…

He stabbed himself.

Once.

Again.

And again.

Blood gushed from his wounds, his body shaking, his cries twisting into laughter, laughter and agony, laughter and horror. His mother never moved. She simply watched. The light in Frank's eyes dimmed. His body slumped forward, his hands slipping from the hilt of the knife. A final breath left his lips.

The room fell silent.

And in the dim glow of the overhead light, his mother smiled.

CHAPTER 15

FAMILY REUNION

J osh felt full after his lunch with the twins. They had just dropped him at his place, and he entered after seeing them drive off. The door closed behind him with a soft thud that somehow made the silence louder.

The comfort of being with the twins—Frank and Frederick—had already slipped away, leaving only the echo of their laughter and the faint warmth of companionship that faded far too quickly.

Now, the house felt colder—emptier.

He stood in the hallway for a moment, not quite ready to move, wishing he were still with them, still lost in lighthearted conversation. Anything to delay this quiet, this aching stillness that always found him when he was alone.

Carol arrived home earlier than usual, moving through the house with restless energy. She scrubbed surfaces that were already clean and rearranged things that didn't need rearranging. The tension in her body was impossible to ignore. Josh could feel it in the air. Something was wrong.

Of course, the murders had the whole town on edge, but this was different. This was personal. He could tell by the way her hands trembled slightly, by the way she avoided his gaze. Then, there was the information and warning that Bill shared with Carol, which put her on edge. People have been talking. Josh is in the hearts and minds of this town, but for all the wrong reasons.

Josh walked over to the dining table, picked up a cloth, and helped Carol wipe it down. She was at the counter, meticulously polishing a glass until it sparkled as if by making it flawless.

"So, when's he coming?" Josh asked, his voice firm, his eyes observing her.

Carol didn't look up. She kept polishing.

"Michael called him. They are friends and expressed his concerns about you. He doesn't want what happened to Kevin to happen to you. So, your father is flying over to have a talk with you."

Josh swallowed. He realized this meant trouble.

The doorbell rang.

Carol stiffened. She set the glass down and turned to Josh, her expression suddenly fierce, determined. "You will behave."

Josh said nothing as she walked to the door, but inside, his stomach churned. Then, with a deep breath, Carol opened it.

Matthew stood there, smiling.

He pulled her into a hug, and she melted into it for just a moment before stepping back, her expression soft. Then Matthew turned to Josh.

"Josh," he greeted, his tone steady.

"Dad," Josh replied, his utterance devoid of warmth.

Matthew strode into the room, making his way to the kitchen counter. He lowered himself onto one of the chairs, his keen vision flicking between Carol and Josh. "Heard you got in trouble with the law?" His voice sounded informal; however, the impact of his words was substantial.

Josh clenched his jaw. Of course, that was the first thing out of his father's mouth.

Matthew, in his late forties, remained sharp and commanding. His crisp blue suit and loose red tie gave him an air of effortless authority. He kept his jet-black hair neatly combed, and his posture stayed as rigid as ever. He remained a man who didn't dance around the truth—he cut straight through it.

Carol, suddenly restless again, turned toward the stove and set a pot to heat.

"Your dad was nice enough to come see you," she said, her voice tight, like she was trying to smooth over the tension that had already taken root.

Josh said nothing. He knew this would not be a simple conversation. But right now, his father's disappointment was the least of his problems. There were far bigger things happening in town that made this little family drama seem insignificant.

Carol placed a steaming cup of coffee before Matthew, forcing a smile. "I got your message this morning, but I didn't have time to—"

Matthew shook his head, cutting her off with a simple gesture. It wasn't important. His attention was on Josh. And Josh braced himself.

Though Matthew presented difficulties, he never shirked his duties. He may not have been the father Josh needed emotionally, but he was practical. He didn't shy away from advising Josh, or offering financial help when needed. Carol was grateful for that. She kept the lines of communication open, making sure Matthew understood Josh's struggles, hoping—desperately—that he would step up when it mattered.

And now, more than ever, she needed him to. She needed him to help Josh stay on track, get him into college, and secure his future. And to figure out this mess.

Matthew took a slow sip of his coffee, setting the cup down carefully before fixing his sharp gaze on Josh. "That wasn't a very nice thing to do," he said, his voice measured, almost thoughtful. "Got your mother all worried."

Josh swallowed hard. His father had a way of making everything feel like an interrogation. "It was a misunderstanding," he said, forcing his voice to stay even. "There was a bank glitch. They blamed me for it."

Matthew didn't blink. "So I heard." The disappointment was unmistakable. Matthew was an easy man to read when he was unhappy, and right now, he wasn't just unhappy—he was pissed. "And the lamp?" Matthew asked, his voice quieter, more pointed. "Was that also a glitch?"

"Matthew," Carol interjected, pleadingly.

Josh clenched his jaw. He wouldn't lie. Not about this. "No," he admitted, locking eyes with his father. "That wasn't a glitch. I took it."

Silence stretched between them.

Matthew inhaled deeply, exhaling through his nose as he put his cup down. His fingers drummed against the counter before he spoke. "It wasn't yours to take, and I want it back."

Josh's heart pounded. He sensed the pressure of his father's request, but wouldn't yield. "I'm sorry, Dad," he said, his voice steady. "But I'm keeping it."

Carol gasped. "Josh!"

Her lips parted, but the words caught in her throat. When they finally emerged, they cracked—thin and sharp—like glass under pressure. "You know it's not yours! You took it without permission—"

Josh cut her off. "I'm sorry, Mom. I really am," he said, his voice raw. "But I can't give it back." He turned to Matthew, eyes pleading now. "It's not safe for you here. It's not safe for any of you."

Matthew scoffed, shaking his head. "Forget the lamp?" he said, incredulous. "Do you have any idea how much I paid for that lamp?" Without another word, he pushed back from the counter and strode toward the stairs.

Josh's stomach twisted. "Dad, wait—" He moved to follow, but Carol grabbed his wrist.

"Josh, stay here," she said, her voice firm but desperate. "Don't make this worse than it already is."

Josh hesitated, his fists clenched at his sides. He turned to see his father disappear into his room; the door swinging open violently. Then he turned back to Carol. "He isn't really here for me, is he?" Josh remarked bitterly. His voice was quiet, but the hurt in it was deafening. "He just wants that stupid lamp."

Carol shot him a warning glare, but it softened almost immediately into something else—worry, disappointment, helplessness. This wasn't how she wanted things to go. She had hoped Matthew would help, that he would guide Josh, not tear into him over something so small.

Upstairs, the sound of drawers slamming and objects being thrown around echoed through the house. Matthew ripped through Josh's belongings, searching for the lamp.

Ten minutes later, he stormed back down, his face red with frustration. "Where is it?" he demanded, his voice sharp, his eyes darting between Carol and Josh.

Josh stood his ground.

"Where is it?" Matthew shouted again, this time stepping toward him.

Josh took a breath, forcing his expression to remain neutral. "I threw it away," he lied.

Matthew's eyes darkened. "You little liar," he seethed, stepping right into Josh's face. His breath burned with rage. "You little thief."

Josh could have fought back and thrown his anger into the fire. But right now, Matthew's behavior wasn't the true issue. Protecting his parents mattered. So, instead, he turned his face away, saying nothing. Carol stood frozen, holding her breath. Matthew's chest rose and fell sharply. Then, without another word, he stepped back, gave Carol a long, hard look, and stormed out the door. Josh didn't move, listening as the sound of his father's car roared to life and sped away.

The house fell silent once more.

Carol turned to him, her expression filled with something deeper than just disappointment. And for the first time that night, Josh wondered if he had just made things worse.

"I wish he hadn't come," said Josh.

"The sheriff was here; it's only a matter of time before he comes with a warrant. Do you have any idea what I am going through?" said Carol. "And you could have been nicer to him."

"Me?" asked a confused Josh.

"Let's see," Carol stated, very annoyed. "You stole his lamp! Then you 'supposedly' stole a car! And then you stole ten million dollars!"

"I told you it was some stupid glitch," Josh said, annoyed.

"And you withdrew a thousand dollars from that glitch?" yelled Carol. "Who do you think will pay for that?"

"I will, of course," said Josh, his voice raised slightly.

Carol took a few steps back and sat on the chair Matthew occupied moments earlier. Her wet eyes stared at Josh, like something slipping from her grasp. She inhaled deeply and spoke calmly, despite her frustrated expression.

"You will?"

Her voice rose a little, tears streamed down her face, her body trembling with anger as she repeated. "You will....? Your father, may God bless his soul, agreed to pay the thousand dollars. A thousand dollars, Josh! And on top of that, the car dealership is threatening to sue for damages."

She wiped her tears roughly, her tone cracking as she continued, "Whether you stole it or not, the traffic cameras don't lie. They show you behind the wheel! Do you think you're so smart and everyone else is stupid?"

Josh clenched his jaw, the sting of her words hitting harder than he'd expected. He turned his gaze away, unable to meet her stare. The weight of his lies pressed down on him—each one crafted to protect, to delay the inevitable—but now they were unraveling fast. The cruel irony, however, involved the truth—strange, fractured, unbelievable—being their only potential salvation. But it sounded more like madness than redemption.

Carol's breath hitched, her emotions spiraling between heartbreak and rage. "Hate him all you want, but when I need him— when you need him—he shows up. He takes responsibility!" Her eyes locked onto Josh, unwavering, filled with disappointment so sharp it cut deep. "I wish you had some of his traits in you."

She turned abruptly and headed toward the stairs, desperate to remove herself from the conversation before her tears consumed her.

"Mom," Josh called after her.

Carol stopped but didn't turn around. She stared up the staircase, her posture stiff, as if forcing herself to hold it together. She felt broken, defeated.

"Please leave this place," Josh pleaded.

That got her attention. She turned slowly, her expression

shifting from disappointment to something far worse—worry. "What?" she asked softly.

"Go to a friend's house. A relative's. Just leave town," he begged.

"And leave you?" Alarm rang in her voice.

"Yes," Josh insisted, his heart hammering in his chest. "Things are only going to get worse."

Carol's eyes narrowed. "And how do you know that?" Her voice held suspicion. "Am I supposed to just abandon you in this mess?"

Josh opened his mouth to answer, but nothing came out. He had an answer, of course he did. But it wasn't one he could give her.

She took a step closer, searching his face with desperate eyes. "Please, Josh, tell me what's going on. We can figure it out together."

For a moment, he wanted to. He wanted to tell her everything. To believe, just for a second, that she could fix this like she always had when he was younger. But that wasn't reality. This was bigger than her. Bigger than both of them. Josh averted his gaze.

A cold resolve settled over Carol. Her jaw tightened, and she straightened her back. "No, Josh," she said firmly. "I won't leave." She walked up the stairs, her decision final.

Josh stood there for a long moment before following. When he reached his room, his stomach twisted. The room had been ransacked. His drawers were overturned, his belongings scattered, his backpack unzipped—exposing the lamp. He exhaled sharply and moved quickly to tidy up. Once the room looked in order, he shut the door, his mind racing.

"Bob," he whispered.

A ripple of energy filled the air, and in an instant, the creature appeared, shifting into human form with his usual greeting. "Aaqa."

Josh didn't waste time. "How come my dad didn't see the lamp? He opened my backpack."

Bob's expression remained unreadable. "I put it away so he couldn't get to it."

Josh's throat tightened. He already knew why.

"You understand what would happen if he took it," Bob reminded him.

Josh cut him off. "I know. You'd kill him."

Bob tilted his head slightly as if amused by Josh's bluntness.

Josh ran a hand through his hair. "I get why you hid it. And I appreciate it. But I need to know—have you had any luck finding the killers? More bodies are showing up, Bob. We need to stop whoever's behind this."

Bob's expression darkened, his voice carrying a dangerous edge. "I am hunting the ifrit that killed your woman friend in the other town." He sneered. "The same woman who enslaved my kind—and whom you so foolishly defend."

Josh's stomach twisted at the accusation. Bob wasn't seeking justice. He was playing a twisted game of vengeance. Josh's silence didn't deter the creature.

"I've located some of his family," Bob went on, sounding casual, similar to a business discussion. "I continue to hunt him, to get closer to finding him. Once I do, I will know who is truly behind all of this."

Josh studied him, suspicion prickling at his skin. "Why do I find it so hard to believe anything you say?"

Bob's lips curled into a wicked smile. "Probably because I am evil."

Josh's fingers curled into fists. "I will banish you. I swear it." His voice was low but firm. "I need these deaths to stop."

Bob remained unfazed. "What else would you have of me today, Aaqa?"

Josh exhaled, forcing his emotions down. "Nothing more. Get back to your hunt."

In the blink of an eye, Bob was gone. And Josh was left alone in the dim, ransacked room, the weight of everything pressing down on his chest.

Carol sat on her bed, sobbing into her hands. Helpless.

It was one thing to have a son who didn't listen. But it was another to have a son accused of theft, of murder.

Deep down, she knew Josh would never hurt anyone. He wasn't capable of it. But how could she convince the world of that? The police, the courts, the people who only saw the evidence, not the boy she had raised?

And what if they arrested him? What if they charged him? What if she lost him forever?

Her mind raced in desperation. Only one person cared enough, only one would let nothing happen to Josh.

She reached for her phone and called Matthew.

MATTHEW SAT AT THE AIRPORT, WAITING FOR HIS RETURN FLIGHT. He was still fuming about the lamp, but the moment he heard Carol's sobbing, his frustration softened.

"What's wrong?" he inquired, his voice immediately gentler.

Carol tried to pull herself together, but the words spilled out in shaky breaths. "Matthew, I—I'm sorry about earlier. I'll find the lamp, I swear. I'll give it back to you."

Matthew sighed. "Don't worry about the lamp right now, Carol. You're clearly under a lot of stress."

Carol took a deep breath, but it didn't help. "They're accusing our boy of stealing. Of murder." Her voice broke. "Josh wouldn't hurt a fly."

Matthew straightened. His tone sharpened. "I'll get a lawyer. We'll sort this out."

Carol let out a trembling sigh, the weight on her chest lifting just a little. A lawyer. That meant protection. That meant hope.

The conversation continued with Matthew for a bit longer before he had to board the plane. Carol wasn't relaxed, but her stress had gone down after talking to Matthew. She walked over to her vanity and started applying lotion to her face. Her fingers trembled, exhaustion heavy on her body. She glanced at her reflection in the mirror, trying to focus on something normal, something routine.

The reflection changed. Her breath hitched. The woman in the mirror wasn't her. She was older—much older. She was wrinkled and weak, her body hunched by age, and her hairline receding. Her face was worn and tired, like life had drained out of her. Carol gasped and stumbled back, landing hard on the bed.

The woman in the mirror was still there. And she looked just like Carol.

Panic surged in her chest. She touched her face, feeling the smoothness of her skin. She observed her hands; they appeared normal. When she turned back to the mirror, the old woman was gone.

But something was still there. A movement at her feet. Carol looked down—and horror seized her throat. From beneath her bed, freckled, wretched, elongated fingers slithered out. The skin was dry, cracked, almost reptilian. The fingers stretched toward her, reaching, grasping. Before she could react, they snatched her ankles.

A searing pain burned into her skin, like fire branding her flesh. Carol screamed. The fingers yanked. She fell forward, her head slamming into the ground with a sickening thud.

Josh heard the scream. His heart stopped. "Mom!"

He ran, knocking hard against her door before bursting in. His breath caught in his throat. Carol lay on the floor. She trembled, her forehead swollen from her fall. Her hands gripped her ankles—Josh's stomach turned when he saw the deep, raw marks burned into her skin.

"Mom," he said, panic seeping into his voice. He rushed to her, gently pulling her into a sitting position.

Carol sat there, shaking. Her eyes were wide, lost. Josh scanned the room. Nothing. No one. But something had been here. Carol sat still on the bed, shaking. The woman in the mirror and the fingers under her bed had disappeared. Carol was dumbfounded. She looked at Josh. "What is going on?" she asked sheepishly. Josh didn't say anything. He felt more furious than ever before.

"What happened, Mom?" he asked with concern.

Carol looked around the room as if trying to find a way to explain. "I saw a woman in the mirror, and then a presence grabbed my feet and pulled me toward the ground. I have lived here all my life. Nothing like this has ever happened. I don't understand."

She stared at Josh to see if he would believe her. Josh said nothing. He got some medicine and bandages and did what he could to help her. She relaxed and eventually went to sleep. Only then did Josh go back to his room.

The moment he stepped into his room, he slammed the door shut. "Bob!"

The air stirred. A shadow shifted.

The creature appeared.

"Aaqa."

Josh was livid. Eyes raging with the thought that the terror that had been haunting this town was finally in his home. He wanted to scream but purposely kept his voice low. "My mother was just attacked. Where were you?"

Bob tilted his head slightly. His expression was unreadable. "I was, as you commanded, hunting the murderers." His tone was innocent—mockingly so.

Josh's hands curled into fists. "You are not to leave this house anymore. Scratch that. You will let nothing happen to my mother."

Bob remained still, his glowing eyes unreadable.

"If anything happens to her," Josh spoke in a low and dangerous tone. "I don't care what your excuse is—I will banish you."

Silence hung thick between them.

Then, Bob smiled—a slow, knowing, terrible smile. "As you wish, Aaqa."

A puff of smoke curled toward the lamp. In an instant, Bob was gone.

Josh stood there, his breathing heavy. His mind raced. He pulled out his phone and dialed a familiar number. Lily. It rang. And rang. And rang. No answer. His gut twisted. His sixth sense screamed at him. This wasn't over.

Josh ran a hand through his hair, gripping it tight. His mind flashed to Kevin, to Lily, to his mother.

This was only going to get worse. And if he didn't do something soon, the people he loved wouldn't just get hurt.

They'd die.

CHAPTER 16

THE SOMBATS

The next morning, Josh busied himself with breakfast when Carol left for work. He considered asking Carol to stay home, but he believed it would be better if she didn't. She would worry, and they would fight, so it's better if she went to work. Her feet improved, but she walked with a slight limp. While eating his cereal, he thought he heard sirens again in the distance. He panicked and proceeded to the window, looking for any sign of the emergency vehicles. He neither saw any sirens nor did he hear anything. Relieved, he continued eating his breakfast.

Josh looked for work. His original plan was to work at the mechanic shop with Kevin, but he decided he didn't want to anymore; the memory of his friend would be too painful.

He put on his jacket and left for the market area. He figured he should see a few 'Help Wanted' ads and see if something might suit him. The market area had wider roads than most of the town, and it seemed to be well-decorated. The shops consisted mainly of small, family-run businesses, along with a few well-known stores. Josh stopped by a shoe store with a help wanted ad and applied. He also saw an opening at a bakery and an ice cream store.

After roaming around and making sure he got his applications submitted, Josh sat in a small snack shop and ate. It was about noon, and he felt hungry. The snack shop was mainly a takeout place with a few seats and an LED screen mounted in the front area. The TV was playing a news channel, but the sound was off.

Josh sat by the windows to enjoy his meal and looked outside to see some stores, the people, and even the cars that buzzed by as he ate. He turned toward the TV and saw the T-Tree house, the home of Frank and Frederick Sombat. His heart sank slightly, and then they showed a significant police presence with an ambulance loading a corpse onto a stretcher covered in a white sheet. Josh turned his head away, tears dropping from his eyes. His phone rang. It was his mother.

"Where are you, sweetie?" she asked, her voice cracking.

Josh did not answer, but she could hear him holding back his tears.

People fixated on the TV and whispered to each other, "Another murder."

"Mom, I will call you back," Josh said, trying to keep it together.

On request, the store manager raised the volume on the television.

"Bodies at the Sombat mansion were discovered today." A woman in her late twenties was talking from the Sombat mansion.

"Cynthia, do we know how many bodies?" asked the newscaster from the studio.

"Leslie, we know of at least one death, possibly more. We don't have enough information as the authorities are trying to contact the family members before they release the details. But around 9:47 AM this morning, someone in the mansion behind me called the authorities, and by 10:05 AM, we had police and at least one ambulance here," Cynthia informed Leslie seriously. Cynthia was wearing a professional woman's suit and had short black hair.

"This town has seen much pain in the past few days, and..." Leslie put her fingers near her right ear as if she was listening to something and continued, "Folks, the mayor will be speaking on these murders; we are going live to this event."

A short, stubby white man with a receding hairline and round spectacles appeared on the TV screen. His expression was grave, his posture rigid—a man of business addressing a town in crisis. Behind him stood the sheriff, his face unreadable.

"The recent deaths in our town deeply sadden us," the mayor began, his voice measured but heavy. "I spoke with Mr. Sombat this afternoon and expressed my personal condolences, as well as those of our department, for this horrific tragedy. Last night, someone brutally murdered both of his sons.

Josh tensed. Some people started turning toward Josh. They looked at him as if they were looking at a runaway convict.

"The investigation is ongoing, so I can't provide many details," the mayor continued. "But I assure you, I have reminded our sheriff that this cannot go on. We must bring the perpetrators to justice as swiftly as possible."

Josh couldn't take it anymore.

He turned away from the store's TV screen and walked out, shoving his hands into his pockets. His head hung low, his vision blurred by unshed tears. The cold air hit his face as he made his way home, but it did nothing to ease the storm raging inside him.

Kevin. Frank. Frederick.

Gone.

Alvira. Pastor Jeffrey's family.

Gone.

People who tried to help him. Those caught in the crossfire.

Josh clenched his fists. There had to be a way to stop this nightmare. There had to be a way to end it. He finally understood.

Bob's warning—the town would think he was responsible if they ever found out about Bob. People were dying daily. Of course, they'd start looking for a common link. And who was that?

Josh.

He understood Alvira's warning now, too—that eventually, he would have to make a choice. Keep Bob, or banish him. Neither option was good. And he understood something else, something that sent ice down his spine. He was trapped.

No way out. No clear escape. Just death, creeping closer every day, taking people he loved.

Josh slumped into a kitchen chair, staring blankly at the table. His phone buzzed against the wood. Tracie.

He swallowed hard and answered. "Josh," she sobbed.

Josh squeezed his eyes shut. "Hi, Trac..." But as soon as he spoke, the dam broke. His voice cracked, and the tears he had been holding back came rushing out.

"I loved them so much," she wept. "They were funny, witty, and stupid." She let out a wet, choked laugh before breaking down again. "Josh, who would do this? Who would do this to Kevin? And now Frank and Frederick? Why?"

Josh didn't answer. He couldn't. His throat felt tight, his sorrow intense.

For a long moment, they just cried together, saying nothing.

"Maybe it's best if you, Liz, and Anthony leave town for a while. Whatever this is seems to target us," said Josh, wiping his tears.

"And you?" asked Tracie, blowing her nose.

"Yeah, me too, but I also got Mom to worry about," said Josh.

"I don't know, Josh. I will talk to Liz. Listen, I gotta go. You take care," Tracie continued.

Josh nodded. "You too."

THE SOMBATS HAD BEEN WORKING ON A BUSINESS DEAL IN NEW York City when they got the news. They flew back immediately, their world shattered. That night, Mr. and Mrs. Sombat stood outside their home, grief-stricken, facing a sea of reporters and onlookers. They weren't ready for condolences. They weren't ready for anything.

Authorities had briefed them, but the explanation made no sense. The servants had found the boys that morning after they never came for breakfast. The forensic report proved even more horrifying. Frank suffocated Frederick, and then Frank took his own life.

Murder-suicide.

But the Sombats didn't believe it. Their sons weren't like that. There were no signs, no fights, no distress. They had spoken to them just hours before their deaths. They had been normal. This wasn't just a tragedy. Something was very wrong.

The press conference was outside the mansion, and a good deal of townspeople brought flowers and candles to pay their respects. The Sombats had been good to the people of this town. They had helped a few struggling families and shared their wealth to better the lives of their neighbors and friends. People genuinely respected and cared for them and were forgiving when Frank and Frederick pulled their silly pranks. Now, the sight of the grieving couple struck a deep chord of sorrow. No one deserved this kind of pain.

Mrs. Sombat stepped forward, standing before the microphone. She was sobbing but determined, a woman of quiet strength trying her best to hold herself together. "Frank and Frederick were my boys," she said, her voice trembling. "They were kind, sweet, intelligent…and yes, mischievous. But they weren't what the authorities were making them out to be. My baby Frank would never hurt anyone." Her composure shattered. The weight of grief crushed her, and she broke down, covering her face with her hands.

Mr. Sombat immediately stepped in, wrapping an arm around his wife as he turned to face the crowd. His voice, thick with restrained emotion, cut through the silence. "Something is very wrong," he said, his eyes dark with fury. He lifted a shaking hand and pointed at the officers standing to the side. "These people...they are hiding something sinister." He paused, his jaw clenched. "My boys were decent. They were not monsters."

The mayor, watching from the sidelines, was already fuming.

William Sanders had made a mess of this.

The deaths of the Sombat boys, on top of Kevin's, Pastor Jeffrey's family, and all the others, had the town on edge. It looked bad. Worse, Mr. Sombat was a generous donor to several charities and political causes the mayor cared about. Having a powerful man's sons murdered under his watch was not good for business.

So, when the mayor demanded answers, Sheriff William Sanders, not the brightest in the department, caved under pressure. He suggested Frank had been the culprit—his fingerprints were all over the murder weapon, after all. And now that Frank was dead, maybe the killings would stop.

The mayor stared at him in disbelief. "And how exactly," he asked coldly, "did Frank pull the skeletons out of Kevin's and Pastor Jeffrey's bodies?"

Sanders had no answer.

Unfortunately for him, this conversation happened inside the Sombat mansion, within earshot of the household staff. The servants relayed everything to the grieving parents, and when the Sombats found out, their grief turned into fury.

Mrs. Sombat unleashed on the sheriff, calling him incompetent, spineless, and stupid. She didn't care about civility anymore.

Her sons were dead, and these fools were trying to pin it on them.

Meanwhile, Mr. Sombat turned his wrath on the mayor himself. "You employ this buffoon?" he spat. "My sons are dead, and this is the best you can come up with? A cover-up?!"

It was an ugly, chaotic scene that deepened the town's unease.

JOSH ARRIVED AT THE MANSION WITH ONE GOAL: TO OFFER HIS condolences. To share in the sorrow. So he waited, hoping for a chance to talk to the Sombats, which didn't happen. They were too grief-stricken and didn't want to see anyone. He wasn't the only one.

Tracie, Liz, Anthony, and Lily were there, too, but Josh didn't want to see them or talk to anyone except Lily. He watched her from a distance, silent as the night wore on until, finally, she started leaving. He followed her to her car, heart pounding. Lily was about to open the door when he spoke.

"Lily."

She froze. Then, slowly, she turned. Her eyes were red-rimmed, her face pale. She looked at him. And then—just as quickly— she looked away.

"You know they're lying," Josh said, voice raw. "Frank had nothing to do with this."

Lily's shoulders tensed. "No, Josh." She turned back to him, her gaze sharp and unrelenting. "You did."

The words hit like a slap, unexpected and brutal.

Lily's expression burned with fury and grief. "You, Josh, are the most selfish human I have ever encountered," she spat. "You refuse to banish that thing because you believe its lies. Because you actually think it's protecting you."

Josh took a step back, hands buried deep in his pockets, searching for an argument—for something, anything—to say.

But Lily wasn't done.

"Ever since you brought that thing here—ever since—we've been losing people," she said, her voice rising. "People we grew up with. People we loved." She was trembling now, barely holding back her tears. "And do you know why? Do you?!"

Josh swallowed hard.

"Because you're a coward, Josh!" Lily yelled, her voice cracking. "You're afraid that if you banish that thing, you might die."

Josh had never seen her like this before.

She shook her head; her tears falling freely now. "It's cost us everything!"

Josh opened his mouth—he wanted to tell her he couldn't banish Bob. That his mother's life was at stake. But she didn't give him the chance. She turned, yanked open her car door, and slammed it shut. Within seconds, she was gone, her Honda Civic speeding down the dark street.

Josh stood there, fists clenched at his sides, his heart pounding. Her words echoed in his mind.

Selfish.

Coward.

He hated her for saying them. And he hated himself for knowing she was right. He walked home silently, his thoughts a tangled mess of pain, sorrow, defeat—rage. But he also realized something else.

This had gone on long enough.

This ancient vendetta, whatever it may have been, cost him dearly among those he cared for. Bob, remaining near his mother, offered no resolution. It was a risk. And then there was Bob himself.

How truthful were his words? How can Bob hunt down the killers if he is protecting his mother? Even he can't be in two places at once! If the other jinns or ifrits are trying to hurt Bob, then getting rid of Bob should be the solution. Josh saw it now.

He saw why Lily insisted on Bob being banished, why this may be the only way to get out of this. Bob's proximity ensured the gruesome murders would persist. And so Josh made a decision, for there was no other decision to make except this one.

Josh entered the house, his body heavy with exhaustion.

Carol remained in the kitchen awaiting him. As soon as she saw him, she stood up and crossed the room quickly to embrace him. "Sweetie, you're shaking."

Josh pulled away without a word and started up the stairs. He felt defeated.

Carol watched him go, then glanced at the kitchen table where she had prepared dinner. She opened her mouth to call after him, but stopped herself. Instead, she let him be.

Up in his room, Josh closed the door behind him and stared at his backpack.

For ten long minutes, he stood there, motionless, as the events of the past week flashed through his mind. Kevin, his best friend. Lily, smiling at him, holding his hands. Frank and Frederick, the greatest of friends.

He swallowed hard and took a step forward. He unzipped his backpack.

And there it was.

The magic lamp.

Josh exhaled slowly. Then, without another thought, he zipped the bag shut, threw it over his shoulder, and headed downstairs.

Carol turned as he passed. "Josh, where are you—"

But he was already out the door.

THE MOONTIDE STREAM, A PLACE SEEMINGLY PLUCKED FROM A dream, was quiet and serene; its waters shimmered softly silver in the pale moonlight. The stream wound through gentle hills, disappearing into the distance like a secret whispered to the earth. A modest pedestrian bridge arched over it, framed by tangled wildflowers and dense greenery that swayed in the night breeze.

People came here for peace, for proposals, for poetry.

But Josh wasn't here for any of that.

He stood at the center of the bridge, hands clenched around the cold railing, eyes fixed on the slow-moving current below. The world around him remained still, the night air heavy with quiet.

He opened his backpack. Pulled out the lamp. For a moment, he hesitated, fingers tightening around its surface. The weight of his impending actions pressed down on him, stealing his breath. Then, with a flick of his wrist, he hurled it into the water below.

Josh watched as the lamp hit the stream, the current quickly sweeping it away. He followed its path until it sank, disappearing beneath the surface. It was done. He stepped back, observing the empty hills. His heart pounded in his chest.

Then he whispered, "Bob."

Nothing.

He clenched his fists. His voice came louder this time. "Bob!"

The air shifted, and the night darkened. A hazy form materialized before him, its burning red eyes glowing like embers. "Aaqa," Bob greeted, his voice low.

Josh's breath hitched. His whole body trembled, raw emotion boiling inside him. Everything he had been holding in—the fear, the loss, the guilt—spilled out in his next words. "I banish you."

Bob was expressionless.

Josh stepped forward, his voice rising with the force of his pain. "Bob! I banish you forever! Do you hear me?! I banish you! Be gone and never return!"

A flicker of surprise crossed Bob's face. His gaze shifted to the water where the lamp had vanished. Then his expression turned dark. Sinister. And he faded into the night.

Josh stood there, chest heaving. He looked around, expecting something—anything. But there was nothing. No presence. No whispers. Just the quiet hum of the stream below.

For the first time in a long time, he found himself alone.

He turned and walked home.

CAROL HAD GONE TO BED BY THE TIME HE RETURNED. THE HOUSE remained quiet.

Josh locked the doors, dragged himself to his room, and collapsed onto his bed. With trembling hands, he retrieved his phone.

> Shadelss143: I banished him.

BlushyRed215: And he left?

> Shadelss143: I threw the lamp into the Moontide stream and told him he was banished. He left. He didn't say anything.

> Shadelss143: You were right. I'm sorry.

BlushyRed215:

JOSH STARED AT THE SCREEN. HE SET HIS PHONE ASIDE AND PULLED his knees to his chest.

And then he cried.

It came without warning, like a dam breaking silently in the dark. His shoulders shook, his breath hitched, and the tears spilled freely down his face. The weight of everything—every lie, every loss, every impossible choice—finally cracked through his composure. Because sometimes, the only thing left to do is break.

A knock sounded at the door.

Josh quickly wiped his tears and turned his head. "Come in, Mom."

Carol stepped inside. She stood in the doorway, watching him. "Are you okay, sweetie?"

Josh nodded. "I'm fine."

He studied her face. Something was off. Her voice sounded soft, her posture normal, but her eyes... her eyes appeared empty.

"Are you okay, Mom?" he asked cautiously.

Carol tilted her head. "Where did you go earlier?"

Josh stiffened.

"I asked you," she continued, "but you never answered."

A problem existed in her manner of speaking. Josh's gut twisted. "I... I needed some air," he lied.

The change happened instantly. A voice—a voice that wasn't hers—tore through the room. "YOU LIE!"

Josh's blood turned to ice.

"You filthy, ungrateful son!" the voice screeched, contorting Carol's face into a horrific grimace before she suddenly returned to her usual self.

She smiled softly. "Why would you lie to your mother?"

Josh's hands clenched the bedsheets. His entire body trembled.

"Bob…" he whispered. "If you can hear me—please, come back."

Carol's expression twisted with rage. "You dare call him back after you banished him?!"

His eyes flicked downward—to her hand. A butcher's knife gleamed in her grip. He looked back at her vacant eyes. That wasn't his mother standing in the doorway. His pulse hammered against his skull. Think. Think.

"Banish who, Mom?" he tried. "I didn't banish anyone."

Carol's lips curled. Slowly, she lifted the knife—to her own throat.

Josh shot to his feet. "Mom, no!"

She smiled—a wicked, soulless smile.

Josh knew what was coming next.

With a desperate lunge, he threw himself at her, wrestling for the knife. But she was stronger. Stronger than he had ever known her to be. She slapped him—hard. Josh stumbled back, crashing against the wall.

Carol grabbed him by the collar, lifting him effortlessly before slamming him to the floor. His vision blurred. A sharp pain pricked at his throat. The knife. She pressed the knife against his skin.

Josh gasped, straining against her grip. "Mom—please. Fight it!"

Carol's face wasn't hers anymore. She laughed. Amused. Delighted. Josh was fighting desperately to save him and her.

But she wasn't going to kill him. She had other plans. She threw the knife to the side, picked him up by his throat as if he were a backpack lying on the floor, and threw him carelessly.

Josh's body slammed against the wall, his skull cracking against it, and his vision went dark.

CHAPTER 17

FORTY-TWO HUNDRED YEARS AGO

The main bazaar in Harappa was bustling during the nighttime. The place was lit up with lanterns and candle lights, and the bazaar was chock full of shops and traders brimming with people. The main bazaar area had a central location that was well-decorated.

In the center was a large circular pool flourishing with flowers and other vegetation. Ropes hung on two poles throughout the area, and lit lanterns were hanging on the ropes that illuminated the area. The center of the pool had a large statue of a man holding a spear. From the center pool stretched four significant pathways that ran for half-a-mile distance in each direction.

The paths had neat cobblestone floors, which would be washed regularly. The edges of these floors had neatly cut grass and then dirt where the shopkeepers set up their shops on either side. Some buildings looked as if they were reaching the sky. Some shops were more than one floor, and the shopkeepers usually lived on the first floor with their families.

There was a lot of hustle and bustle; it was hard to hear oneself think. People were laughing and chatting, and some were arguing with shopkeepers as they haggled for prices. The shopkeepers were calling out to the crowds, inviting them to try their goods, promising them the best and cheapest products. Others offered a taste of their goods for free or at a significantly discounted price.

The shops were mostly made of clay and some bricks. They were lively shops filled with textile products that decorated the shops. From bronze armor to weapons, household materials to ornaments, sweets, spices, meats, fruits, and vegetables. People found everything in the main bazaar. There were even magic shops, shops that could read your future, shops that sold herbs to cure your ailments. Immediately around the pool were inns and places to eat and drink. People from near and far came to Harappa, for its well-known bazaar, and it showed the place was buzzing with people.

Later into the night, the buzz of people would die down as most started returning home. There were guards near the pool and at important intersections around the bazaar. These guards were armed with knives, swords, and spears. They wore leather armor to protect themselves. Although they didn't interfere with the bazaar's daily activities, the guards castigated anyone breaking the law. People understood shops were closed and went home late at night.

Harappa was more than a well-established bazaar. Outside the bazaar were homes where most people lived, administrative buildings, and a judicial building. There were a few small baths, and large portions of the land were set up for cultivation. In the summer, the area was green, with grass and vegetation multiplying under the summer sun, new flowers blooming, and the buzzing of bees and other animals reaping the benefits of a nice summer.

Our story was about one such summer evening. It was very late in the evening, and the bazaar was empty. A few late stragglers were winding things up, smiling at the guards as they stared at them. Lanterns slowly diminished throughout the town, and the place went dark. In this darkness, three figures of men appeared, heading toward the outskirts of Harappa as they slowly disappeared into the large grass. Using only their insight into the area, they walked in complete darkness. Summer nights tend to be cooler than days, which could be brutally hot and dry in this region. The full moon played a game of hide and seek as it hid behind the clouds. The three men were mindful of when they moved in the moonlight as they knew eyes could be watching.

Meanwhile, the city of Harappa continued growing darker as more lanterns and candles were put away.

All three men had white cloth wrapped around their waists to their knees. Their chests lay bare, solely embellished with necklaces of beads, a few of which held carvings. The man at the very front had a headdress with carvings around it. The leather headdress featured carvings; two layers in front, one in back. They went barefoot and slowly left the city.

Abu, so named, guided the three men. His given name faded from memory; his age exceeded the usual lifespan. His body and face were full of wrinkles; he had milky white eyes and receding white hair growing from the back of his head and running over his shoulders. He had a stick in his right hand, which had a serpent's head, though he did not seem to need the stick the way he walked. He held a small leather bag in his left hand. Power emanated from this man; his old age fooled no one, and most people in Harappa knew to steer clear of him. The most influential men and women called upon him; even then, they were mostly cautious.

Two men stood behind Abu; one was in his mid-fifties, the other in his early thirties. These men, like Abu, had a piece of cloth wrapped around their waist up to their knees and were naked above their waist. They, too, had necklaces around their necks, with carvings on them, but they did not have a headrest. The man in his mid-fifties went by the name Vikhnath; the man in his early thirties, Pinu. All three had a serious look, but Pinu's face seemed concerned.

It would be an insult to call Abu a master sorcerer. Such titles were used for those who wanted to prove themselves. Abu's purpose held far greater importance. He had lived his life and then a few more lives, delving deeper and deeper into the dark arts of sorcery. He handsomely paid for orphaned boys, showing a strong preference for them. He would then train and later sacrifice these boys so he could grow his understanding of the dark magics. All the boys called him Abu.

Vikhnath and Pinu were two such boys. Vikhnath was orphaned at a very young age when he was but a babe, and through the years, he had stood the tests and tribulations that were thrown at him and many other young boys and men. Many perished, but not Vikhnath; he was considered Abu's most loyal and capable apprentice. It only made sense that he would accompany his master on this most important mission.

Pinu was another story. He came to Abu at the age of seven. A rival faction killed his parents, and they took Pinu and his sisters prisoner. Pinu was sold to Abu; the sisters were of no interest to Abu; he deplored the idea of women and wanted nothing to do with them. Pinu proved a strong and capable sorcerer, but he remembered his life with his family. This made him weaker, for life under Abu presented harsh and painful circumstances. Pinu desired a family of his own and had fallen for a girl in Harappa, though he had not spoken to her. People were generally uncomfortable around those associated with Abu, and many knew upsetting Abu meant bad omens for their entire family. Pinu knew that to have this family, he needed to find a way to distance himself from Abu, something Abu was aware of. And so, it didn't make sense why Abu had chosen Pinu, as Pinu's interests lay elsewhere, and this was a mission of great importance and almost fatal danger.

Vikhnath would dare not question his master, but he had indirectly tried to offer other candidates to Abu instead of Pinu. But Abu paid no heed, as Abu's plans required someone like Pinu, an aspect Vikhnath failed to see.

Abu's real objective was to shed this body and become immortal. He was tired of bandaging it repeatedly to squeeze a few more decades out of it. While no army anywhere in the world could stand up to Abu, death was the immediate enemy Abu needed to conquer. After this, he figured he could deal with the world's armies. And so, he hatched the most impossible mission: to conquer the one thing that may grant him eternal life. And for that, he needed a few scapegoats. The idea of Pinu was to distract his enemy and give him an alternative so Abu could buy more time. Little did Vikhnath know that he, too, was part of the same sacrifice.

The creature Abu wanted to defeat was ancient beyond years. And mighty powerful! Magic alone would not be enough, for this creature was created of magic. This would be a game of wits, and Abu would have to outsmart this creature. This is where Vikhnath and Pinu come in; they are very different in their loyalty and motives. At no time must the plan be given away; like chess, Abu must anticipate his enemy's moves to win. Pinu would crack almost immediately; Abu knew this. And the monster will devour him the moment it senses his weakness.

Vikhnath's resilience, however, posed a formidable challenge, making any attempt to break through significantly more difficult. All creatures go after the weakest link; that is natural. But with intelligence at play, the game mustn't be given away, and the creature must never know that both Pinu and Vikhnath are sacrificial lambs and that the real fight is with Abu. If these two create enough distraction, it may give Abu enough time to finish the ritual.

Abu had spent decades studying the enemy, dissecting their secrets, unraveling their power. He had seen his peers wield mighty jinns like weapons, bending them to their will. But an ifrit?

That remained elusive.

The game of cat and mouse always began with a name. Names held power. And power demanded sacrifice—brutal, unforgiving sacrifice.

To the outside world, Abu seemed invincible, a sorcerer of immeasurable strength. But that was a deception. His power was not innate; it was earned, stolen, ripped from the throats of the unwilling. His methods, honed to perfection, had reached the peak of human understanding of magic. And his knowledge? Paid for in suffering.

Entire villages of jinn had perished under his cruelty.

Locked inside massive glass jars, the spirits writhed in torment. Abu stood before them mercilessly, demanding what they dared not utter—a name.

The white smoke that once danced freely within the jars darkened, shifting to ashen gray and then to a sickly black. It twisted and convulsed, forming tortured faces that flickered in and out of existence.

Some jinn screamed. Others begged. A few, stubborn to the end, fought back, lashing against the glass with their spectral forms. Their defiance only enraged Abu.

In his fury, he would sometimes shatter the jars.

The moment the glass fractured, a blinding white fire would erupt from within, filling the air with searing heat. But their freedom was an illusion. The flames flickered violently for mere seconds—and then vanished.

Extinguished. Forgotten.

And those foolish enough to seek vengeance for their fallen kin?

They, too, found themselves trapped—condemned to the same fate, their cries of agony joining the chorus of the damned.

For jinn, revealing one's name to a human was the greatest of sins—a betrayal beyond redemption.

To surrender a name meant eternal disgrace—not just for the individual, but their entire bloodline. Even if, by some miracle, an enslaved jinn escaped Abu's grasp, there would be no sanctuary for them. No place to hide from the wrath of their kind.

Many chose death over dishonor.

But pain, genuine pain, has a way of breaking even the strongest wills.

And then one did.

A jinn, writhing in agony, its form barely holding together, could endure no longer. With a final, rasping breath, it hissed out a name before vanishing into nothingness.

"Kruh Za'din."

Once Abu had the name, the remaining tasks became easier—except for the battle itself.

Both Vikhnath and Pinu had been trained for this moment. For nearly a decade, they practiced committing to memory the sacred chants that would lure the creature. Abu explained to them that the ritual had three parts. But what Abu had not told them was that three rituals would not be enough.

There was a fourth. A secret step that only he knew.

The invocation would be the most challenging part. Simple words and chants would not suffice. It demanded unwavering focus, flawless recitation, and sheer force of will.

Their training had begun long ago in a dark, candlelit chamber, where shadows flickered against ancient stone walls. Abu would stand at the front, his voice low and deliberate, chanting the verses. With each uttered line, the words glowed red and seared onto the walls, burning like firebrands.

Then came the second verse. Again, it etched itself into the stone, pulsing with a sinister energy. The disciples were expected to observe, absorb, and remember. Writing or repetition was beneath them—failure was not tolerated. And for those who failed, the punishment was merciless.

Many an orphan had perished under Abu's hand, their minds broken, their bodies discarded. But Vikhnath and Pinu? They never forgot. Their memories were honed to perfection, and their discipline was unmatched. Abu had chosen them for this —a mission unlike any other.

When their training neared completion, Abu revealed the process.

Three stages.

- Stage One: The Call. The ritual summons all creatures of power, drawing them like moths to a flame.
- Stage Two: The Selection. From the gathered entities, a single name must be invoked. The right name. The true name.
- Stage Three: The Binding. At its most dangerous moment, when the ifrit unleashes every deception and horror at its disposal, it must be trapped within a chosen vessel. This stage is the longest—and the most treacherous.

But there was a fourth stage.

A stage Abu had kept hidden.

The Binding of Flesh.

To merely imprison an ifrit was not enough. To control it, to wield its power, it had to be bound to a human soul.

Abu's disciples were well-versed in capturing the jinn. They understood the brutal nature of subjugation—break the spirit, threaten its existence, and it will submit. Some jinn would fight, battling for freedom until they triumphed or perished. Others, recognizing their captor's power, would surrender without a struggle.

But an ifrit?

No apprentice had ever witnessed its capture. No human had ever controlled one. And now Vikhnath and Pinu were about to step into the unknown. Abu's game of chess had begun years ago. To outmaneuver his true enemy, he first needed to outmaneuver his students.

They had to believe they were playing their destined roles so that when the enemy probed their thoughts, it would sense only conviction, only certainty. Abu himself was seasoned enough to mislead those who tried to read him—but Vikhnath and Pinu?

They were not.

So, he fed them three stages of the ritual.

- The Lure. A call to the hidden, the powerful, the ancient.
- The Name. A challenge, an invocation—one that would enrage the creature, forcing its attention on the invoker.
- The Cage. A trap, a prison, a final act of subjugation.

Vikhnath was given the second stage. He would speak the creature's name. He would bear the brunt of its fury. In its boundless wrath, the ifrit would see Vikhnath as the greatest threat.

This was by design.

Abu intended to protect Vikhnath—but only to a point. If the ifrit sensed Abu's true power too soon and turned its attention toward the real master of this game, everything could be lost.

The plan was simple.

- All three would chant *The Lure,* calling forth the unseen.
- Vikhnath alone would utter *The Name,* believing himself chosen and the ascendant disciple.
- They would repeat the process, over and over, until the ifrit appeared.
- Then, together, they would weave *The Cage,* sealing the creature away.

Vikhnath swelled with pride, convinced he had surpassed all others. Even the master had refused to invoke the ifrit's name—but had chosen him to do it. He was the decoy. And he never even knew it.

Besides the invocations, there was a matter of protection. Abu had prepared a special talisman that each person would hold in their hands. As they invoke the incantation, these talismans would create an invisible shield to protect them from anyone outside the field. These talismans were imbued with the rarest and most potent magic Abu could muster; he was confident it would hold. The shield would stay in place until the creature was sucked into the holding object or the cage. At this point, the shield will come down so the creature can enter the object. With all of this explained, Abu showed his promising students the chants to be used.

THE LURE:

MASTERS OF THE EARTH AND MASTERS OF THE SKY

You claim to be exalted, and you claim to be high
Yet your name I invoke, as I testify
To my command, you shall forever abide

THE NAME:

KRUH ZA DIN, YOU CANNOT ESCAPE

Kruh Za din, for I know your name
Kruh Za din I command, I dictate
Kruh Za din appear in body and flame

THE CAGE:

KRUH ZA DIN, I COMMAND YOU SUBMIT

For here, you have neither power nor will
Submit to me, and in an evil prison built
Bound forever to my power and wit

CHAPTER 18

OF SACRIFICES AND REWARDS

Vikhnath and Pinu had practiced these chants for nearly a decade. The only thing that needed to be added was the name. Now that the name was in place, it was time to carry out the mission. The men slipped through the tall grass, avoiding the moonlight when they could. They did not speak but kept walking, and when they were far away from the populated areas, they stopped hiding. Tall trees were everywhere around them, the beginning of a vast jungle. The sounds of the night animals and insects resonated. Abu observed the night sky, blind as a bat; his magic had given him more incredible senses than young, healthy men. He turned to his assistants, who were standing there looking at him.

"We stop here," Abu croaked. He opened his leather bag and drew out six stones. He handed two to each of the apprentices and kept two for himself. Then, from his bag, he drew out a lamp; this was the cage. Made of glass, this item was made with materials Abu acquired from traders from the West.

The lamp was elongated and straightforward, yet it gave vibes of great power. Abu poured his malice and ill intent into this lamp, and this lamp was pure evil. Abu placed the lamp in the center of a circle that he drew in the dirt. He directed his apprentices to sit around the lamp within the circle. The men were placed, so the three made a triangle with the lamp at the center.

"Remember, when the being arrives," started Abu, "press hard on the talisman in your hands and stand with your hands stretched. The creature will read you and deceive you; do not falter. We have the three stages; carry them out, and it will trap the creature forever. He is strong, but together, we are stronger. Keep your focus, and we shall be victorious."

And the ritual began.

All three of them chanted the first stage and stopped.

> *Masters of the Earth and Masters of the Sky*
> *You claim to be exalted, and you claim to be high*
> *Yet your name I invoke as I testify*
> *To my command, you shall forever abide*

Vikhnath chanted the second stage.

> *Kruh Za din, you cannot escape*
> *Kruh Za din, for I know your name*
> *Kruh Za din, I command I dictate*
> *Kruh Za din appear in body and flame*

Then, all three chanted the first stage again and stopped. Vikhnath again chanted the second stage.

And this continued until the sounds of the jungle disappeared; all creatures big and small had either died, runoff, or were dead silent. The clouds swallowed the moon, plunging the world into a darkness unlike any other. Then, from the heavens, crimson rays descended, slicing through the night like veins of fire. Yet the three men did not falter, their voices steady, weaving ancient words into the fabric of reality.

The moment the moon returned, it was wrong.

No longer pale and silver, but blood-red, casting a grotesque glow upon the land. The rivers and lakes no longer shimmered with moonlight—instead, they gleamed like pools of spilled blood, staining the city in its reflection.

Still, they chanted.

The Harappan city was waking up; brief flickers of light could be seen from the distance; people were coming out of their homes and turned to the red moon in fear and gloom; some looking at it as an abomination. Many took it as an omen and hurried back into their homes. Others prayed, and yet others observed. Abu sensed the red moon and motioned Vikhnath to stand. As Vikhnath stood up with his arms stretched, so did Abu and Pinu. Pinu could feel his hands draining as the talisman started drawing blood from them. He tried to keep his concentration and continued chanting with the other two men. From behind a large tree, eyes were staring at the men. There was a sense of darkness, emptiness, and despair. Pinu, for the first time in many a year, was feeling fear. This was not some child's fear. This was the feeling of defeat, of the inevitable reality of death itself, staring straight at you. And then, from behind the tree, a woman revealed herself. She was looking at Pinu. It was his mother.

"How long I have searched for you, and here you are."

Vikhnath's throat ran dry as he watched Pinu take slow steps toward the apparition. The ritual was still in motion, the air thick with magic, but Pinu…Pinu no longer cared.

His mother stood there, radiant, just as he remembered her. The soft smile and warmth in her eyes were so familiar and real. It had been years since he had seen her face outside the realm of dreams, yet here she was, standing in front of him as if she had never left.

He felt like a child again, lost in the darkness of the past, crying out for justice, for answers, for a second chance. And now he had one.

Was he really going to care about some stupid ritual when his lifelong dream was standing in front of him?

Vikhnath wanted Pinu to remember this was a deception, but he could not break the chant. Abu, on the other hand, was showing no emotions. He did not want the ifrit to see how delighted he was to see his plan fall into place.

"Look, I even found your sisters; we are all together now; we only need you," she continued, and two lovely young girls emerged from behind the tree and approached their mother.

"Brother," the young girls said with a smile, "we have missed you so much."

Pinu smiled; a few tears dropped from his eyes. He opened both his hands and let go of the talisman. With lightning speed, the mother turned into an extensive set of jaws and cut Pinu right in the middle. Then, she and her daughters disappeared.

Cracking Vikhnath was not going to be this easy; all his life, he had been around Abu, and his desire to please Abu had all but crushed any desires the man might have had otherwise. Putting the focus on Vikhnath and offering nothing to confuse or break him with was Abu's masterstroke. Wolves and snakes of all sizes were now abundant around the area, howling mad; some wolves were twice the size of ordinary wolves, their eyes glaring red, angry, and bloodthirsty. The wolves ran into the two men, but the men did not falter, and as these wolves got near, they dissipated. The protective ring was powerful, and both serpents of all sizes and wolves failed to cause a dent in the men's armor.

The men changed their stage as they now had the creature's full attention; they started chanting the cage.

Kruh Za din, I command you submit
For here, you have neither power nor will
Submit to my will and in an evil prison built
Bound forever to my power and wit

The creature was livid to see the insects call him and think they could subdue him. It was time to show the creatures high and low what they had reaped! A large dark arm, visibly bloody under the reflection of the red moon, descended from the sky and landed near the jungle, squashing large trees like ants.

The ground shook, sending shockwaves to the city and flattening several homes. Screams and panic filled the air as the Harappans tried to escape the night's insanity. The ground under the two men opened, but the men did not care; their chants continued.

And just like that, where the men stood, the ground healed itself. The Talisman were glowing white, and a light started emitting from the hands of the two men. The creature's hand firmed against the soil as a massive face emerged from the sky. The face was one of wickedness and cruelty, the large red eyes piercing into the men below. The face descended closer to the men, and the jungle resonated with the sound of the massive ifrit.

"Insects of dirt and filth," the ifrit yelled. "You dare invoke my name!" Its eyes focused on the two men, his words resonating for miles in all directions. Some Harappans fainted, others screamed that the end of time was upon us, yet others ran looking for shelter. The creature moved a little closer, and his voice was even louder. "I!" it yelled again, "invoker of the darkest words, keeper of the smokeless deeps."

The city was buzzing with running and screaming people. The creature turned toward them, malice showing in his face as a blazing ball of fire descended at the center of the town. Upon impact, it burst into a fireball and burned everything within its large radius.

The sky screamed.

"I AM RAGE!"

"I AM DEATH!"

"I AM CHAOS!"

"I AM RUIN!"

It dropped its other arm near the city and moved its face closer to the town. The city rattled again with more buildings shaking, some cracking, others breaking. The creature opened its mouth, and the sky roared. Men and women were sent flying to their deaths, others just vaporized, and yet others cowered behind broken walls and cracked buildings.

The creature turned its attention back to the men and swept the broken trees it had crushed, sending them flying toward the two men. Everything vaporized into thin air as it got close to the men. The hands of these men were now emitting bright white light. Even though the fists were closed, the hands were glowing white. The talisman was sucking blood out of the hands, and the talisman was also glowing hot. Vikhnath was disciplined to tolerate burning, but the blood drain was far more significant than Abu anticipated, and it was draining Vikhnath. He was feeling weak and faint. But his desire to please his master was a powerful motive for him to keep going.

The creature sensed Vikhnath's weakness but also realized that the actual power behind this game was Abu. It raised itself into the sky and brought its hands near its face, closing its massive fists. The sky turned a color of orange, and huge red fireballs descended from the sky.

The scene was apocalyptic, something the race of men may have never witnessed before or will ever witness again. The massive red balls descended randomly, but as they got close, they changed course and headed straight for the two men. The fireballs burst over the two men, the shield drawing even more blood from their bodies. Vikhnath crashed to the ground because of immense blood loss, and the wolves descended on him, tearing him limb from limb.

"You will die here today, old fool. You are no immortal. You are nothing," the jungle echoed, every tree alive and looking at Abu with a most sinister look. Abu was reciting the chants from the third stage, the cage. The trees kept yelling and screaming that Abu was the deceiver, the liar, and he would die today.

They said this is written in the skies and the stars, that Abu's end of time comes tonight no matter what happens. Alone and with no one to mourn, he will be forgotten tonight. But Abu was relentless and focused intensely on the job at hand. The fight, however, had taken its toll; Abu's magic was draining fast; he needed to capture the creature soon, or he might end up like Vikhnath, or worse.

What was explained to the disciples was only some of what would happen tonight. Abu had indeed withheld a lot, and it was now time to trap the mighty ifrit. Massive spiritual armor appeared in the night sky and tore into the being, trying to trap it. The being's will was powerful, and it broke these armors and sent its pieces flying through the night sky. These armors resembled body chest pieces, but they were not physical. They were spiritual and made of light.

Abu rose into the air, suspended, his arms fully outstretched. The talisman was burning hot, parts of Abu's arms and his hands had turned to molten lava because of the heat, and just like lava flows after a volcanic eruption, so were Abu's hands behaving. Abu's eyes were glowing, and his chants were louder, invoking powerful ancient magic unheard of for eons.

Glowing white rods appeared in the sky, encircling the creature and preventing his magic. These rods started draining the creature as parts of his whitish-black smoke seemed to be pulled into the rods. The rods were trying to move closer to the creature, entrapping him. This was when pride and arrogance turned to fear and despair as the creature looked at Abu and realized that an ancient and powerful master strategist was at work.

Battles drain armies, and they also drain great generals. The best generals usually know how to use this moment; to win, the general must think fast. The creature descended to Earth, transformed into a snake, and tried to hide in the world's cracks. But the cage matched the size and position of the creature. It transformed into an eagle and attempted to fly away, but it was futile. The cage continued to match and trap the creature until the creature was nothing but a bowl of smoke, trapped from all corners by the cage.

The jungle, once a cacophony of whispers and screams, had fallen into a deathly silence. Even the air felt still, as if the world held its breath.

The ifrit roared—a sound rattling the earth's bones, shaking the trees, and cracking the stones beneath them. The very fabric of the night seemed to tear open, revealing glimpses of something beyond human comprehension—shifting landscapes of fire and torment, cities of ash, and skies filled with swirling darkness.

Abu's breath came in ragged gasps as he watched the ifrit's ending struggle. The beast's massive hands carved deep trenches into the soil, the earth itself trembling under the force of its resistance. But it was inevitable.

The ancient lamp hovered like a hungry beast, its glow intensifying as it devoured the ifrit's essence. The golden runes encircling it pulsed rhythmically, their patterns shifting and twisting as they tightened their grip on the creature.

The ifrit let out a thunderous roar, a sound that cracked the very air. The jungle, once alive with fury, had gone eerily silent —watching, waiting. Even the spirits that had mocked Abu moments ago seemed to shrink away in fear.

This was no ordinary binding.

The lamp's pull grew violent, relentless—and the ifrit's form disintegrated. Its fiery eyes, once filled with rage and defiance, now flickered with something else. Desperation.

"I curse you, Abu!" The ifrit's voice boomed through the clearing, reverberating through the very fabric of existence. "You think you have won? You think this is over? I will burn inside you. I will rot your bones from within. YOU ARE DAMNED!"

Abu's jaw clenched, his molten arms shaking from the strain. He ignored the creature's threats. He knew the power of fear, the deception of the last words.

"No, stop this!" it said, no longer loud. "This cannot be; it cannot end like this! I will… I will give you immortality if you let me free, human," it pleaded. But Abu had other plans besides just immortality.

The creature threatened and pleaded as it continued to be swallowed by the lamp. Abu fell to the ground, the talisman scattered around him. He was on all fours, panting, but the chants continued. As the last of the creature's essence was drawn into the lamp, it cast a worried glance at Abu. Abu's shield was down, drained, and he wore an evil smirk, knowing he had all but won.

The creature's eyes locked onto Abu's, and in that instant, it saw. Not just the sorcerer standing before it, but something older, something fouler. A relic of ancient darkness, a shadow carved from time itself. Beneath the molten glow of Abu's gaze, the ifrit glimpsed the depths of his malice, the sharp, calculating edges of his cunning, the cold and merciless hunger that drove him.

The realization struck like a death knell—this was not just defeat. This was damnation.

The ifrit saw the future unravel before him: an eternity of agony, his very essence torn apart, piece by wretched piece, to fuel the insatiable hunger of the sorcerer. There would be no mercy, no respite. Abu would strip him down to nothing, not just enslave him but unmake him, twisting his power into a tool, a mere extension of Abu's will.

Desperation surged through the ifrit like a storm, but he was no mindless beast. He was a general, a creature of war; even in ruin, he would not surrender, not like this.

Abu was close—so close—to victory. The ifrit could see it in his smirk, in the flickering hunger in his molten eyes. The binding was all that remained, the final chain to strip the creature of his last shreds of will.

But the ifrit still had one move left.

With a final, frantic gesture, his clawed hand cut through the air, reaching out—not for Abu, but for the jungle. The night itself seemed to shudder. Then, in a blink, the ifrit's form twisted into smoke, pulled into the depths of the lamp.

He was gone.

And Abu, standing alone in the crimson glow, realized—too late—that something had changed.

Entire trees, ancient and towering, were ripped from their roots and flung through the air like spears of vengeance. The jungle itself had risen against Abu.

With his talisman lost and his magic nearly spent, he fought desperately, breaking trunks apart mid-air and shattering branches with the last remnants of his power. But he was slowing. The toll of the battle weighed on him, unraveling his strength.

And then—a single branch.

It found its mark, piercing his neck in one swift, merciless strike. A choked gasp escaped him, eyes wide with disbelief. For all his cunning and power, it had come to this—a moment of weakness, a single misstep.

His frame trembled, then stilled. The great sorcerer, feared and revered, crumbled where he stood. Decades of dark magic unraveled in an instant, his very essence scattering like dust upon the wind.

The jungle fell silent. The night bore witness. And so ended an era—the fall of one of the greatest human sorcerers and the mightiest of ifrits.

THE THUNDEROUS COLLAPSE OF TREES SENT THE LAMP HURTLING through the air, its polished surface catching the faint glow of the dying moon. It tumbled, weightless for a moment, before vanishing into a deep fissure—a scar in the earth left by the ifrit's fury. The golden runes shimmered one last time, tightening their grip, sealing the ancient terror within. And so, the mighty ifrit was imprisoned, waiting in a silent rage for the fool who would one day set him free.

Orange rays emerged on the horizon. No, this was not another bad omen. It was the sun rising. Many in Harappa were crying, others rejoicing. The end of time had been thwarted for yet another time; the Harappans will get to see another day. But all was not to be celebrated; some people started looking for their family members and their friends, and others were trying to help their fellow citizens. Religious figures began walking among them, reminding them of the fragility of life and that the end of time may still be just around the corner.

CHAPTER 19

FORTY-TWO HUNDRED YEARS LATER

Josh awoke on his bed, staring out the window. He was gauging his surroundings. For a moment, he wanted to believe it was all a dream, but the eerie sense of hopelessness and despair reminded him that this was not something he could ever wake from. His head throbbed from the fall earlier, a sharp, pulsing pain radiating from the swollen lump on his forehead. But that was the least of his worries. A deep, instinctual terror clawed at his gut, whispering that the worst was yet to come. The night sky was dark as the moon hid behind the clouds, occasionally peeking out in anticipation of things to come.

The room was pitch black. He sensed great evil around him, and parts of him were frozen in fear. Something moved next to him, and a hand rested on his shoulder. He recognized the fingers. There was a ring on it, the kind that Lily wore. Josh slowly turned toward the left side of his bed. There, lying next to him and gazing at him, was Lily.

Lily's red hair was tousled and wild, spilling everywhere. A sinister smile spread across her face, and a menacing glint appeared in her eyes. Josh felt Lily's hand grab his shoulder as Lily slithered over Josh and rested on top of him. She smiled wickedly and said, "Hi."

A wicked red gleam flickered in Lily's eyes, burning like embers in the night. As the moonlight slipped through the clouds, it cast pale illumination over her form, revealing the horror that she had become.

Josh's breath caught in his throat. The face staring back at him was barely human. Deep, jagged scars marred her skin, twisted like grotesque carvings. Her once-smooth complexion was ruined, the flesh torn and warped as if time and suffering had ravaged her beyond recognition. Swollen veins bulged beneath her skin, pulsing grotesquely, as if something vile coursed through them.

The Lily he remembered—the young, beautiful girl—was gone. In her place lay something wretched, something broken beyond repair. Her skin was cracked, the fissures filled with congealed blood and oozing pus. Her once-vibrant red hair was now a filthy, tangled mess, matted with dirt and decay. The rags that clung to her frail frame reeked of filth, the stench of urine and rot thick in the air, curling into Josh's nostrils and making his stomach twist with nausea.

"Say something," Lily whispered lovingly.

"Please get off of me," Josh whispered.

Lily's ice-cold hands clamped onto Josh's face, her grip unnaturally strong, her nails biting into his skin. Her touch sent a jolt of revulsion through him, but before he could recoil, she leaned in, her decayed breath washing over him like a wave of death.

"But you *lusted* for me… am I—"

A second voice, deeper, inhuman, erupted from within her, a guttural scream that made Josh's blood curdle.

"NOT PRETTY ANYMORE?!"

The sound appeared monstrous—an unholy fusion of beast and man, layered and discordant, as if multiple voices shrieked at once. It tore through the room like a wailing banshee, rattling the very air around them.

Josh remained paralyzed, his mind scrambling for answers that refused to come.

Lily's lips twisted into a semblance of a smile, her mouth stretching wider than it should. "Kiss me," she cooed, her voice sickly sweet, yet dripping with malice. Her tongue—long, dark, and serpent-like—slithered out between her cracked lips, writhing as she drew closer.

Panic surged through Josh's veins like wildfire. With a desperate burst of strength, he shoved her—hard. Lily tumbled backward, hitting the ground with a sickening *thud*.

Breathless, Josh sat on the edge of his bed, his whole body shaking. But then his gaze fell beyond her—and his stomach dropped. Lying there, twisted and motionless on the cold floor… was a headless body.

His mother.

The realization crashed into him like a tidal wave, drowning him in horror. A strangled sob tore from his throat as hot tears spilled down his cheeks.

Lily observed as if she was waiting for this moment. A sinister smile on her face, she watched Carol's headless body with pleasure as she heard Josh sob. It was as if the last few days were nothing but a buildup to this moment, to break Josh absolutely and completely.

Josh's tear-filled eyes locked onto Lily's twisted form, his sobs ragged and broken. A storm of emotions raged within him—grief, terror, and something even worse…*love*. Somewhere beneath the decay, beneath the horror, she was still *her*.

Wasn't she?

His fingers dug into the bedsheets, gripping them with white-knuckled desperation, as if holding on for dear life could anchor him to sanity. But there was no escape. No waking up from this.

Lily tilted her head, observing his torment with something almost like amusement. Then, in that same haunting, lilting voice, she whispered, "All is not lost, my love."

Her tone dripped with mockery, twisting the endearment into something vile.

"With me, the possibilities are *endless*." And then she *smiled*. Not just any smile—but one brimming with malice, with cruel anticipation.

Because this was just the beginning.

She had barely *touched* the surface of the agony and suffering she had planned for him. And Josh heard what he wanted to hear but wished he hadn't.

"Sweetie," came a voice—soft, familiar, *impossible*.

Josh's breath hitched. His body tensed.

Slowly, he turned to his right…

His grip on the bed sheets loosened as he arched backward in horror. A severed head, blood still dripping from the jagged stump of its neck, floated in the air, just inches from him.

It was his mother, smiling at him. Time had ravaged her. The rich, black waves of hair he remembered were gone, replaced by brittle strands of white hanging in clumps from her withered scalp. Deep wrinkles carved into her sallow skin, pulling her features into something wretched, something… wrong.

"I'm fine, sweetie," Carol's head cooed, her voice warm—so disturbingly *normal*. "Don't you worry about me."

Tears welled in Josh's eyes, spilling over as he stared at the grotesque vision before him. His lips trembled. His whole body quaked. The disbelief, the grief—it exceeded limits, all of it felt excessive.

"You, Josh," she continued, her expression eerily blank, "have been the greatest gift of my life."

Josh couldn't take it. He turned away, squeezing his eyes shut. "Stop," he whispered, his voice cracking. "Please."

"I have never been prouder of anything than you," Carol finished, still smiling, still *so wrong*. Her lips curved, yet behind it lay no warmth, no genuine emotion, just an empty, soulless mask.

Josh sat on the bed, pulling his knees to his chest, rocking slightly as his breath came in short, uneven gasps. His mind was unraveling, breaking apart under the weight of it all.

"Please," he choked out, voice barely above a whisper. His fingers dug into his arms as he squeezed himself tighter, trying to drown out the surrounding nightmare. "You won," he admitted, hollow and defeated. "You got everything you wanted."

His voice broke as he lifted his head, eyes dull with resignation.

"End this farce," he pleaded. "Kill me. Just *kill me*...and leave everyone else alone."

"Not everything. Not yet, Aaqa," Lily said, looking at Josh. "But you are right; we can be a little civil." With that, Lily frisked her finger. Carol's head flew through the window, and Lily burst into maniacal laughter.

Josh turned toward Lily in total disbelief, staring at Lily's broken face.

"BOB?" Josh asked in agony.

"Aaqa," Lily responded, smiling wickedly.

"That's not possible. I banished you. I threw the..." Josh stopped as his sights fell on his side table. The lamp he had thrown into the stream a few hours ago rested on the side table.

"Banish," Lily said, the words dripping with disdain.

Then, the thing inside her erupted.

"*BANISH?!*" the unnatural voice shrieked, distorting the air itself.

"*YOU FILTHY INSECT!*"

The room trembled, the walls groaning as if the sheer force of the sound could rip reality apart. It was rage—pure, seething fury—but beneath that fury, something else flickered. Something small, but undeniable.

Fear.

Josh's breath came in ragged gasps as he stared at Lily, his grief momentarily eclipsed by something raw and burning— *anger.*

Lily's eyes widened ever so slightly, her lips parting as if to taste the shift in his emotions. And she *smiled.* She *relished* it.

"You were so wrapped up in your little *fairy tale,*" the voice slithered, smoother now, eerily calm, "that you never understood the truth."

Josh's hands curled into fists.

"I was never yours to *command,*" it continued, a dark amusement creeping into its tone.

Lily's head tilted, her bloodied grin stretching wider.

"The fool who put me in that lamp… he never finished the ritual," the creature purred. "He *trapped* me, yes, but I was never bound. Never owned. Never controlled."

Josh's breath hitched.

"I am too *ancient,* too *wise* for such pathetic tricks."

The room darkened, shadows stretching unnaturally.

"I *underestimated* him. That was my only mistake." Lily's voice was her own now, smooth, triumphant. "But I *denied* him his ultimate prize… and he *died* for it."

A wicked, victorious grin spread across her face.

Josh was no longer afraid; his rage and stupidity were overpowering his fear.

"I freed you. I believed you!"

"*Freed me?*" the demon spat, its rage shaking the very air.

Josh felt the floor tremble beneath him, the weight of something ancient and *furious* pressing down on his chest.

"Your *kind imprisoned* me!" the creature roared, its voice splitting into echoes, overlapping in a horrifying cacophony. "I spent *four thousand years* inside that *cage—aware* of every agonizing second!"

The neighborhood flickered to life. Lights blinked on, one by one, as distant murmurs and hushed voices filled the night. But the demon didn't care. Not anymore. It no longer needed the shadows, the deception.

Because no one could stop it.

Any magic that could *truly* harm it had been lost to time, buried beneath centuries of dust. Even if the entire town gathered at its doorstep, they would accomplish *nothing*.

Josh's breath came in sharp, shallow gasps as a bitter realization twisted deep into his gut. His lips trembled before he bit down, trying to suppress the wave of agony crashing over him.

"So… there were no *enemies*," he murmured, his voice breaking. "You made that up."

The rage inside him surged. His fists were clenched so tightly that his nails dug into his palms.

"You were the one killing everyone," he said, his voice shaking with fury. "You killed my *mother*?"

A slow, wicked smile spread across Lily's bloodied lips.

"I did," the voice confirmed, smooth now—calm, even. *Savoring* his pain.

Josh's breath hitched. "You killed my *friends*?"

The demon laughed softly, almost mockingly. "I did," it admitted, with no remorse. *None.* "But I wasn't alone."

Josh's stomach twisted.

"That little *fiasco* at the magic shop?" The demon chuckled through Lily, eyes glinting with malice. "That was *my* doing. I *tortured* another jinn into revealing itself, forced it to play along in our little magic show." It leaned in, its grin stretching impossibly wide. "After *four thousand years* of misery, I *deserved* some entertainment."

Josh's whole body shook.

"And then…" the demon purred, its voice dipping lower, eyes dark with cruel amusement, "…there was that *fool* who thought God could save him."

Josh froze.

"He *sensed* me," the demon mused, almost nostalgic. "And then…his daughter came."

A slow, wicked shiver ran through Lily's body as if the creature inside was *reliving* the moment.

He could barely breathe. Everything—all of it—had been nothing but a sick, elaborate game. And he had been *powerless* to stop it.

"You know he begged me for mercy," Lily said, looking at him.

"You lie," said Josh, his body shaking and tears falling.

"Oh, but he did. His spirit was strong but broken," she continued.

"YOU LIE!" yelled Josh. "it's all you do!"

"Then there were those two friends, desperately trying to cheer you up." Lily laughed.

Bitterness and regret tore into Josh like jagged claws, leaving him hollow and raw. The truth crashed down on him, merciless and sharp—what a blind, arrogant fool he had been. And worse, those who had trusted him, who had stood by him as friends, had been the ones to pay the price for his mistakes.

Even now, even knowing this argument represented a crumbling, hopeless thing, he clung to it with frantic desperation. He needed to prove a point, anything, if only to ease a sliver of the crushing guilt that consumed him from the inside out.

"I saved you from eternal damnation; I freed you from the lamp! I believed you!" Josh said, angrier at himself than at the creature.

"And I spared you when I emerged, so we are even!" said the creature unnaturally.

"Did we not tell you that the creature is evil?" said two voices coming out of Lily. One sounded like her, while the other echoed an unnatural voice.

"Did we not tell you to get rid of it?"

"DID WE NOT TELL YOU NOT TO TRUST IT?!"

"Why?" Josh whispered, his voice raw. His vision blurred with tears as he stared at the nightmare before him. "What did you *gain* from this?"

For a moment, there was silence.

"Nothing," the creature said, its tone eerily calm.

And then the room *exploded* with a sound.

"AND EVERYTHING!"

The walls trembled as the demon's voice tore through the air, rattling the windows, shaking the bed beneath Josh.

"Do you think I spent four thousand years in that lamp thinking about reason?" The being sneered. Its laughter was deep, guttural, inhuman.

"Would you not come out and have a little fun?"

"Would you not deserve it?"

Josh's body sagged in defeat. His face was soaked in tears, his breaths coming in ragged gasps. His pain was unbearable, but his mind had made its choice. "End it then," he pleaded, his voice shaking. "Lily had nothing to do with this. Let her go. Take me. Kill me. Do whatever the hell you want—but end this!"

Lily's lips curled into a wicked smirk. "End this?" she mocked, tilting her head. "Oh, Aaqa... why would we do that?" Her grin widened, stretching her decayed face into something unnatural, something almost hungry. "We are having so much fun."

Josh flinched at the name.

Aaqa.

She was playing with him now, digging into his soul with words alone.

Lily's voice dipped into a taunting whisper. "Besides... death is finite." She sighed, almost wistfully. "And we cannot go there. But life?" Her eyes gleamed. "Life means we get to watch." She leaned closer, her breath cold against his skin. "We get to see you and your kind suffer."

Josh squeezed his eyes shut, his whole-body trembling.

She had taken everything from him.

"Now," Lily purred, "I will break you."

Josh's stomach twisted as a fresh wave of fear crashed over him.

She wasn't finished. Not even close.

"You will obey me," she said, her voice thick with anticipation. "Not because of some ancient magic, oh no. Not because I control you." Her wicked grin widened. "You will obey me simply because you fear me."

Josh's breath hitched.

Lily paused, savoring the moment. She smiled—a slow, cruel, knowing smile. "I will be the Aaqa," she whispered, "and you… my slave." She laughed, a wild, manic cackle that shook her entire body. Her head jerked back, her filthy, tangled hair whipping in all directions as she convulsed with glee.

"And this body," Lily continued, moving her hands over her body, "will do very nicely for us. We know you have lusted for it, and we have lusted for it. And we have enjoyed it in so many ways you cannot imagine." Insane laughter rang through the room.

Josh could not hold back his rage; his anger, pain, loss, and despair were all coiling up inside him. But the creature was not done; Carol's headless body stood up, all bloodied, and it started burning. "She won't need that body, will she?" asked the demon in amusement.

Josh lost all sense of reason and lunged at Lily with full force. Lily and the creature in her were on the ground, Josh on top, punching Lily's face with full force. There was very little he could do to that face that wasn't already done unnaturally by the creature.

"Get—" punch.

"Off—" punch.

"HER!" punch.

Josh's fists connected repeatedly, the sickening crunch of bone and flesh filling the air. But the thing inside Lily only laughed. A deep, manic cackle, as if Josh's strikes were nothing more than a light tickle.

Her head snapped back with each blow, her face a mess of blood and twisted delight, her mouth curling into a gruesome grin.

With unnatural force, Lily drove her legs into Josh's chest, launching him across the room. He crashed into the wall; the impact rattling his bones before he crumpled to the floor.

Before he could move, she was on him.

Her fists rained down, each hit harder than the last, the raw power behind them beyond human. Josh felt his face split, blood pouring from his nose, his vision swimming as pain exploded through his body.

Lily vomited.

A violent, gut-churning eruption, thick and putrid, splattered across Josh as he lay on the floor. The stench was unbearable. Lily stood over him, her body shaking with laughter, hands on her hips as she bent down, her face inches from his.

"We have defiled this body," she cooed, voice thick with mockery. "And we welcome you to join us."

Josh trembled, his fury rising. His hands curled into fists, his entire body shaking as vomit dripped from his face. With a roar, he lunged.

Lily barely had time to react before he slammed into her, his raw anger propelling them both across the room. Her laughter never stopped ringing in his ears as he drove her backward.

Straight into the wall.

The sitar.

The instrument hung from three large nails, and a thick metal rod connected the top two, supporting the weight of the ancient piece. Josh's father had given it to him. It was more than just a relic—it was a memory—a piece of a life that had been stolen from him.

With all his strength, Josh forced Lily against it.

The impact was brutal.

The sitar snapped, the metal rod ripping free from the top nails. And the nails plunged into her back. Lily's body went rigid. A horrific, gurgling sound escaped her lips.

A thick, black smoke poured from her body.

Josh stumbled backward, chest heaving, watching as Lily's lifeless form hung there, impaled, her face frozen in a grotesque expression of twisted agony. The smoke hovered in the air, shifting and writhing like a living shadow. Then it laughed. A slow, knowing, delighted laugh.

Josh's hands trembled as he approached Lily's body, his heart breaking. He gently cupped her bloodied face, pressing a soft kiss to her forehead, his lips lingering as silent sobs wracked his body. Carefully, he lifted her off the nails, cradling her as he lowered her to the floor. His tears fell onto her pale skin, his breath hitching as he collapsed to his knees, his body shaking uncontrollably.

Above him, the creature watched. It did nothing. It simply floated, observing. Savoring his suffering.

And the more Josh broke, the more it relished the moment.

Josh moved back and sat on the floor, his hands in his hair, tired and broken. He was resting against the bed and continued crying. He thought of his mother, a great weight on his shoulder. She deserved so much more; all that was good in the world was in her, and to see her end like this.

Josh started sobbing helplessly as he turned to Lily. He loved her so much. But she was looking back at him. He had closed her eyes, thinking she had passed away, but there was still life in those eyes. She was a mess; she was wretched, smelling of piss, with broken, disgusted skin. But there was beauty in her, or maybe Josh's love for her made her look like that to him. While tears flowed from his eyes, he looked at Lily and said gently, "I am so very sorry."

The smoke seemed to cringe a little. This display of affection did not sit well with it, so the creature decided it was time to restart the pain.

"Aww, she lives; good, I wanted at least one night with the three of us!" A husky, sinister voice resonated in the room. "Come now, Master, this is truly pathetic," said the smokeless evil. "Did I not offer you a multitude of them? Did I not say they would worship you?" mocked the evil creature. "But," continued the sinister voice, "you only wanted this FILTHY RED BITCH!"

Josh did not care about the creature's nonsense; he was in emotional hell. He looked at Lily, whose lips trembled a little as if she was trying to say something back, but words would not escape her lips. Josh noticed Lily's eyes; they looked at Josh and then at the lamp. They looked at Josh again and looked at the lamp. It seemed words weren't necessary, as they communicated on another level. Josh stood up, his fists tightly clenched. He was shaking from head to toe, tears still flowing from his eyes. Josh went to the sitar, and he broke the metal rod off the bottom nail.

The creature crackled again. "That won't do you much good against me, but maybe I can give you an object to hit." And then the smoke disappeared. Lily rose; it was apparent that her body was completely broken, and everything that was happening was happening unnaturally. Lily rose slowly, waiting for Josh to unleash his anger on her. And then there was the laughter, the insane, maniacal laughter, resonating throughout the room.

Josh stood beside the side table, raising the metal rod with both hands. As he swung the rod toward the lamp, Lily's body fell to the ground. The room resonated with a loud "NOOOOOOOO," and something rushed from Lily to Josh at lightning-fast speed. It hit Josh so hard that he went flying out the window.

But the damage was done; the lamp lay in pieces. Smoke filled the room, and two boulder-sized eyes glared at the broken lamp. Gone was the arrogance, the sense of entitlement, and the smug idea of immortality. In its place was a creature in pain and fear, desperately looking around for a way out, defeated a second time by a race he considered filth, the dirt beneath him.

Everything unraveled in a sudden, sickening blur.

The room exploded as if a bomb had been placed in it, and most of the house caught fire. A massive hole appeared in the roof, and a streak of white light with an orange hue shot into the night sky. The neighborhood awoke with the sounds and screams coming out of the house. People were clicking their phones and taking pictures or making videos. Sounds of sirens from police cars and ambulances were making their way toward the neighborhood. Outside the home lay a head and a body some distance away.

The first responders sprinted toward the house but skidded to a halt just steps from the wreckage. Debris littered the lawn like broken bones, smoke curling from the burning house. But it wasn't the fire that rooted them in place—it was the severed head lying grotesquely in the front yard.

For a moment, they could only stare, frozen, horror etched across their faces. The sight was so wrong, so nightmarish. It clawed at the edges of their sanity. One of them gagged; another whispered a prayer under his breath as if that could somehow erase the image seared into their minds.

As they lifted the faint, barely conscious Josh onto a stretcher, their hands shook—not from the weight, but from the unbearable thought of what else they might have to touch. The head seemed to stare back at them, an accusation, a curse. Every instinct screamed to leave it behind.

Firefighters eventually put out the fire and cleared the area, but the damage remained extensive. Whispers rippled through the town, each retelling more twisted than the last. People grew more uneasy, eyes darting nervously at every shadow, voices dropping to hushed tones when the topic came up. The uncovered truth seemed to fill the air with dread.

And yet, what they didn't realize—what they couldn't know—was that the nightmare, at least for most of them, was finally over.

CHAPTER 20
CONNECTING THE DOTS

Rosetta stood next to a bed, sobbing. With a wet tissue in her right hand, she kept wiping her tears with it. Her lips trembled as she occasionally uttered, "Lily," lovingly. In front of her was a bed with tubes and important medical instruments. On the bed lay Lily—part of her face was bandaged, and her body was covered in a white sheet.

Following the incident, they admitted Lily to the hospital, where she fell into a deep coma. The doctors were trying to figure out what happened, and while they seemed determined and professional, privately, they were lost.

Josh's home's top floor burned down, and Carol's body, which was lying in Josh's room, burned completely. The wood and the home's furniture had all burned, and everything in Josh's room turned into ashes, except Lily. There wasn't a single burn on her. Her skin showed signs of exposure to intense heat, but her hair, skin, organs, and everything else were completely intact, as if she had never been exposed to the fire. When the firefighters found her, she was completely naked, as all her clothes had burned, but her body was fine.

She had scars, broken bones, and damage done to her body by the ifrit. Everything she went through before the fire was visible, including the large nails piercing her body. One nail barely missed her heart, and she had lost a large amount of blood because of her injuries. But the fire could not harm her. This baffled the doctors, who were mostly men and women of science. But what happened here was very unscientific.

Outside her room, visitors and friends stopped by, frequently checking on her and her mother. Some people brought food, others had flowers, and yet others came with well wishes for Lily and her mother. They wished this nightmare would end and the good people of this small town could return to the normality and peace they once had.

Josh Cox lay in another room on a floor in the same hospital. He, like Lily, was badly injured with broken ribs, a broken pelvis, and deep scars all over his body. He had lost a good amount of blood as well. Physically, the doctors expected him to recover; he was young, strong, and healthy. But emotionally and mentally, this man was more broken than probably anyone else in this town. There was no one in his room sobbing and wishing him well, no one outside the room waiting for him. The only two individuals who were outside were police officers guarding the room.

Too much had gone wrong, unexplained—too many deaths around Josh Cox. People started realizing these unexplainable events were all somehow connected to him. Josh's friends, Josh's mother, Josh's girlfriend, Josh's house, and so on. The latest chapter that happened in his home with his mother dying and Lily in a coma seemed to verify their fears.

But things were shaky. There was no murder weapon, there was no motive. And the strange light that burst into the night sky only convinced people that something sinister was at play here, that Josh probably got himself involved in something he didn't understand.

But what?

Josh's father was informed of what happened, and he flew back to deal with the situation as best he could. He stopped by and tried to talk to his son, but he just lay there staring at the TV, which was not even switched on. Matthew was shaken; he had issues with Carol and Josh but never imagined something like this would happen. Like everyone else, he couldn't make heads or tails of the situation.

The incident, by now, had gone national, with the 'girl who lived' being the latest national news. 'An entire floor burns to ashes but not a single burn on Lily Higgins' was trending. All this unwanted attention made the townsfolk uncomfortable, especially the mayor, which also meant the sheriff. Matthew worried but understood and told Eric Masterson, a family lawyer friend, to do what he could for his son. Eric promised he would.

The breaking of the lamp saved many more lives than could be appreciated. Bob or Kruh Za din would not stop tormenting Josh and Lily. As a master ifrit, his reach was far more significant than a single house or a city. He easily removed the elderly

Alvira Adisa from the Magic Beans shop when he felt it was necessary. But for all his wickedness and cunning, he failed to understand the man who put him inside the lamp.

Abu, as mentioned before, was ancient. And with longevity comes experience and an opportunity to learn from mistakes. As arrogant as Abu was, he was no fool. He was very aware of the danger he was putting himself in. He also knew that just because he expected things to work a certain way didn't mean they would. And given that there was no record of anyone capturing a master ifrit, this was uncharted waters, and anything could go wrong.

And it did. Abu failed to anticipate the last-ditch effort by his nemesis, and he paid for it with his life. But where Abu failed, Abu also succeeded, for Abu devised a master plan to make the lamp part of the struggle and battle. He created three powerful spells and magically sealed them on the lamp.

The first spell was to ensure that the lamp was unbreakable. There was no point in risking so much if the lamp broke and the prize was lost, which was why the lamp lasted this long.

The second spell ensured that only those who willed magic from the lamp could use it. Rubbing the lamp did nothing if the intent to drive something from it was not there.

The third spell was probably the most important one. It nullified the first spell if the lamp's owner wished to destroy or break it. Abu realized that if things went wrong, as a last resort, he wanted to destroy the lamp if he felt the creature was uncontrollable.

The above three spells were why the lamp could stand the test of time and worked only for Josh after going through so many hands. The spell was also why Josh's will to see the lamp destroyed caused it to shatter, though it may seem like it was the rod that did it. Kruh Za din never knew this until he saw the lamp shatter. That was when he realized how the master strategist had beaten him again!

CHAPTER 21

THE CURSED DAGGER

A well-shaven man who looked beyond his years sat on a bed in the dark, staring at the wall in front of him. He had woken up from a nightmare and had no desire to go back to sleep. When this happened, Josh would stay awake, lost in thought, staring at the wall before him.

The last few years had been interesting for Josh. Some wanted him prosecuted, but the evidence was still circumstantial. The case dragged on. The only actual argument was that Josh was usually around those who died, his mother used as a prime example. Then they tried to depict him as mentally ill—unstable. People wanted him gone. They did not want whatever he had in their neighborhood or in their town. When the jury barely reached a verdict of not guilty, the judge overruled them. To the judge, Josh posed a threat to society, and he needed to be locked away for the greater good.

But the town's opposition to Josh wasn't the only issue. When called to the witness stand, he openly confessed to killing his mother. He did this because there was no way to explain what had happened. The idea of his mother being remembered as a psychopath who took her own life was far more painful to him. Whatever she was, she was a sincere and honest woman who sacrificed much of her life to do the right thing. And the right thing was Josh. That was the final respectable action he could imagine for his mother, so her memory wouldn't be blemished. That and he had nothing to live for. Everything that mattered was lost—Lily was in a coma, and his mother and his friends were brutally murdered. And deep down, he couldn't deny that this was his fault.

Josh spent three and a half years in jail, but thanks to social media, things were on the verge of transformation. A documentary on the town's strange events revealed something sinister and unexplainable: the town's inability to handle or even understand the situation. Statements by Kevin's father and mother and Mr. Sombat shed light on how the town rushed to judgment.

"I don't believe that Josh or Kevin were in any cult for a second. I don't, it's not true," Sybil Morris told the interviewer.

"They were goofy kids, looking for mischief and fun," added Michael Morris. "But Josh would give his life before seeing Kevin hurt."

"And Kevin would do the same for Josh," interjected Sybil. "They couldn't find the actual murderers, so they put Josh behind bars."

"What about the confession by Josh Cox?" asked the interviewer.

"They started going after his mother. The boy lost everyone who mattered to him," said Michael Morris.

Sybil Morris wiped a tear. "Josh did the only decent thing he could do. He didn't want her name tarnished."

Matthew Cox did not hold back his rage at how this all played out. He told the interviewer that there wasn't a shred of evidence against his son, and his mother's memory was all that mattered to him after she passed away. When the interviewer asked why Carol would take her own life, a visibly upset Matthew got up and left the room.

Prominent lawyers throughout the country started showing interest in the case. During the next elections, a new mayor was elected, and with a new mayor came a new sheriff. The case was reviewed, and it was thrown out for lack of evidence. Josh Cox was released from jail as a free man.

After his release, Josh went to his house. The insurance company reluctantly agreed to pay the cost, and the house was rebuilt. Mr. Morris, a veteran real estate agent, played a signifi-cant role in convincing the insurance company to honor their deal. Josh did not want the house; Lily was the only reason he was there. She was all that remained.

Lily awoke from her coma a few months after the incident. And immediately, she wished she hadn't. Usually, with incidents of demonic possession, the victim has no memory of what happened. Lily was not so lucky. And whereas evil deeds can be committed on a woman's body, Kruh Za din ripped into Lily's soul and thoroughly tainted it. Not only did Lily remember the horrific pain of abuse in body and soul, but she also remembered the sickening joy and satisfaction it brought to Kruh Za din. These reminders tore away at Lily's existence day in and day out. And then came the constant nightmares. In most of these nightmares, she would live through the events of that one night repeatedly. And it was breaking her.

Sometimes, she would eat so much that she would get chubby. Other times, she wouldn't eat for days, and she would be all bones, her face weary and tired. She had lost her sense of purpose; she only existed to escape life—a tormented life. All of this started taking a toll on her. She could not hold jobs; she was frequently sick, tired, and completely lost. Rosetta started sleeping with Lily to wake her from her nightmares. And even at work, Rosetta's mind was constantly on Lily.

After his release from jail, Josh had only one thing left—Lily. She was his final link to something genuine, something that had once been like home.

One morning, as Lily walked toward the hospital where she now worked alongside her mother, she saw him. Josh stood there, waiting.

Her steps faltered. Her body tensed, a shiver running through her as if the ghosts of her past had reached out to grab her. She didn't look at him, but she knew—knew he was watching, hoping. Her breath hitched, her vision blurred with unshed tears.

Josh's heart pounded. He clung to a sliver of hope, praying she'd turn to him with something—anything—but she stood frozen, drowning in a storm of agony. Memories slammed into her, each one sharper than the last. The screams. The loss. The nights that had stolen pieces of her soul. And now, standing before her, was the reason it all happened.

Josh saw it in her eyes when she finally turned to him. This wasn't the Lily he once knew, the girl who had been soft, kind, full of light… no, her eyes burned with fury, with hatred so raw that it cut through the air between them. Silent tears traced down her cheeks, but there was no sorrow in them—only rage, only pain.

His throat tightened. His fists clenched at his sides as the truth settled like a stone in his chest. There was nothing left for him here.

Without a word, Lily tore her gaze from him and walked past, leaving him standing in the wreckage of what could never be repaired.

She knew—God, she knew—Josh never wanted this for her. She knew he had suffered too. But none of that mattered. Not anymore. This wasn't a place where logic held meaning, where people found comfort in justifications. This was about one thing —pain.

Josh had become its symbol.

Pain filled each breath, each step, each sleepless night, as her body and mind suffered from memories too dark to speak of. The shadows that had stolen her life had faces—merciless, inhuman, evil beyond comprehension. No one without that experience would ever grasp it. No words, no reason, no explanations succeeded in making it logical.

Lily didn't need understanding.

She just needed to survive.

And that meant walking away.

Lily hated herself.

She despised the way her own body had betrayed her, how it had been used—defiled—for the twisted pleasure of an unspeakable evil. She loathed the memories that refused to fade, the ones that haunted her in the dead of night, whispering that she had been powerless, that she had been nothing more than a vessel for its cruelty.

She hated life for what it had given her. For ripping away the people she loved, for leaving her with nothing but shattered pieces of who she used to be.

But more than anything—more than herself, more than the nightmares—she hated him for bringing that thing into her life. For ignoring her when she pleaded, when she begged him to get rid of it. For his arrogance, his selfishness, his blindness that had cost her everything.

After this brief experience with Lily, Josh sold the house. He moved to another state and found work in a warehouse. He rented a small single-room apartment with a kitchen and a bathroom. He, too, had his share of nightmares. Kevin would occasionally show up, and Frank and Fred would join him. He would see their skeletons being ripped from their bodies, and the screams of his friends would wake him in agony. But the worst part was when Carol showed up. There was so much regret, even in his dreams. Things he never said to her, how much he loved her, how much he missed her. Why didn't he listen to her when he should have, the many times he could have been a much better son? And for the way it ended for her. Mountains of regret were bearing down on him, day in and day out. His nightmares were breaking him, but his days weren't treating him much better.

There were sleeping pills that helped; there was also another medicine that was prescribed to him. But then again, science and logic were used for something the medical folks did not understand or believe in. These bandages sometimes helped, but most of the time, they left him in agony. On days when the nightmares didn't happen, Josh felt a bit more relaxed. He would go in early to work and sit at the cafe near the warehouse. He would order coffee and a bagel and enjoy it quietly before heading to work. On days when the nightmares happened, Josh would not eat at all; he would work and work until they closed the place down for the night. And then he would come home and sit, staring at the wall, afraid to sleep.

Matthew tried to keep in touch with his son, but he wasn't getting anywhere. He paid for and tried hard to find a psychiatrist who could help him. He did not know what to do or how to help. And he missed Carol now that she was gone. He missed her, and he wished he had been better to her. Sometimes, he confided in Josh, and the father and son would connect in tears for a few minutes. But Matthew did have a life of his own, a wife, and two daughters now that he needed to care for. And with time, Matthew's visits turned into phone calls, and then those also disappeared.

The last week had been good for Josh. He had no nightmares and slept pleasantly. Today, he stood before the cafe, waiting for his turn to order. He looked at a croissant and figured it looked tasty. *Let's switch*, he thought and ordered his regular coffee, but instead of the usual bagel, he picked up the croissant. There was a seat outside the cafe, and he sat down and started his breakfast. The road was noisy, people were rushing everywhere, trying to finish last-minute errands before starting their day.

In the distance, a black woman with round spectacles was watching him. She was standing next to a zebra crossing. This was a busy part of town; people were moving between roads when possible, and cars were rushing to work. But she stood stationary, fixated on Josh. He had not noticed her; he continued to eat his breakfast calmly.

The woman had a large bag hanging on her right side. She started crossing the road and walked toward him. She got to him and pulled up the chair before him; Josh looked up and cringed. It was Sheila Adisa, Alvira Adisa's daughter. Josh had first met her at the Magic Beans shop with Lily.

He slowly lowered his head and stared at the table. He was holding his coffee in his right hand, and he shook a little.

Sheila placed her bag on the table, and with a serious look, she spoke. "You are a hard man to find."

Josh had spoken to Sheila twice before. The first time was when he visited the Magic Beans shop with Lily. The second time he talked to her was about two years ago when Josh was released from jail. Sheila was one of the first ones to come knocking on his door. She sat down and started asking him questions, which made him feel very uncomfortable.

She was desperate to know everything—every detail of that terrible night. Her voice trembled with urgency as she pressed Josh, reminding him of the hole her mother's death had left in her heart. She needed answers, and he had a responsibility—to her, to her mother's memory—to help Sheila find the truth.

Josh hesitated, the weight of the past pressing down on him like a heavy stone. Reliving that night was agony, but her determination was relentless. Piece by piece, she pulled the story from him—what Lily did, how the lamp shattered, every fractured moment. Josh tried to protest, his voice tight with frustration, reminding her he couldn't possibly know how the lamp broke —he had been thrown through the window before it happened. But she wouldn't let it go. She wouldn't stop until she had every fragment of the truth.

Sheila met Lily after Lily gained consciousness. Lily, like Josh, was very reluctant to delve into the past. Surprisingly, Sheila knew how to touch Lily's emotions so that she would reveal her most painful memories. This helped Lily as well. Unlike the psychiatrists, who may be professional but did not believe in the supernatural, Sheila did. And as Lily opened up to her, she felt as if a weight had been lifted from her shoulders. The few meetings Lily had with Sheila were helpful, but with time, Sheila's visit had little to do with Lily's recovery; she appeared to be focused on something more significant: information.

"You remember me, Josh, don't you?" she said, focusing on him.

Josh was still looking at the table. Sheila's glare intensified, and she said, "I met your friend, Lily, after I met you last time."

Josh looked at her. His wet eyes seemed to have a glimmer of hope. A bit of the old Josh was still there.

"Good!" Sheila remarked. "Now that I have your attention, let's discuss the matter at hand. And mind you pay full attention; lives are still at stake."

Josh stared at Sheila, still holding onto the table, but Lily's name had sparked his curiosity and concern.

"Do you remember my mother?" she asked.

Josh nodded.

"My mother explained the two planes to you?" she asked seriously.

He nodded.

"Good, I have spent the last few years trying to piece together what happened when you smashed the lamp. While we would like to believe the creature is dead, I don't believe it is true. In the world of jinns, they exist as free creatures, as we do here on our plane. They go about their daily business like we do, and the only restrictions are the restrictions of their societies. With me so far?" she asked.

Josh continued to stare at her.

Sheila continued. "Then there are jinns who become tainted and are considered 'bound.' If a man captures a jinn or any member of their species, the jinn is bound. For that jinn to exist anywhere, it must always be bound to something. And if it isn't, it can't exist freely, so it gets banished. The banished plane is a separate plane from the two planes of existence. The banished plane, or the forgotten plane as it is referred to, is a never-ending place, where the primary purpose of the bound entity is to find an escape. An escape doesn't exist unless someone can rebind the creature to something in one of the two planes. I believe your ifrit is now roaming through the endless abyss of the forgotten plane."

Sheila took a moment and then continued, "I am not the only one interested in, err..." She paused. "Bob, is that what you called him?"

Josh nodded again.

Sheila shook her head slightly and returned to the conversation. "Your Bob is probably the most powerful entity ever to have crossed mankind. And mankind, as you know, is power hungry. The hard part of finding and binding this creature is already done. The only thing left is to figure out its name and rebound it to something on our planet. And your Bob inadvertently took care of that. Possessing your friend Lily created a secondary binding source; the only thing missing is Bob's real name and the magic to bind him to her."

Josh was listening to her intently. While he had tried to move on from his horrific past, he would not be naïve and allow any more pain to be inflicted on Lily. If there was something he could do to protect her, he would.

"I take it you care about Lily?" Sheila asked.

He lowered his head. He knew how he felt, but didn't care to share it.

"Anyone who can control this Bob of yours through Lily will have immeasurable power," Sheila continued. "And Lily will cease to exist. This creature will completely consume her and use her body for his purposes. I fear that, eventually, someone will figure out how to make this work. Humans are tenacious, and some of us are already looking for ways to bring him back. They don't realize that the creature will consume them, Lily, and everything else. For example, two hooded figures are following me; they were by the shoe shop the last time I saw them." Sheila made a gesture with her eyes to point toward the shop.

Josh glanced at the shoe shop; sure enough, two individuals were standing there. The moment they noticed Josh looking at them, they turned away. Josh recognized them; he had seen them before. He had seen them around town a few times while looking for work. They always avoided eye contact with him, but he found their presence peculiar. They were always covered, and their hoods hid most of their faces, but he recalled seeing them near the Sombats' home, too. When Josh was walking home from the Sombats' the night Lily yelled at him, he heard footsteps following him. But he was too broken to confront them, so he ignored them.

Sheila continued. "Those two are from the 'circle of dandelions,' a cultist group obsessed with dark magic. And there is nothing darker and more powerful than your Bob."

Sheila's expression twisted into something unreadable as she locked eyes with Josh. A shadow of hesitation flickered across her face before she finally spoke.

"The Circle of Dandelions is deeply entrenched in blood magic, masters of bridging the two planes. They felt it when you brought that creature back into this world. They've been tracking you ever since." Her voice was steady, but there was an urgency in how she leaned toward him, willing him to understand the gravity of the situation.

Josh exhaled sharply, rubbing his face as if trying to scrub away the weight of her words.

"So," she continued, taking a slow, measured breath. "Are you willing to help me put an end to this? Once and for all?"

Josh truly looked at her for the first time, the silence stretching between them like a taut wire. Then, finally, he spoke. "What do I have to do?"

Sheila didn't answer immediately. Instead, she reached into her bag, pulling out something wrapped in dark cloth. With deliberate care, she placed it on the table and began unwrapping it. The fabric fell away, revealing a dagger—its wickedly sharp blade gleaming under the dim light. The moment Josh saw it, he shivered. It was almost identical to the one he had stolen from his father long ago.

Sheila's gaze softened, but her voice remained firm. "This is going to hurt," she warned. "But you have to understand, one life, or even a handful of lives, is nothing compared to what's at stake."

Josh's hands clenched into fists as he stared at the dagger, his mind racing.

"Lily Higgins must die," Sheila said, her voice barely above a whisper. "And she must die by this dagger. This dagger is the only thing that can ensure that the creature never returns."

Josh's world tilted. His knees buckled, and he collapsed into the chair before sliding to the ground, his breath coming in sharp gasps. "No... no, no," he mumbled, shaking his head in disbelief.

Sheila took a step closer, but her presence only seemed to make it worse. "Josh, listen to me. Lily is already as good as dead. People are planning to take her—cults that will hunt her relentlessly. If you do this…it will be an act of mercy."

Josh jerked backward, his eyes locked on the dagger as if it might leap at him. "NOOO! NOOOO!" His scream tore through the air, raw and primal.

Heads turned. Pedestrians, on their way to work, stopped in their tracks. A murmur rippled through the breakfast crowd waiting in line. Sheila stiffened under the weight of their stares, quickly wrapping the dagger back in the cloth and shoving it into her bag.

Josh kept moving, stumbling backward, his voice rising. "NOOO! NOOOO!"

And then—the sharp blare of a horn.

A bus.

The screech of tires.

A sickening thud.

Gasps and screams erupted from the crowd as Josh was flung through the air like a discarded rag doll. He hit the pavement with a bone-jarring crash. His body lay twisted, unmoving. People rushed toward him, their faces blurring together as darkness crept in at the edges of his vision.

His lips moved, trying to say "No, no, no…"

Until there was nothing but darkness.